THE DEATH OF
ALAN BELL

ADAM BUNKER

'All say, "How hard it is that we have to die" - a strange complaint to come from the mouths of people who have had to live.'

-Mark Twain

1. APRIL

i) A late and inadequate introduction

There are 270 stations on the London Underground. They serve over a billion people a year - a billion people who solemnly hold onto the passing minutes and passing stations before they arrive broken at the office every morning. Because they are told to. Over a billion people a year agonisingly claw and carve the air out of every conceivable corner of every carriage, spread evenly between every one of 270 stations, piling in just to save waiting a further three minutes for the next carriage on their way home. It gets tiresome, and it never bloody ends.

As best as I can calculate I've been to (a rather unlucky) thirteen stations.

Today, as is the same every morning, my suit hurts. I don't wear suits well. They're tight, sharply angled and I feel as though I've been welded into mine like a feeble-bodied medieval knight. The station - again, same as every morning - is populated with an assortment of people who wouldn't be out of place in an asylum: those who have gone or will eventually go mad and probably commit a series of heinous crimes in the process. The kind of madness presumably brought about merely by virtue of having spent half their lives being meticulously welded into suits. A frankly worrying absence of thought seems to keep most of them preoccupied, and as they stare blankly into the pit below the rails I begin to worry - as always - that any one of them will hurl themselves in just for something interesting to do. Or that one will push me under for similar reasons. Others (the ones with enough in the way of facial expression to suggest an active brain) glance around at each other sheepishly and gingerly, forming misguided impressions of everyone else just as I do. Presumably they're hoping I don't hurl myself in front of the train.

The invisible piston splits in half as it hits the masses. It wraps us in tight morning air and we amble onboard.

Seated now, staring intently at my fists. The bulb above my head is flickering as though it's in agony. It's obviously trying to be as professional as its peers - as healthy - but its attempts are foiled by an obvious and embarrassing disability that it can do nothing to help. I can sympathise. That said, I think it'd be best if someone just put it out of its misery because in all honesty - when all possible poetry is taken out of the situation - it's just very bloody annoying. It makes the carriage dark and that's useful neither in the morning *nor* in the evening.

I suppose the worst that could happen at the moment is that it could cause someone to fall asleep and miss his or her stop. If that happened, they might arrive late to work for 'just about the last time', get sacked and, having no one to turn to about their possibly insurmountable debts, end up chucking themselves under the next train*.

*Note: *In the busy world of the London underground where everything apparently needs an unsympathetic nickname, these unlucky sods are called 'one-unders'.*

This wouldn't be good, obviously, because it would cause delays. Said delays could lead to more unpunctual employees and therefore many more one-unders. If anything, it's just irresponsible to leave the bulb flickering due to the obvious and calamitous potential for bringing about mass suicide. Of course, there's a strong possibility that this is all just be abject conjecture. Either way, the bulb is annoying and I wish it would die swiftly.

I'm sorry; I don't mean to talk about the inevitable subject of death so early on, but I reckon I can be forgiven due to the circumstances I've recently found myself in.

This morning was supposed to be the morning I give my letter of resignation in at work, but now that I think about it I can't for the life of me figure out why. If I don't give in my notice - as in, if I simply stop turning up - then eventually someone in HR will realise I'm not there and I'll be fired. The reason we give in our notice is obviously so we can have the opportunity to quit before this happens, but it's just occurred to me that the reason I am leaving this job and the reason I won't be applying for a new one are one and the same, so I just don't think I'm going to go.

This isn't exactly coming out in as ordered a way as I'd hoped it might. The nonsensical ramblings from page one until now might already be becoming annoying, but I'm afraid that's very much going to be the order of the day due to the insurmountable fact that I am an idiot. If you *are* struggling to keep up, I think you should probably stop reading and do something useful with your time instead. I fail to think of anything in the coming pages that won't make you disinterested, confused or angry. I won't judge, trust me. If you are intrigued though - in much the same, inevitably fatal way that a fly is intrigued by the heavenly blue flicker of an electric lamp - then let me tell you this: If you are reading this it means I am almost certainly dead. I am dead, I am deceased, and in a similar mode I am no longer living. Today is Monday the 29th of April and last Friday I was told that I'm dying. I have as close to a year to live as a doctor can genuinely promise without compromising his professionalism, which is just about as much time as it takes to write a half-decent book. Or half a decent book. ...I suppose we'll soon see which.

**

I think it's amazing and somewhat absurd how quickly and to what extent you become faux-philosophical when faced with death - even someone with nothing substantial in the way of philosophical education and an almost profound lack of general knowledge, such as myself. To prove this, I'm getting off the train at the next stop. I've no idea what I'm going to do with the rest of the day, but I'm certainly not going to work.

I quite feel like grabbing the attention of everyone on this train and telling them to take the day off with me. As inwardly unstable as they all look, I'm sure they've got families or loved ones somewhere. They should probably go and see them. They should probably go and roll around in some grass, have some casual sex or at the very least enjoy a cold pint. They all think (as I did only last week) that they have to go to work and do their jobs for seemingly very important reasons. I can't pretend that dying gives me enough authority to tell society to quit work, but I do feel compelled to tell all of these sorry-looking, institutionalised souls not to bother. I doubt there's much chance that they'd all simultaneously abandon the working world just because I say so, anyway; you need to be dying to appreciate that level of apathy.

Reorganising everybody's perception of purpose this early on probably isn't a very good idea either way, because, at the very back-end, I suspect it's somebody's job to replace the flickering bulb above my head.

ii) Paying to sit down

Right then... I'm going to try from now on not to be so predisposed to society's claustrophobic effects. Even though I'm not sure what that actually means in practice. If I was a bit more poetic I'd probably burn my tie as a metaphor for it being the proverbial noose around my neck for the past 29 months, but the short length of time I've had to come to terms with my death (those three days I was talking about) hasn't exactly graced me with the level of cynicism needed to perform such a wasteful act. Newfound cod-philosophies on life not-withstanding, my current thought process has weaved itself into something along the lines of: 'It would be a waste of a bloody good tie, and I might need it if I have to attend a formal social occasion, such as a funeral.' On that score, it is a very nice tie so I wouldn't really mind if it was the one I wear at my own.

I left the flickering bulb to its own devices and got off the tube at Hyde Park Corner. My mobile phone is switched off.

The park is endlessly huge and busy every day of the year, but today being a Monday morning (and a brisk April), it isn't brimming. There are still a few flexitime suits pacing about on their way to work and the inevitable beat of joggers trying - for some reason I don't think I'll ever understand - to improve themselves. They look a bit like a disorganised army as they pass each other. You can see them right across the park from some places, like headless chickens trying desperately to regroup.

I'm sat on a deck chair writing this exact word (the word '*word*' in that case) and am trying not to focus on the fact that it clearly isn't deck chair weather. This helps though, as it means that the area isn't being policed particularly well. Call it cheap, but I refuse to pay for the privilege of sitting when I have a perfectly good rear-end capable of doing the job itself, given any suitably sized section of ground with which to do it on. (Read: I have an arse). This is the primary reasoning behind my game of '*See how long I can sit in the deckchair before the haunched Portuguese man asks me for £1.50.*'

... It's not the catchiest of names, I know, but it's still very much a work in progress.

It's quite windy, which is a shame. The top layer of the Serpentine is constantly being scooped up and blown along a few centimetres as if it is skin being shaved. This produces a fine mist of ripples that dash along the surface, being chased only by the hazy swells that precede it. The whole thing is quite hypnotising, and I can feel myself falling gently asleep despite the cold air running about my ears.

***

And now I've woken up, which is usually the process that immediately follows falling asleep. It's a generally flawless system from which I've benefited many times in the past. Waking up means I can at least deduce that I'm not yet dead, which is always a fairly nice realisation to have, but more so now than ever before. Some 40-odd minutes have passed.

As a would-be writer disillusioned by his own past failings, I realise that this book (with all the poems, lists, ramblings and spurious accounts that will follow) is my last chance to create something that'll make my 26 years on earth memorable to anyone and something that (I hope) will pump through the veins of London forever. This is every writer's ambition of course: to live forever as a permanent and resonant voice within the habitat he or she was raised in - regardless of the societal changes time weathers upon it. I like to think that to live in the world is a man's privilege, whereas to leave a mark on the world is his purpose.

To that end, dear reader* (both friend and stranger), I promise that - barring any legal or moral limitations - I'll try and make the next 12 months as interesting as I can. Although I can't guarantee any miraculous or breathtaking events. This book is currently about nothing as much as it is about everything. If you take it upon yourselves to make a literary leap of faith you will have my eternal thanks, but you have to understand that at the same time I'm just a man living a limited life in a city. I'm not boundlessly rich or endowed with super powers. I've no mortal enemies or secret missions to carry out. I've actually no bloody idea what I'll fill a book's worth of pages with in truth, but I know that I've got to at least try before I go. If you want, you're more than welcome to come along for the journey. I'll try and keep in mind during the next year that there's a difference between 'going off the rails' and deciding that the rails just aren't the right place to be.

First of all, I have decided not to tell anyone about my illness. This probably seems an odd decision given the endless amounts of delicious sympathy I could have access to, but the result of my (three days of) thinking has been that it's best if no one knows. Misguided as it may be, the reason for this is that I don't particularly want any special treatment in the coming year, nor do I want to see everyone acting differently around me. I don't want it to influence any of the events that happen over the next twelve months and I'd like all the relationships in my life to play out as they would normally. It'll all just culminate in a swirling, steadily worsening vortex of sadness otherwise, and that's something I'm keen to avoid. Therefore, everyone will be kept in the dark. More importantly, telling everyone seems like it would be very emotionally draining work and, frankly, I'm loath to upset the status quo.

I'm also choosing not to write about the physical effects, treatment, or symptoms of my illness; firstly because they will not be that evident, existent, or evident (respectively), and secondly because if you want to read so morbidly about death I suggest you look at the tragic life stories section of your local book shop. There are plenty of choices. What I mean is this: you don't need to know what it is I have. There's nothing you, any doctor or I can do about it, so the only difference it would make is that you'd have another word to add to the list of words you're unsure how to correctly pronounce. Like 'patriotic'. Consider this The Secret Death of Alan Bell.

I was awoken - in case you were wondering - by the Portuguese man insistent on receiving his £1.50. I probably would have given it him this time, but for a lack of change in my wallet. I still have no idea what I'm going to do with the rest of the day. With that thought, an overwhelming sense of freedom has just gripped me and my suit doesn't feel quite so tight. Now, I presume, is the time to draw up one of those lists of things to do before you die, and (as is my understanding) place 'swim with dolphins' proudly at number one. Is that really the best thing we as humans can possibly do on this planet? Is larking about in the sea with some overgrown fish the pinnacle of our existence? I think I'd like to prove otherwise. I don't even particularly *like* dolphins; they all seem like they're plotting something horrible.

If I was to sit and write one up I don't think my list would be very sea life-heavy, especially as all I can think of doing now is getting very, extremely drunk. I've never been drinking in a pub on my own before (let alone this early in the day). Maybe that should be the first thing ticked off the list?

*Note: *I must stress that when I say 'dear reader', I don't mean it in a patronising, sat-in-a-wingback-chair-wearing-a-dressing-gown-sipping-brandy kind of way. It's just that I've no idea how else to address you. Don't worry; I'm not so naïve as to think that just because I'm dying I'm any better or wiser than the next person. That won't stop me preaching unfounded advice, of course, but it'll help if you understand two things:*

1) I genuinely don't know what I'm talking about.

2) I'm going to be doing it whilst calling you 'dear reader', whether you like it or not.

iii) The girl with no name

As morning drips through window slits,

The girl with no name won't rise

The man she loved just thinks and sits;

 Digests her with his eyes.

They loved enough to fix the world,

Emblazed with moonlit skin,

Bed sheets liquid, creased and curled,

Absorbed by gills and fin.

Their bodies break, and split apart,

peeling thighs from hips,

the last time that they'll share a heart,

Enveloped in her lips.

Stay there girl; sleep in peace;

Not knowing good from bad,

His parting is the best release;

she'll know the love they had.

As morning drips through window slits,

The girl with no name won't rise

Sleeping beauty's name befits;

 In alcohol's disguise.

iv) Pie-type things

I left the girl there - in her own bed - wondering firstly how many people across the country were doing the same thing every morning, and secondly what on Earth her bloody name was. My best guess would be Suzanne. She looked like a Suzanne.

Potentially, that girl you meet in a pub on that idle Monday could turn out - if such a thing exists - to be your soul mate. The two of you could be cosmically bound together by the powers of fate and destined to be each other's 'one.' If that were the case then I could have just walked out on the best thing ever to happen to me, without even being able to remember her blasted name. Not that it makes much difference now of course. For the rest of you though, it's an interesting thought.

I'm probably over-thinking things; that was my first ever one-night-stand after all. Another thing to cross off the list, and another notch on the bedpost of my own moral ambiguity.

I got home just in time to hear the hurried end of an answer phone message. The voice stopped talking too quickly for me to recognise who it was, a plight not aided by the jingling of my keys and the slamming of the front door – a noise that echoed off the barren walls so palpably that you could almost see the sound waves bounce. My front room is bare, and the answer phone is the only thing plugged in. There are boxes *everywhere*.

I don't know if you've ever moved house, but there seems to be the paradoxical problem that there are never enough bloody boxes and, at the same time, the things seem to multiply before your eyes like bacteria. There's one pile in particular that worries me most, since it's building up in an alarmingly organised fashion and is starting to resemble the central business district of a thriving city. I can't remember putting them there and I can't for the life of me remember what's in them. The stress is probably just getting to me, but all the same I think I'll leave the pile to its own devices and hope I move out or die long before its public transport system starts developing a problem with flickering bulbs.

Whilst I'm on the subject of contumelious observations regarding modern living, I *hate* the pitch of answer phone machine beeps. I fully accept that the noise is designed to grab your attention, but have you ever noticed how many beeps we have to put up with these days? Your phone beeps, your answer phone beeps, your watch beeps, your microwave beeps, your computer beeps, your alarm beeps, your TV beeps, my toaster beeps (because it cost far more than a toaster should), and now even this book is beeping. Why is it always beeping? A beep is an urgent and stressful noise. If it's not 'beep' it's the equally sharp and painful 'ding' or 'ting', which I'm sure manufacturers think are all rather inoffensive, but to be honest there's a myriad sounds in the universe that have the potential to alert you while not poking that part of your brain which makes you hurt at the same time. Maybe I'll spend the next year designing machines that make the sound of crisp snow crunching beneath your feet, or of the ocean lapping at the shore. I reckon that'd be a pretty satisfying way to be told that your ready-meal is done.

At any rate, I had to make the answer phone beep at least three more times before I could hear the message hidden within.

'You have one new message.'

'Hi Alan, it's Tim. Either your mobile's been switched off all day or you just hate me. We were wondering if you wanted to come round for tea tonight? Jenny's making some sort of pie-type thing. Let me know. Cheers.'

Tim and Jenny - for those unsure - are my best friends, and have been since university started seven years ago. He's in career limbo; she does costume-related things at the BBC. I would tell you more about them but I'm terribly aware of the fact that any writer worth his proverbial salt should reveal details drip by drip. It would be no good if I were to start detailing their entire existence, warts and all, as soon as they make their very first appearance. And by 'no good' I mean 'irresponsible', both because there are some stories I feel you should have to earn through blind persistence, and also because - save for any extraordinary events - I only really have a limited amount of things to talk about. Thus, I'm going to try and stagger information so as to keep you reading. If this annoys you then I'm sorry, but I'll make it up by promising to tell you a very interesting anecdote involving myself and a banking error in a few chapters' time. For a more instant payoff however, the next paragraph will start with a fascinating insight into my culinary tastes.

I like pie-type things. I especially like home-cooked ones, not least because their preparation doesn't involve the sharp beep of a microwave reaching climax. It's three o'clock now, which is about the time that a person who hasn't had lunch is trying to stave off hunger. Three o'clock, however, is not a good time to eat for the following reasons:

•It is halfway between a good time for lunch and a good time for dinner.

•If you eat at three o'clock you will be hungry at about midnight. This isn't good for me because I really like cheese, and if you eat cheese before you go to bed you'll have nightmares.

With the looming threat of nightmares in mind I returned the call and arranged to go round for dinner; resigning myself to fight the hunger until I was allowed to be let loose on the pie-type thing. (This is already getting to be an action-packed read, isn't it?). Their house is in Palmers Green, which is a place inconveniently equidistant from two tube stations and requires a considerable walk from either. This was only really a problem because I don't like buses, I'm lazy and because today has taken a turn towards the inexplicably freezing.

***

Tim answered the door wearing a green pinnie; his slender frame being wrapped up and hidden by doileyed fingertips. He looked like a peacock who hadn't fully read his mission statement. My alarmed expression must have alerted him to the fact that he still had it on because he suddenly seemed to jolt and then frantically rip it off, as if it were an especially frilly snake trying to constrict his lungs. All very funny to witness.

"I was helping with the cooking."

"Oh right. I didn't realise you had to be a flamboyant homosexual to cook these days."

"Just get in."

Tim's hallway was just as barren as mine, and there

seemed to be a splinter faction of the box city growing there just as there was in my living room. He and Jenny are fairly clever people, but I noticed that one of them had thought it would prove useful to label nearly every box with the word 'stuff'. I really don't see how that would help anything, ever. Unless they are looking forward to the surprise of discovering which specific brand of 'stuff' each box contains as a reward for a successful move. My boxes aren't labelled, but I think that's more productive because, in theory, I could pack another box or two in the time it took them to write "stuff" on all of theirs. I didn't bother bringing this up though.

Jenny was in the kitchen sporting an equally effeminate pinnie. I have never been to a shop and had the compulsion to buy a pinafore, mainly because if you have full control of your limbs or any hand-eye coordination at all then it's pretty easy to avoid throwing food all over yourself. I therefore find it confusing that these people had bought (at least) two, coupled with a very real desire to wear them.

"God, you two love to wear pinnies," was the most eloquent sentence I managed to put together on the subject.

"There's lots of flour involved in making pie, Alan. It's messy work feeding freeloaders like you," said Jenny, rolling out the pastry.

"That may be so," I replied, kissing her on the cheek, "but I can't imagine you both needing to be involved in the flour-throwing process at the same time. If you've got some sort of flour/pinnie fetish then it's none of my business but it would be polite to finish before company arrives. At any rate I'm not a freeloader... I've bought a bottle of Tesco's finest."

I'd always been taught to bring some alcohol when attending a dinner party. It's incredibly rude to bring food as it implies that you won't like the cooking, but alcohol implies that you are both thankful and willing to share. Also, bringing a bottle of wine to a dinner party made me feel like a grown-up. Also also, I promise not to write the word 'pinnie' again in this chapter.

"Lovely stuff," Jenny said. "May is coming, by the way - so you can actually meet her before Friday."

Explanations are owed, I feel. Tim - having always expressed an interest in doing so - has also just quit his office job, but to pursue a career as an actor and not, I assume, because he's dying. What this means is that the two cannot afford to stay in their current house on just Jenny's salary. I was interested in moving, as was their friend May, whom I had never met. As such, the four of us are to move into a house in Tufnell Park together on Friday. we have only signed a contract for a year which, as it turns out, is fairly convenient for the simple reason that I'll stop being alive around the time that it runs out, and is also good for me because I don't have to spend my last year living alone - even if it means living in a housing situation essentially the same as the TV programme *'This Life'*. As odd and alien as it is moving into a house with someone I've never met, I'm not that bothered about it at the moment because it's taking a backseat to the more important moral issue of moving into a house with three people and not telling them that I'm dying. C'est la vie.

"Ah that's cool," I said, because it's acceptable to say the word 'cool' until you're about thirty. At thirty you must stop and say something slightly more conservative like 'good' in its place. If I could teach you nothing else, it would probably be that.

Tim and Jenny flitted about the kitchen as I sat at the table sipping a glass of wine thinking about the word 'cool'. They've been together for seven years but still consider each other with affectionate touches every time their paths cross. They act as a couple just created; still intrigued by each other's forms and graces, and it always makes me happy to see such an unflinching kind of love. What's most unusual to me about it is that, in the absence of proposals, engagement and marriage, they now find themselves - having lived alone as a couple for four years - just as willing to move into a shared house as would be any two young singletons. 'Unusual' is probably the wrong word actually; I think it's bloody fantastic.

They had me hypnotised for some time watching various bits of chicken, mushrooms and things that I've no inclination to name being dunked in the pie dish when the doorbell rang. This time Jenny went to it, presumably because May was more her friend just as I was more Tim's. Suddenly I felt very nervous. I felt like a man on a blind date, or one who was about to meet his arranged bride for the first time. It didn't help, of course, that this was to be another person for the list of people I must lie to about my health.

Jenny returned with her guest. May entered the kitchen with a bottle of white wine clutched in her tiny hands. She stood in the doorway, favouring me with a few darting glances and waited for a formal introduction. The awkwardness of the situation made it drag, and after what seemed like a length of time far too long to recover from, Tim stepped up.

"May, this is Alan. Alan, May."

I stood and said a very British hello, kissing her on the cheek. She smelt nice. She couldn't have been more than five feet five to my six foot. Her rounded face was framed with long, black hair. It sounds funny to say - almost chauvinistic - but she clearly hadn't made a huge effort with her hair or make-up. Thing is, she clearly didn't care, and it gave her an air of confidence that made her markedly more attractive than if she had cemented her skin under layers of foundation. Her face was incredibly natural and almost milk white. She sat down as Jenny handed her a wine glass. I poured her a glass from my bottle and was repaid with a soft 'thank you'. When she spoke her voice would fluctuate wildly. Throughout the night words would sometimes escape her as a calm, ladylike, almost vapourous release. Others in a much more girly pop of excitement, often brashly erupting into a rapturous laugh.

I don't remember much-worth of anything from the rest of the night (save from the quality of the pie), because - far from being the adults we tried to be - we ended up racing each other to a wonderful state of thick, heavy drunkenness. Wrapped up in the warmth of laughter and wine, however, and as the gravy seeped through our bloodstreams I remember taking in May's form through blurred eyes and thinking: 'You might very well just be my favourite thing here.'

v) **Dropping spiders**

I've been thinking about the whole 'list of things to do before you die' thing. After looking at some suggestions on the internet I've decided to detail some of the ones that I most definitely will *not* be doing before I die. These are as follows:

<u>Buy everyone in the pub a drink:</u>

No. On one website I found this was number one on the list. It actually nestled *above* swim with dolphins, and I have absolutely no idea why. This seems like an ill-thought-out, last-ditch attempt to gain friends or some such vein nonsense, but to be honest, it just seems like nothing but a very expensive waste of time. I know you can't take money with you but there are many better things to spend it on whilst you *are* still kicking about than pints for barflies. These people (who are obviously never going to say no to a free pint) might manage to inflate your booze-buying ego for a while with drunken shouts of "legend!" or similar empty praise, but once you've left they're really not going to give a single flying fuck about you. They certainly won't be filling seats at your funeral on the basis of one drink. What a waste of bloody list space.

Hugged a tree:

What? Why? I just don't understand the things some people want to do with their time, I really truly don't. "Yay; hugging a tree is fun... oh wait now I'm covered in wet bark... and there's a poisonous caterpillar on my arm. Brilliant."

Changed a nappy:

I'm starting to get the impression that some of these are just things to have experienced rather than the podium of life-changing events the list ought to be. Wipe green faeces off a baby's arse? No thanks.

Held a Tarantula:

I don't like spiders, especially big ones. Having said that, I've heard that if you drop a Tarantula on its back from about a metre it shatters like glass. This I think might actually be worth doing just to try that out. But then if I'm going to say that I might as well say I want 'Drop a Tarantula' on my list instead, to save it from being more like a set of instructions. I'd bloody love to smash one - evil little bastards.

Touched an iceberg:

It seems like the necessary travel involved to achieve this would be a long bloody way to go just to touch a piece of ice. I have enough trouble with defrosting my freezer because the seal's broken. It's not coming with me when I move.

Have the honour of meeting Michael T. Weiss and chat for awhile:

Someone had this on their list. I searched for Mr Weiss on the web and found out that he played Dr. Mike Horton on 'Days of our Lives.' I'll say no more.

Live abroad:

Doesn't it really depend where abroad is? I mean I do regret that I'm not going to get to really travel the world, but this person's 'abroad' might mean London, in which case I'm one up on them. I grew up in a small town and then moved here for university. Having lived somewhere else already means I can happily say that I have experienced two different ways of life, and that I know I'll be happy to spend my last days in London. I've always been the kind of person that's interested more in the smaller experiences in life than the big adventures. I'd rather read a text message than a newspaper, and I'd rather relish and appreciate one more year of normal life than see the rest of the world without being able to properly take it all in. Besides, I've just signed that contract on the new house.

See Area 51:

Bit ambitious, this. I think that if you're going to have this on your list it should either be the last thing you have planned (because you would undoubtedly get shot to pieces) or you should have the list entry before it as 'become the president of the USA, thus gaining clearance to Area 51', which isn't something I'm too keen on either, to be honest. Seems like quite a stressful job.

2. MAY

Baked Beans
Bread
Orange squash
Token item(s) of fruit
Fresh Chicken / Sausages
Beer / cider (whatever's on offer)
Wine
You're out of gin.

Things learned:

- No matter how much you safeguard them with what's advertised as strong tape, some cardboard boxes simply lack the required enthusiasm to carry your unending shite from one room to another. If they get wet, this problem worsens tenfold.

- The whole thing about lifting with your knees not your back only applies to those not dying in a year. Screw you, health and safety.

- To an extent, how to make a chicken pie. Current chance of ever using this specific nugget of culinary wisdom: incredibly slim.

Favourite Text:

Jenny: "May thought you were really nice so that's all cool. In other news, Tim's been flicking me in the back of the head all day saying I deserve it for making him drink wine. Please come round and do whatever it is men do with each other. Not the pub. x"

i) Sofa cushions don't have Oyster cards

Yesterday we moved into the new house. As surprising/miraculous/implausible as it sounds, a group of four quasi-adults who know nothing about anything managed to disassemble their lives and move them all to a new location in just one day and without too much trouble. And by 'without too much trouble', I mean nobody died.

As a child I was always willing and able to tune out when adults started discussing mortgages, bank accounts, interest rates etc., safe in the knowledge that at some point someone would sit me down and teach me all about how to be a grown-up. I bloody wish that *had* happened, because if I'd been taking notes on these boring conversations then by now I might to some extent have an understanding of how the world around me functions. As it is, when it comes to organising things of any real importance I tend to leave everything to someone else. Thus, the move was mostly choreographed by Tim and Jenny.

The problem with that is that, while I'm basically a

child in an adult's body, they really aren't much more clued up themselves. We'd decided that we could all share one moving lorry, as this would be the cheapest option and Tim was convinced that they were "quite big these days, so all our stuff should get on no worries." This was ambitious in the first instance, but I'll get to that in a bit. Basically, May lived furthest away from where we were moving to and they lived closest, so theoretically the route should have gone like this:

➤ May's flat – Cup of tea, then pack her kettle and mugs onto the lorry.

➤ My flat - Pick up my all-encompassing pile of boxes.

➤ Tim and Jenny's house – Pick up their all-encompassing collection of pinnies.

➤ New house – Unpack mugs, boxes and pinnies.

➤ Get drunk.

Nothing ever goes this smoothly, though, and due to the fact that (for some ill-conceived reason) Tim was in charge of booking the lorry, he got it wrong and it turned up at his house first. At ten o'clock then - when it was supposed to be at May's house - Tim and Jenny started loading all their things onto the gargantuan lorry. It then went past me and on to May's, where they loaded her stuff onto it.

In the confusion, nobody rang me to tell me the plans had changed.

This extra hanging about probably wouldn't have bothered me too much if it weren't for the inconvenient fact that I am dying, and therefore don't count 'waiting around for a lorry' as a particularly good way to spend three hours of my final year on Earth. This is especially annoying when EVERYTHING you own is either *in* a pile of boxes or *under* a pile of boxes, meaning there is literally nothing to do to keep yourself occupied. No TV, no internet, no music, no food. If you ever find yourself in a similar situation - and everybody refuses to answer their phones - I defy you not to question first of all if you have the right moving day and then, ultimately, whether your friends have just been figments of your malicious imagination all this time. All I knew was that I was sat on the floor in a barren flat with nothing to do, while I waited blindly for a lorry that might or might not ever turn up. As the minutes disappeared I felt increasingly like a complete, utter mental.

At about half-three the lorry finally rolled up outside and Tim got out with two burly-looking removal men - burly being an understatement because they were both bigger than I'd have thought physics should rightly allow. I was about the size of their thumbs.

This was probably just as well, though, since it's startling just how much shite one person can own, and especially handy when almost all of it leans towards the 'heavy' end of the 'annoying to lift' spectrum. My particular pile of shite had taken me a frustratingly long time to organise and sort out, and the collection of boxes that had been scaring me a few pages ago had now collapsed under its own weight - no doubt causing untold damage to the civilisation built up around it. Tim and I pretended to help by carrying hollow things like lamps and cheese graters as the burly men took hold of my wardrobe and bed single-handedly. Their aptitude for the task at hand made me realise and appreciate that there really is a job for everyone out there: these lads were clearly never going to be doing anything *but* shift furniture. No discredit to them; they did their job well (despite being noticeably annoyed at the hugely illogical route Tim had them take), but people this big were never cut out for the weedy office world; they're purpose-built. One was bald and had massive cauliflower ears that drooped right down to his neck, where an illegible tattoo cracked over his skin like armour. He looked a bit like how I imagine the Big Bang must have looked if it was from Ealing Broadway. His esteemed colleague just looked like a brick wall.

We got to a point when all that was left was my lounge sofa. I had pushed it up against a wall in the front corridor the day before and stacked its cushions neatly, but that was as far as I was prepared to go because I'm not exactly what you'd call 'strong'. What happened next isn't exactly interesting, but it did lead to an interesting set of events, so to spruce it up and speed things along I'll try and write it in a jaunty little verse. This is more for my own amusement than yours, but bear with me:

The burly men came in for the chair,

And carried it away,

They didn't see the cushions there,

Much to my dismay.

I'd told Tim I would get the train -

Meet him at our abode,

Now I had an extra strain -

Carrying cushions down the road.

Bearing in mind it was rush hour, I wasn't that thrilled about the prospect of getting on the tube with six sofa cushions forced between my arms. Stacked one on top of each other they came up way past my eyes, meaning that - unless I could think up some clever way of convincing them to no longer exist - I would have to walk about London blind, dressed as the chap from the Michelin adverts. In a hopeless effort to plan the most efficient way of transporting them with only the two upper limbs I was born with,

I wasted about five minutes of my soon-ending life just limply staring at the things, feeling sorry for myself. A text from Tim explaining that he'd see me at the house and 'well done for a successful move' didn't really help things, but it did snap me into a sort of action.

***

It is amazing how scary the world *sounds*.

When all you can see is a collection of horizontal zips, the car horns and general bustled hustle hits your ears in a pretty daunting manner. It's also amazing how hard it is to walk about town with a window of vision no bigger than about four postage stamps on either side. Nobody in our polite British society said anything of course (or if they did I couldn't hear them), but I could feel their eyes on me - staring at me and trying to work out what possible set of circumstances could have led me to such a pain-in-the-arse existence.

I enjoy people-watching. It doesn't matter where you are in the world, it is *always* the case that if you spend more than about thirty seconds in a built-up area you will always clap eyes on one or more of the people I affectionately refer to as 'mentals'. You can usually spot mentals a mile away because they will invariably have something on their person that clearly separates them from the rest of normal human-kind. This, for instance, could be a particular item of clothing; something that challenges all usual definitions of the word 'acceptable' with regards to why it would ever be *made*, let alone bought and then ultimately worn. Often it's coupled with curiously developed facial hair - even the women. Some mentals wash their hands with the ever-changing fashion scene and get it in their heads that we are all in a bygone decade, wearing full outfits ripped straight from the seventies or eighties. Others carry around singular shopping bags from shops that don't exist for at least 50 miles or have long since closed down - the contents of which protrude and bulge in shapes that could almost definitely match up with parts of a human corpse. Mentals are never a normal size, always growing into misshapen bodies of polar extremes (both in terms of height and width), and - crucially - they will sport a more than worrying expression that ventures down one of two routes: either they've seen nightmarish things the likes of which you couldn't possibly imagine, or they are essentially the living dead.

The point is that when I spot one of these mentals I usually make good sport of trying to work out what's in the bag, where they've been or where they're going. It's fun to think about where they live, or to ponder just what it was in their life that has given them that look of terror and confusion. What I'm getting at here is that yesterday - barring the unusual facial hair and *visibly* pained expression - Tim had unwittingly relegated me to the status of a mental in the eyes of all those in the high street. In fairness to the British public, I think even *I'd* find it hard to come up with a back-story complicated enough to explain why *anyone* would be stomping about town with six sofa cushions.

I don't want to talk about how much of a struggle crossing the road was because it was a bloody nightmare and, frankly, I'd rather forget it entirely. Instead, I want you to try and imagine a broken man standing at the little turnstile-type doors at the entrance of the tube, before duly lobbing six large sofa cushions over it with all the enthusiasm of someone who's just been fired from the DFS warehouse, but who still has to carry out their last day regardless. This wasn't dignified. This especially wasn't dignified because I then had to then swipe through it as proudly as I could before stooping over and trying to reassemble the pile - picking them up from the mucky, greasy floor. All this happened at rush hour, remember, so on the opposing side of the gate where the escalators met street level at least fifty tired and bemused commuters bore witness to the ridiculous sofa dance on their way home.

I was now *definitely* a mental. The Definitely Mental Death of Alan Bell.

The tube was the least eventful leg of the journey. I was travelling *into* London at such a time that it was basically empty, and my cushions managed to sit three to a seat - admittedly a fate only marginally better than the floor. I'm still not really sure how I got to the station in one piece, seeing as it was nigh-on impossible to see where I was going and the outside world is limitlessly dangerous. But as my embarrassed face calmed out of its rose-red state I realised that that was probably the last time I'd walk through the high street at Turnpike Lane for a long time. Possibly ever. Shame, then, that I couldn't really take in the sights.

When I reached my stop I made my way carefully up the escalators by feel. The dark air whipped at my cheeks from the only two angles it could attack. My arms ached. The thinly-aired streets were all but empty and I was thankful to be under cover of near-darkness. I was, however, fully aware of the fact that - whilst I could walk from my old flat to the tube blindfolded - I was shaky on this new route to say the very least. It didn't matter though... I had come this far.

Actually, at the time it really didn't matter. On my journey I had transformed. I had met every challenge before me and by this point I had become some kind of cushion-carrying soldier of fortune. I was God of all things furniture. I had risen through the ranks from inaptly-built budget removal man to a regular scientist of sofa physics. I was locked in an epic bout with tiring arms and lacklustre vision and - damn it - I was going to win. I set off in the direction of the house knowing that in a mile's time I was going to be sat with an fresh beer in my new and final home. I was going to be sat on this sofa and - mark my words - it would be the comfiest sofa ever stitched into being.

The only thing is (and this is a big problem), is that when it's dark and your vision of an unfamiliar area is largely blocked by a wall of cushions, every time you hear someone cross your path your heart jumps and you pray to god that it won't be (A) a murderer, (B) a bigger murderer or (C) a big murderer with a more than partial interest in living-room upholstery. I tried to reassure myself that we had moved to a nice area, and such people were confined to the gritty slums of a fictitious Dickensian London, but it was always in the back of my mind that London is London and big murderers lurk just about everywhere as a result. I was busy scaring myself stupid with this less than helpful notion when my thoughts were interrupted by a voice. The voice belonged to one half of the four feet that had just passed me, and it was probably the worst thing I could have heard given the already ridiculous circumstances.

"Alright, mate?"

Chavs. Two dirty little London scallies that should rightly have either been in jail or in bed. I wasn't their 'mate'. I doubt they were even each other's mates. They were probably just hanging about together to work out the best way to nick each other's wallets.

"Fine, thanks," I mumbled, not stopping for a second.

"You what?" he said, so shocked at my reply it was as if I had just made his mother out as a whore. She probably was, to be fair.

I stopped and turned around, ending side-on so I could at least see their faces. I'm at that age now where I find it impossible to tell the difference between an eight year-old and an eighteen year-old, and anything carbon-based in between (as these were) just falls neatly into the indistinguishable bracket of 'child'. One of them had a BMX at any rate, so I suppose they'd have to have been quite young. …Or they'd just robbed someone quite young. They were both wearing baseball caps that were perched in a near vertical position on their heads, presumably to keep their overly big hoods from falling over their wasted little eyes. I took a deep breath and stopped.

You may already think that I have a somewhat negative view of today's kids. I'll have you know that this isn't out of abject, unfounded ageism, though. It is because I feel there exists in the world a certain sect of people who - through no fault of their own - are quite simply not born normal. Quite different from your everyday 'mentals', they are born angry, aggressive, and cruel. These people may learn to surpass these tendencies in later life, they may not, but what is for sure is that when married with the completely mad amount of hormones teenagers have to deal with, this antagonistic nature can and does manifest itself as something which is basically the purest of evil. These days this evil tends to manifest itself in the form of chavs, a sect of sub-society that wears something of a uniform to make it easier for us to pick them out. At any rate, it appears that they make it their sole aim in life to make everyone else's as shit as possible, and it seems to increasingly be the case that every single child I see *is* one of the little bastards. Ageism schmageism; kids today are evil.

These two, as I had feared, were clearly out looking for trouble. I sighed heavily.

"I just said I was fine. You asked me if I was alright and I said I was fine." Then I did something silly: I carried on talking, and I used words with more than one syllable. "Am I to assume," I continued, "that you weren't merely interested in how I was doing? I thought you were extending a friendly greeting, and reassuring me that we do in fact live in a nice world where people look out for one another. Now I take it you weren't, though, so I'm just going to go. Bye."

I stayed looking at them for just long enough to register their faces changing from mindlessly aggressive to even more mindlessly aggressive, then turned round and carried on walking. I realised that trying to talk back intellectually to the physical embodiment of misplaced rage, while carrying ungainly soft furnishings, was a stupid idea when I suddenly heard racing footsteps from behind, followed by the sensation of the load in my arms swiftly lessening. It took me a minute to recover from the shock of what had actually happened, but those cheeky little bastards had nicked - and subsequently biked away with - one of my sofa cushions without even saying a word. With only my basic use of the English language I had bamboozled them into thievery. And so the degeneration of Britain's youth continues, albeit with slightly comfier seating.

When I finally got to the house Tim greeted me with a bottle of beer and a worried look on his face.

"I think we've lost the cushions for your sofa, mate."

I stared at him blankly, trying to work out how to even begin to tell him the absolutely absurd set of trials I had been through, bearing in mind that this chapter is quite long and I'm no good at storytelling in the aural form anyway. I'm sure you'll understand then, that - instead of telling him how being robbed by parasitic scallies had ultimately caused me to drop every last cushion in the street out of sheer self-pathos - I simply shrugged, took a sip of ice-cold beer and said:

"Err... I'll go to IKEA tomorrow."

ii) Stealing small items

This house makes some odd noises at night. Things clank and clunk worryingly, and every now and again animals of unknown evolutionary origin make busy noises up in the roof. I suppose it's one of those things I'll get used to and come to depend upon to lull me to sleep. Or at least I hope this is the case, as 'I'll sleep when I'm dead' has never been in my repertoire of mottos. Speaking of sleep, I had to do what little I managed on the floor last night as my room doesn't yet have a bed and my sofa is recently bereft of cushions. I knew before we moved that I'd be sofa-bound for a while, since our new landlord clearly isn't a big believer in beds, but in truth I don't think I quite realised what a pain in the arse buying one of the things would actually be.

My new room is a warm shade of cream that nicely radiates the shadows of the few items of furniture I do have – a bedside table and a rickety old wardrobe. The deep red blind has to be actually taken off the wall and rolled up and down like a scroll, but I don't see the point in ever having it up because what waits behind is a yard of windy nothing bouncing off the brickwork of the opposing house. I'm not complaining of course, especially as my input in finding this house was as minimal as it could get. I tend to enjoy letting everything get sorted around me, giving a placid thumbs-up to whatever gets organised or agreed upon by the masses. As long as I'm being told what to do by people I trust, I'll do nigh on anything for an easy life. It's probably the reason why I haven't been overly angry at fate for painting me with a terminal illness; I'm too laid-back to not just go along with it.

All my stuff sits in boxes that lean against the far wall - inch for inch the same pile as was in my last house. For whatever reason it doesn't scare me anymore. If anything it just annoys me. I foresee that unpacking is going to be more trouble than packing because I have a real problem with knowing where to start with such things, and as such I imagine it'll be a case of doing half of one box before getting distracted by the promise of another.

In England, as is the case in a large part of the western world, modern humans purchase their furniture in a place called IKEA. I suspect that no matter what time period it is that you as a reader find yourself in, this is probably still the case. I fear that it would take something of a very organised and well-funded rebellion (led by an abundance of pure common sense) to overthrow the Swedish giant. ...and I say common sense because there is literally nothing logical about the way the shop works.

This morning - as Tim and Jenny stayed and sorted out the various communal areas of the house - May and I trotted off to IKEA. This was primarily to get a few items for our bedrooms (including a bed), with a secondary mission of trying to create a makeshift sofa based around the shell that remained from mine. I have my suspicions that this situation was Tim and Jenny's construction as a way for me to spend some time getting to know May, but I was glad for it. We got up early for lack of sleep in our new abode and hopped several busses to the big blue behemoth of a shop. It's a strange looking place. Instead of the welcoming warmth and smooth lines of most shops, IKEA looks like an angular alien mothership that's fallen from space and been painted sky-blue so as not to draw attention, while E.T and his mates fix the engine.

"I really, really, really hate this place," I said as we began our ascent. It was like being willingly swallowed by a huge whale; a huge, *evil* whale.

"I've never been to one. It does look a bit … imposing though."

Bless her: she was looking around in a kind of awe, and clearly had no idea what was about to happen to us - no idea that she was being escalated face-first into a world of unmitigated frustration. I then proceeded (out of duty) to tell her in detail everything I thought was wrong with the multi-tiered shop from hell.

"Basically," I started, "if you want to shop online then you shop online, and if you don't then you do as we're doing and physically go to a shop. Fundamentally the two experiences *should* be different…"

We were walking through the showroom at this point, and she was half listening to me whilst finding it increasingly funny that the Swedes had found it necessary to give every item a name, instead of just a product number. She joked that she wanted to buy a spade called 'Doug', and with that I lost my point and started to have fun.

I was saved in this instance by good company, but I'll continue my point to you, dear reader. In a real, actual shop, one is supposed to be able to take the object one desires from the shelf and then bring it to the till and pay for it. IKEA, quite to the contrary, has for some reason tried to set itself up as if it was a website… except in the real world. What I mean by this is that it is divided into three parts. First of all there's the showroom, where every item of large furniture they sell is arranged in a sprawling maze. There are small fake bedrooms and offices that look impossibly clean and precise, the idea of which is to entice people into buying pretty much everything on show. The place is so big that there's usually a restaurant stuffed in the middle of it so that you can eat just enough to sustain your weary organs for another few hours of shopping. If you can call it that. It's more like being paraded round an overly proud friend's house and marking down all the things they own that make their life better than yours.

To the first time IKEA shopper, anyone who in possession of a brain or anyone used to the functions of a normal store it's all far too big an ask to understand what the hell's going on. On my first trip I actually tried to pick up an armchair from a faux living room and put it in my trolley, almost knowing that what I was doing was wrong but waiting haplessly for somebody to tell me so. What you're supposed to do (and you're meant to figure this out by yourself) is write down the little code attached to each item on a bit of paper as you go round.

This would be all well and good if there were any members of staff around to inform you, but the place is such a ghost town that if it were open twenty-four-seven it wouldn't be at all hard to hunker down and live in one of the little bedrooms. There are plenty of empty information kiosks stocked with pencils and notepaper, but I think ideally what's needed is a short seminar at the entrance to the showroom, much like the aeroplane safety instructions before a flight. As it is, I find it a bit too much to expect people to pick up their pencil and paper and actually know what to do with it without just assuming they've entered a pub quiz. It's like mixing shopping with a particularly obscure murder mystery, wherein nobody actually gets murdered.

Once you've decided what you want to buy, you have to go into a big warehouse and get it, but I can't for the life of me understand why. This kind of manual labour is the part of shopping usually done by the people that actually work at the shop. I have no idea how IKEA has managed to convince people that if they want a bed, they have to go and carry it to the till themselves, especially considering most shop warehouses would require you to wear a hard hat and fill in at least eighteen pages of health and safety forms before you were even allowed to enter. The place is filled floor to ceiling with generic flat-pack bollocks that has a tendency to be the most awkward thing ever to have to remove from a shelf, but you do it anyway because:

A) There's no one around to help you

B) Once you've got that far, it's fairly impossible to leave without buying *something* out of pride.

So you pick up Freda, your pine-finished queen-sized double bed, load it onto a trolley yourself, then wander off to find the slats (which they make you buy separately), and then finally the mattress.

May and I between us had one full trolley, and three large rollers full of beds, chests of drawers; strange gravity-defying DVD racks and wardrobes. I'm not one of those people naturally capable of controlling/ steering/driving a shopping trolley, even when it's empty. When you've three of these laden, wheeled death-carts, steering capably becomes somewhat trickier still, and a secondary priority to just not killing anyone or tearing down the whole shop. Neither is the kind of legacy I want to leave this planet with. What made it worse by far is that May apparently has the arm strength of a malnourished baby, so I had to do most of the legwork myself – the result being that I looked like a stressed out shepherd performing a rain dance. In Hell.

At any rate, one nearly broken bone, several dented boxes and one terrified child later we somehow found our way to the till. There were (approximately) ninety million people in the shop when we were there, and only two open tills. By this point I think May had found out the hard way exactly why nobody likes going to IKEA, as she turned to me pretending to cry and demanding that she wanted to go home. She did this very loudly, which was funny until people around us started looking at me as if I'd just beaten her up.

I think what I'll do now is explain the third part of IKEA's nonsensical shop format, and *then* explain how we accidentally got one up on them. I've got a stream-of-consciousness type thing going on now so there's no sense in stopping.

Thirdly then, once you've maimed several other shoppers and paid for your fifteen tons of low-grade MDF, it becomes frighteningly apparent that you've not only bought more furniture than you'll ever need but also that - unless you're with Bruce Banner and someone makes him very angry – you won't be able to get it home.

IKEA realises this and courteously provides a delivery service that you have to cart everything over to, after having paid. I'm having trouble putting into words how soul-crushingly annoying this is. Nobody but me seems to have realised that, whilst to some extent you'll have spent your time as a consumer, you also spend the bulk of your time in IKEA actually *working* for the swines. Think about it: if it was a website, you would place your order, drink away your debt worries and go back to sleep - all from the comfort of home, while some burly warehouse operative is paid to pick up your order and trudge it to the back of a van for delivery. IKEA - having hit upon an idea that precisely strikes that marvellous balance between laziness and genius - gets us to do it for them, and for some reason nobody argues. I suppose more than anything I'm just a tad jealous at having not come up with the idea myself, but it still baffles me as to how they've managed to get away with it all this time under the thinly-veiled disguise of providing relatively cheap products.

The furniture is cheap because it is consistently and unflinchingly shit.

I think if I had more time on this planet I might've opened a garden centre where customers are required to come in on a daily basis and water the plants for a year before they're allowed to buy them.

However: forgetting the fact that for one long morning/afternoon I came out of my early retirement to accidentally work under IKEA's employ, we did have a bit of a result. Due to the overwhelming surge of angry people at the till, the checkout girls weren't too keen on doing their job thoroughly, meaning we were hurried through without much in the way of personal service. Our cashier, Keisha, hastily scanned everything she could see, but that's not say everything we *had*. And so it was that we learnt one handy loophole in IKEA's otherwise flawless business plan: if you hide the slats for your bed down the side of the mattress then as far as Keisha, the security guards and the Swedes in general are concerned, they don't exist. This worked twice with slats and once with a lamp, each obtained completely gratis thanks to the staff's lack of enthusiasm or training beyond an ethos where line-of-sight is king.

I class free slats(x2) and a lamp as an alright compromise for a day's hard graft, so I'm almost willing to forgive the big blue shop for all its misgivings. Almost.

Maybe, in this time of instant gratification - when kids 'don't know they're born' and everything is a mere button click away - having a torrid time purchasing furniture keeps people in check with reality. IKEA might be doing society a service, because as May quite rightly put it:

"You bloody well earn your furniture, don't you?"

I'm still not sure where I stand, but I do know that for all the hardships and frustrations that getting our furniture caused, I had a very addictive time in May's exceptionally addictive company.

Oh, and in terms of the sofa mission: we gave up entertaining the notion of salvaging the cushion-less one, so we bought a new one entirely, along an exorbitant amount of supplementary cushions – the plan being to make a huge cushion pile in the corner of the living room and sit in it like contented, misshapen cats. Sorted.

iii) Someone to blame

Dying a predictable type of death as I am, I suppose it's only normal to develop a greater interest in religion. I consider myself fairly agnostic and, as such, I'm open to the idea that there might well be something enormously big out there (or bigger than Chiswick, at least), but there also might not. Trying to comprehend the confusion cocktail that is outer space - how big it is, how we're just hanging there inside it and basically what it *is* in the first place – usually leads the fragile human mind to the convenient conclusion that someone or something must be behind it all. More to the point I think we like to look for someone who's *responsible* for it - someone to blame for the whole thing. This is only natural.

I seem to have recently developed frequent mood swings about the unfairness of being cut short - sometimes feeling punished, sometimes feeling very at ease. At the time of writing this I'm in a good place, quite nonchalant about life and death (I swear that quite often the latter seems to be the easier option of the two), so I reckon this is as good a time as any to talk about religion as I see it in the modern world without getting too emotionally attached to the subject.

Having just researched it (my aforementioned 'greater interest' extends to looking at one website), apparently there are 22 major religious groups in the world, including 'non-religious, atheistic or agnostic' as one set. As far as I'm concerned, in real, everyday life there are only about four. Maybe five at a push.

I was raised as a Christian, and remained one up until I saw the film *Robin Hood, Prince of Thieves* starring Kevin Costner. You might wonder just how upset I'd have to be with a historically inaccurate portrayal of a medieval vigilante (with a thick American accent) for him to remove my faith in God, but rest assured it wasn't Costner's smug performance that did it. What *did* first turn me away from the church (at the tender age of nine) were the rather grubby onscreen actions of a certain cinematic Bishop. The Bishop of Hereford was played in the film by the ironically-named Harold Innocent and – though I appreciate that the film in question wasn't exactly based on fact - it did open my tunnelled eyes to the seedy, money hungry origins of the world's most popular religion.

Hang on: I think I may've jumped the gun a bit...

According to popular belief, God appeared. Following a prolonged stretch of boredom in the company of nothingness, he vomited up the Heaven and Earth and birds and bees. As is my understanding. In biblical times - a period of history void of any discernible proof to the contrary from science's corner - that must have seemed a fairly watertight theorem for the whole 'where did we come from?' conundrum.

My problem with all this though, is that Christianity seems shoot itself in the foot with too many magic tricks and a boat-load of dogmatic hypocrisy, all of which might've floated 200 years ago but just doesn't wash now. This maybe oversimplifying things, but I reckon that it's simple human nature to look to the skies for answers. This means that if enough people around you explain away difficult questions with "God did it" as you grow up, you're fairly likely to believe them. God in the Christian sense has a fairly captive audience, then. He's got the competition all sewn up. Or at least he would have if it weren't for all the unnecessary smoke and mirrors that do nothing but tarnish his believability. The paparazzi were out in full force when Jesus came to visit so we still have lasting testament to his japing about on (and with) H2O, as well as fixing every disease under the sun and making one fish into thousands of fish - which today is pretty hard to swallow. To me, it just screams 'please believe me; I'm bloody magic, I am.' If he'd just appeared and spread God's good word through nothing but persuasive speech-making, that'd be easier for me to get along with.

Things get worse at the Robin Hood stage. It turns out that the organised side of Christianity is (or at least was) run by the kind of people God wouldn't even gift a second interview. It seems to me that, for all its apparent goodness and divine credentials, the church is a business like any other; its history is so corrupt that any adult with half a brain still under its spell must be so intensely god-fearing that they'd be too scared to actually *go* to Heaven in case they broke anything. By far my biggest problem with Christianity though is that, if such an unendingly wise, loving and all-knowing God existed, I doubt he'd be so dogmatically strict as to punish me to an eternity of hell just for not going to church every Sunday. If I were so benevolent as to be able to create an entire planet and stock it full of people; if I were so powerful and all-loving as to gift someone 70-odd years of life, I'd probably rather they went out and enjoyed themselves instead of endlessly kneeling down in a big building and asking me for their forgiveness. But then God does work in mysterious ways. Or so I'm told.

I always thought Judaism must be a reasonably convincing religion since Jesus *was* Jewish, while simultaneously being the poster child for Christianity. Actually, that's more confusing than anything else; I can only presume that the two religions share enough values for some sort of merger to seem viable. Of course, this is working on the assumption that the saying 'a problem shared is a problem halved' works if you exchange that first 'problem' with the word 'religion'. Which it probably doesn't.

According to popular stereotypes Jewish people are very good with money, but in a much less cutthroat way than Harold Innocent and his corrupt pals. In truth (at the risk of upsetting both Christians and Jews), the two aren't all that far removed from one another. In both faiths there is only one God. I've never been that sure whether this is the same God as Jesus' dad or whether the two are colleagues or rivals, but it doesn't really matter; I don't think that becoming a Jew at this stage in my life would offer me anything that'd be worth either a medical procedure on my special area *or* giving up pork. For me, the final nail in Judaism's coffin is that the letter 'J' doesn't exist in the Jewish alphabet and no one seems to have noticed. This means followers should really call themselves 'Ewish'. It's a fundamental literary oversight too big for me to overcome.

I could bang on and on about every religion in the 22-strong list, and I don't mean to favour some over others, but quite frankly I don't feel like I have the time. I'm dying at a speedy rate and explaining the ideologies of all the world's major religions would take many more words than I intend to write in the entirety of this book. Suffice to say, most religions do the same thing: they teach us to be nice to each other, to live good lives and give us something to aim for after death. The intricacies of each specific set of beliefs don't really matter when you break it down like that.

Whether it's eternal paradise that awaits you or the chance to do it all again in a different guise, the point of life in the eyes of most religions is to be a good person and to love those around you. Karma says 'do good things and good things will happen', the idea of reincarnation says do bad things and you'll end up as a tree*. Nobody wants to be a tree, so the incentive is to live a nice life full of nice deeds. It's all very simple. Dogmatic, yes, but pleasingly simple all the same.

*Note: *Admittedly, I never quite understood this. One of the possibilities of reincarnation, based on how well you've done as a person, genuinely is to come back as a tree. Whether you get promoted or relegated after that depends on how nice you've been as a tree, but how can a tree be good or bad? I'm not debunking the reincarnation idea completely, but the short answer is: it can't; it's a tree.*

So, at the end of all of this existential pondering, what do I think? I have to say that, although subscribing to one concrete ideology may give me a nice feeling of belonging and membership, I still think being agnostic is the thinking man's religious choice as it's the theological equivalent of hedging your bets. Either way I end up being right. I think I'll always have a view of organised religion as being a form of crowd control. In the days where people went around killing each other for fun, suggesting that doing so would land you in Hell for infinitum was a good way to make any civilisation's populous start behaving slightly better. In medieval times this started to get stretched and skewed until taxes and all sorts of other misgivings could be justified as 'God's will', and I just don't think that that's right. I don't think any sort of god, with all the power and compassion in the universe, would really condone scare-mongering.

I get confused as to how a being so loving and caring could in turn be so vengeful and angry. In that regard, my biggest hang up with religion is where it prevents you from having all the different kinds of fun that an atheist life lets you enjoy. If a god created pork, why not eat it? If a god made the day beautifully warm, why not wear as few clothes as you can? I'm not claiming to in any way understand the inner workings of a god, but why would one make things and then tell you not to interact with them? Maybe that's just my 'live for the now' mentality breaking through, but I think still it's a fair point.

I think I believe in the soul. 'I think I believe' is as strong an opinion as I'm prepared to put forward but I definitely think the idea has legs. When I close my eyes and try to grasp what my very 'self' is, I find it impossible and depressing to consider that everything I am as a person is merely the summation of bone, carbon, tissue and electrical signals. Our personalities - everything we love and hate - can't just be made up of physical matter, can it? It's obviously a self-serving and egotistical notion to believe that your existence will carry on after you die but that 'being' - of myself and of everyone I know - seems far too special a thing to just disappear into the ether and cease to be after death. Even if it carries on as mere energy, that soul must go somewhere, surely?

I dunno.

And that's the point, of course; the absolute best thing about theologising is that nobody actually knows *anything* for sure. This, in theory, puts me on a level playing field with someone who's studied religion and beliefs their entire life, and I find that incredibly exciting. It means that no one is wrong, no one is right and everyone's able to make up his or her own mind. I'm quite certain that no one's ever going to find out for sure either way, just as I'm sure that the secrets of the universe are far too beautiful and intense for the human brain to be able to comprehend without instantly melting - but that shouldn't stop you thinking about it for yourself.

On that note, I strongly believe that science and religion shouldn't be at odds, even if many people would try and convince you otherwise. Einstein was a big believer in God. He didn't try to debunk religious theory, just to use science to unravel God's plan. If science has proved the Big Bang, the existence of dinosaurs and the evolution of man, why can't religion make out that God did it all? The two needn't be at odds. If anything, the more science finds out and explains, the more crazy and god-given it all seems.

In closing, I wouldn't dream of telling anyone what to think, believe or trust in with regards to the mysteries of life. Moreover, I feel it'd be hugely irresponsible of you to read anything I say and treat it as actual advice, seeing as I know literally nothing about anything. If I could do just one thing, though, it'd be to encourage you to ignore anything anyone's ever told you, strip back all your beliefs to a point where you can start again and then make up your own mind. If you invent your own religion in the process, who's to say you're wrong?

The best part is this: if all religion does turn out to be completely wrong, you'll never know about it; you'll just be very, completely and irrevocably dead. Amen.

iv) **White lies and red busses**

Something that I didn't really expect to happen, happened last night. It seems to me that this is happening more and more often as of late, although offhand the only other example I can think of is that I didn't expect to be diagnosed with a terminal illness... and that happened.

...Such is my point.

Some exposition is required, I think, as I'd rather tell you the preamble than just blurt out the thing that happened, in much the same way thriller movies don't often tell everybody the big twist until they're good and ready.

Actually that's a bad example because, short of breaking into the movie studio and pilfering scripts, there isn't much the general public can do about the situation. This is different as the book is clearly already written and I'm more than a bit dead, which makes my power over you fairly minimal. I regret to admit, dear reader, that there wouldn't be much standing in your way should you choose to skip ahead in a fit of impatience and find out what's happened ahead of time. If you do want to do that, I can save you a lot of time messing about with last night's happenings by just telling you that right at the end of the book I die a death.

As further means of stopping you from skipping through the tripe, I've just decided that I want to weave some element of dramatic irony into my retelling of last night's events. This is a technique employed in thriller movies, whereby the audience know that Mr X is a murderer, but the other characters don't. I don't have any murders, but what I'll do is let you in on the story of that banking error I mentioned a few chapters ago. The way this'll work is that you and I will know something that Tim, Jenny, May *et al* don't – something aside from my illness, that is – that'll come into play during the following retelling of last night's events, as I lead up to the main thing that happened. Follow?

Basically, for this to work I need to ask you to shoot forward and read the last little bit of this chapter, and then promptly report back to read the bit below this, without having read anything else in-between.

This serves the dual purpose that if you *were* impatient and skipped ahead without my telling you to, then you must have no doubt been confused by said last passage, and also that it gives you a reasonable indication of how long the chapter is. This means that if you think you should really get to bed or have something pressing to do then you're probably going to be in a better position to be able to make the right decision, with the help of an understanding of your own general reading speed...

It's both a punishment and a service, which I have cleverly dispelled upon you from beyond the grave.

I will write **Start Here** in bold where you have to start so it's east to spot by scanning... Ready?

Go.

Now that you're back and fully up to date with the ins and outs of my professional relationship with Nancy Turner (whom I've never met, previously heard of, or indeed spoken to), I should probably explain that the bank has never taken any money from me unfairly, and that I have absolutely no idea what they're on about.

What I do know, however, is that shortly after I received this letter they took the liberty of depositing my account with quite a large sum of money. And a further £150 on top of that.

I don't think it's really necessary for me to put the exact amount, but suffice to say it's enough with which to live comfortably for a year.

Please bear this in mind during my retelling of last night's events, as the groundwork for the dramatic irony is now firmly in place. It would be a terrible shame for it to slip past you after all this hard work just because you've been a lazy reader. In fact; never mind: I'll probably just remind you when we get to it anyway.

Right, I'll begin the story of last night... Now:

Yesterday was Tim's birthday. He turned 27, which is an age that seems quite old even to a 26 year-old. It's also the age that I'll be when I die, which is actually quite nice as there are a lot of fairly well-respected famous people who've died at this age, and I reckon it wouldn't be a bad club to end up in.

I've gone off track again; this isn't about me, it's about Tim.

So Tim turned 27 yesterday and the lucky bastard had it land on a Saturday, meaning everybody was in to make a fuss over him all day. Having a fuss made over you on your birthday is invariably amazing. Everybody seems to act as if you've done something really extraordinary and deserve rewarding, when in truth all you've done is managed to eat, drink and breathe enough in a year to not die. Doing enough consuming and respiration to not die is a really easy task when you've not got a terminal disease, I'll tell you that for free.

We started the day by being reluctantly woken up by Jenny and forced to cook him a surprise breakfast in bed. I didn't really mind because I'm the kind of cook that will eat at least two thirds of everything that is designed to end up in the dish, during its preparation.

Accordingly, he ate the breakfast and we all drank some champagne, which at 9.30am is a very posh thing to do. The breakfast consisted of bacon, scrambled eggs, toast, coffee, orange juice and bubbly. Nobody needs three drinks at once, but one presumably feels obliged to indulge in such opulence on a 27th birthday.

May said that she once went to a posh meal out with a friend's parents' and she ended up with *five* drinks at the same time because she didn't want to seem rude by turning them down. I think this is probably what was going on in Tim's head, since he seemed a bit stressed out at having to keep his three in a fair circulation. He was undoubtedly very appreciative at the same time, though.

In-between watching him take in mouthfuls of scrambled egg (a bit awkward because nobody likes to watch someone eat, in the same way that nobody likes to be watched whilst *they* eat), he made his way through a small collection of presents that were piled up at the foot of his bed.

Jenny had bought him a new watch - a pretty handsome looking thing that he put straight on and promptly told everyone the time with. This is the age-old trick of trying to seem as appreciative as possible at having received a gift by using it instantly, even though there is very little need to do so. When I was about ten I did this when my grandma gave me a super-soaker for my birthday.

This is a tactic that I now try to avoid.

He had a few cards and fewer actual presents - as is the way of things when you get older - but he did seem to do quite well in terms of clothing vouchers. I'd had a conversation with him a few days prior to ask him what he wanted.

"I dunno. Anything, really," he answered.

Logically, I took that to mean a coffee mug with a special compartment for biscuits and a T-shirt that read 'Sorry girls, I'm gay'. Admittedly they're both fairly poor presents, but that'll teach him for being so unhelpfully ambiguous.

All this happened without anyone verbally mentioning the fact that Tim was quite clearly all naked and hairy underneath his covers, which I gather was a universally pleasing omission from the otherwise cheery and hair-free conversation.

All four of us hung about for most of the day, doing as close to nothing as we could manage, save for watching *Match of the Day* (or whatever football programme it is that's on on a Saturday) with Tim and trying to track down who it was that finished all the champagne. Probably the damn animals up in the roof, because it definitely wasn't us. The plan for the evening was to meet a big group of our friends in Covent Garden for a night of mid-to-late-twenties-style drinking and dancing.

This (if you remember) is where the element of dramatic irony we cleverly set up a little while ago comes nicely into play. Basically, for the whole moving house debacle I had intended on booking two weeks' holiday from work so I could get settled and remember how to correctly 'do' house sharing. From the glory days of my studenthood, I remember the appropriate response to such a living arrangement is to get very drunk a lot of the time. This holiday was all planned long before the bank (for whatever reason) decided to give me a large sum of money, and before the doctor (presumably for reasons relating to his professional reputation) told me I was dying, which both resulted in me giving up work all together.

I was standing with Tim and our friends Ross and Hugh in one of the few bars our group graced last night, when he asked me:

"When are you going back to work, Al?"

This put me in something of a bind, seeing as not telling people I'm going to die has meant that I've also not told them I've quit my job. The fact is, even though I'm sure the bank's mistake has put out some unfortunate namesake of mine (and themselves, obviously), I'm guessing that - overall - my circumstances are probably a little bit worse. What *this* means is that, instead of telling the bank they've cocked up, I'm taking the moral low ground and keeping every last penny. I'm sure this wouldn't go down particularly well with my friends. Without knowing about my health they would just think I was a thieving bastard. It would no doubt spark off a lot of 'helpful advice', which would uniformly suggest that I should come clean to the bank lest I end up in jail.

I really don't think that any jury in the world would convict a dying man for keeping money that the bank accidentally gave him, but as far as everybody else knows I'm the picture of health. Therein lies the problem.

At any rate (back to the dramatic irony), my reply to Tim's question was:

"I'm actually... err... not."

I'd like to think this was rather restrained, considering we were all at the stage of drunkenness where everybody shouts slightly louder than they need to and your vision feels heavy. At this level of intoxication I usually find that attention is something my brain suddenly decides it needs a lot of, and, given the circumstances (a room full of my loved ones), I think it's nothing short of a bloody miracle that I didn't just blurt out that I probably wouldn't be here for Tim's 28th.

"What do you mean?" Hugh asked.

"I- I might have quit."

In an ideal world this wouldn't have drawn any further questioning and we'd have moved on to talk about something else. Like today's football result. Or the fact that it was Tim's birthday.

"You quit?!"

Bugger, thought (the rather smashed) I. I'm really not very good at lying on the spot, especially after a few drinks. Now I'd started down a windy road of mistruths that I'd not only have to make sound convincing, but also remember once I'd woken up the next day.

"Basically... I hadn't mentioned anything, but one of my uncles died just before we moved. I think he'd always taken a bit of a shine to me, 'cos he left me, like, fifteen grand in his will. I just reckoned that I'd been given the chance to do what I've always wanted - to be able to sit and spend the time writing a book for a year."

Jesus Goodfibbing Christ. Now I was on a role. I'd spun some sort of super-lie that didn't only cover my tracks on the whole money/work fiasco, it also covered the fact that I'd spent the majority of the last week or so frantically writing. I also had a dead uncle, the existence of whom in the first place none of my friends had any chance/intention of checking up on. It was nigh-on perfect, and I'd done it whilst drunk.

"Oh shit... sorry mate. I thought you looked a bit

upset recently," said Tim. Thus, my lie had also covered the presumably perturbed look that contracting a terminal condition had spread across my face.

"Yeah sorry man," said Ross. "Still, that's a quality lifeline for this book of yours."

They were all saying sorry, but more than anything else their faces suggested that they were happy at the thought that one of their mates had been given fifteen grand. Which is fair enough, since none of them had anything morally invested in my fictional uncle's health, anyway.

"Yeah," I said. "It's just a shame really, because he lived up north and I hadn't seen him in years."

Then *why*, I suddenly thought, would he bother throwing fifteen grand at me? I realised I'd better keep schtum from then on about the sensibilities of this (for some reason) northern faux uncle, and tried to change the subject. To no avail.

"Yeah that's an odd bad/good news situation, man... What's the book about anyway?" Hugh interjected. "Or is it a big secret?"

As you and I know, dear reader, it is a pretty bloody big secret. As much as my drunken head wanted to jump onto a table and proclaim to the world that this was a book about my last year on Earth, I had the wherewithal to know better. Not least because I'm fairly sure that Tim finding out that his best friend is dying would probably put a bit of a downer on his birthday.

"Yeah, it's a bit of a secret at the mo, sorry," I finally said, tapping my nose. "Right 'scuse me chaps, I'm gonna go chat to Miss Cooper.

It's at this point that I should confess how I've been hitherto pretty poor at conveying/noting the following:

- Myself and May have been getting on famously since we moved in.

- We have very much the same sense of humour.

- I find her quite attractive.

With these things understood, I'll carry on with the main point of me writing this chapter: the thing that happened last night.

I walked over to May, who was on her own getting a cocktail at the bar. She was wearing a blue dress with black tights/leggings (I can never tell the difference) and knee-high boots; her jet black hair was down and straight. To my fuzzy head she looked very, very pretty.

I ordered a drink too and we both started talking about the bartenders, who looked to be competing with each other over who could take the lengthiest amount of time to make a drink. They both insisted on lobbing the bottles and glasses around to excess - bouncing them off their shoulders, knees, eyeballs and the like.

"Is it wrong that I really hope they drop all the bottles?" she asked.

"Depends. If by 'wrong' you mean 'right', then yes."

"It's all just faff, innit? I could have made my own drink about eight times by now."

Firstly, I have to let you know that when she says 'innit', its not in a bad, chavvy way – it's in an ironic, endearing way. Secondly, just after she said this she turned and looked at me with a smile.

There are two things I look for in a woman (in terms of appearance, that is. Because you're meant to say 'personality' first), and they are: nice eyes and a nice smile.

This human girl has the nicest combination of the two I have ever come across in one real life person. Her smile is wide, happy and massively infectious. Her eyes are a shiny hazel-green, and they have that bottomless, reflective twinkle that means they smile just as hard and merrily as her mouth. It's all framed with a milky, pale sea of skin that does nothing but make a spectacle of the colour in her lips and pupils. I wish I had a picture, actually, because I've heard they're more productive than words (to the power of

1000, no less). I would draw one and stick it in the book but my drawings are what could generously be described as 'poor' and ungenerously as 'offensive'. I once tried to draw a picture of a semi-naked woman for GSCE Art, and my teacher (Mr Carr) wrote 'This needs work Alan, please see me' on it. Our meeting basically consisted of him discouragingly questioning why I had chosen to take Art in the first place, for the best part of an hour and a half.

At any rate, May and I stayed together for the duration of the time in the bar. Other people came and went, obviously, and we spoke and drank and laughed with them too, passing each other chance smiles as we did. When alone, we took the time to engage in serious debate regarding the following:

> Whether May's boots were bigger than those worn by a woman across the bar

> What ever happened to Sooty

> How everything in Brighton is painted green (Apparently)

> What fire actually *is*.

All topics remained somewhat inconclusive, save for the boots issue - which we decided was probably a draw. The woman across the bar was a fair bit shorter than May but her boots went up well past her knees, making it impossible to tell. Following this lively debate we all trekked towards the dance floor to move up and down to the sound of a covers band. During this the two of us began a fairly strange drunken game/exercise-in-idiocy, the rules of which comprised solely of trying to sporadically yank each other's hair as hard as possible without first getting blocked. Regrettably, I think it's best compared to the kind of childish flirting you do when you're about eight... but flirting it undeniably was, and it was undeniably very fun.

All this was no doubt the subject of much gossip amongst everyone else we were with, as my hands were wrapped warmly around her at various intervals, and more importantly her hands were letting them be. For a real lack of any better way to describe it, it felt extremely 'nice', and extremely exciting.

When it finally came time for everyone's liver to receive some respite and go home it was too late to catch the tube, so we had to walk to Trafalgar Square to hop the night bus. Central London at night is a strange circus of the bizarre, the annoying, and the regrettably likeminded. It reeks with tourism, it oozes crime; both brash facets of society litter and lace themselves around landmarks hundreds of years old. The air is in turn surprisingly crisp and stubbornly grey, making cutting a path through the hordes of people akin to playing rugby in a viscous jelly: you take two steps forward and one step back.

Last night, however, I didn't really notice any of this. I was walking to Trafalgar Square with May's delicate hand squeezed firmly in mine. We walked behind everyone else, I think because she was shy. We actually didn't say that much to each other, but glances back and forth suggested that we didn't particularly need to. Having done that awkward step onto a crowded night bus, we took a seat behind all our friends on the back row.

The night bus is hell. The night bus crawls with noise, jerks about incessantly and stops and starts far too often. It lurks through London as if it polices the place, swallowing up the infirm, the unwanted and the scum from the streets. These imps then use it as a soapbox from which to pump out their god-awful music, their fowl misuse of the English language and - more often than not - the contents of their stomachs.

But again, I didn't really notice. As we lurched ever closer to home, my hands began to gently stroke and explore May's. Her hands did the same, and our faces leant just close enough for the fibres of our skin to whisper to one another. Finally, but at the same time completely out of nowhere, our tired, sticky, drunken lips met in a long, warm kiss.

That, dear reader, was the thing that happened last night. May and I flirted a whimsical path towards kissing one another. We kissed several times on the walk back from the bus to our house, each one warmly plucked from the air amid the dark secrecy of the back of the group.

She didn't let me stay in her room, and I'm glad.

I was glad not only because it might have further confused things, but also because it proves my theory that she is that thing which is so rare these days: a nice, honest, beautiful girl with morals and class. She's what I look for in a woman. We kissed a fuzzy kiss to part ways before entering the house, and then we both retired to our separate rooms.

I haven't seen her today as she's been out with Jenny, but I so desperately wanted to. ...Almost as much as the coward in me never wants to see her again.

Start Here.

A couple of weeks ago, something very fortunate happened in relation to the fact that a dying man who doesn't want to tell anyone he's dying should have the right to an early retirement. I received a letter from the bank that said the following:

Dear Mr Bell,

As a valued customer, we sincerely regret the unfortunate series of debits that our system accidentally drew from your account *over the past 18 months. We hope that this misconduct on our behalf has not deterred you from banking with ********* in the future, and are writing to you to explain that our bank relies on an ethos of a fair and reliable service – something that, in the first instance, is built on a strong relationship with our customers.*

As such - as was discussed on the telephone – we intend to repay you in full for any money that was unfairly taken within the next five working days, and also to credit your account with a further £150 to show how much your custom means to us.

Kind regards,

Nancy Turner

Senior Customer Relations Manager

********* Bank

Now Go Back.

v) **A bit of a smooch**

"So what are you going to do once this year of writing is over then?" Tim asked.

We were sat in our lounge. Yesterday - as expected - neither Tim or myself surfaced before midday due to large amounts of alcohol reeking large amounts of havoc with our souls. I oozed into the lounge like a giant slug at about 2.30pm, where I found Tim sunk into the pile of cushions as if he were melting.

"I think I'll go travelling," came my response.

After an interrogation the night before, my brain's seemingly decided that the best way to deal with my somewhat complex situation is to needlessly create and perpetuate lies upon lies upon lies. Travelling was an excuse that came to me in a flash of inspiration in the toilet of the bar we finished up in, as for some reason someone had drawn a Brazilian flag on the cubicle door. "...Spend some time in South America, I think."

Brilliant Alan. Well done. It's just as bloody well

that no one had drawn a picture of a man telling his friends he's dying, because apparently I'm extremely impressionable when it comes to toilet art.

Actually - at the risk of losing your interest in this gripping narrative - I just want to point out that, contrary to how things have been going recently this was never supposed to be set out as a diary. As it happens, this chapter and the one that preceded it have been written just a day after the events in each respective one have taken place. I think this is because instead of writing what happened on Saturday and Sunday in one chapter, it makes more sense to keep your interest by breaking them up slightly.

Not only that, but writing what I deem to be two perfectly good chapters in one night seems like far too much work for an unpaid writer. As such, you'll get what you're given and either carry on reading or give up. I'm still dead, and therefore not likely to be offended unless you literally rip the pages up and use them to burn my grave (or something nonsensically violent to that effect).

What I can do is offer you two things. The first is that I can tell you what I'm doing right now* - so as to rest this 'past tense' diary stuff for a while - and the second is to promise not to write anything more after this chapter for a few days. Thus, I'll hopefully have a lot to talk about and won't be able to split it all up again without falling massively behind. Be warned, though: my memory's nowhere near powerful enough for me to start writing about events that happened more than about three or four days ago.

What I'm doing now is writing about what happened yesterday.

So, back to the scene at hand: a very hungover Tim and a slugular me nursing the floor in our lounge at about 2.30pm (yesterday).

(Which was Sunday).

"Ah that's cool," he replied. "So you don't think you'll want to renew this contract, I take it?"

"Probably not, mate."

Definitely not, mate. I'll be quite unhelpfully dead by the time contracts need signing, sorry. I really wish my friends didn't have such an interest in my wellbeing/future, sometimes. Questions after questions genuinely make me want to chuck in the towel, tell them I'm on the way out and take up a nice cosy place in a nursing home. Bloody friends and their bloody empathy.

Tim was nursing a rotten hangover and took several trips to the bathroom to eject the offending chemicals. After the second time - vomit noises ushering their way down the hall towards the lounge - I thought I should ask him about *his* life, seeing as any further questioning aimed my way would most likely result in an increasingly bad series of events that'd end with me being stoned to death by the townsfolk. Or something.

"So are you nervous about tomorrow?"

Tomorrow, which is now today (Monday – such is the unrelenting passage of time), Tim was/is to have an audition for a play that's meant to be going to the Edinburgh Fringe Festival. I've just realised that I forgot to ask him how it went, so in the unreadable gap in time between this paragraph ending and the next beginning I should probably send him a text.

Good, done. At any rate, Tim's response yesterday was something along the lines of:

"A little bit, yeah. I've not had an audition since just after Uni."

"What are you going to perform?"

"Not sure... something from *The Entertainer* I think."

"Do you not have anything prepared?"

"Nah, I still know a few audition monologues off by heart."

This surprised me. I think to an extent I'd just thought that Tim's acting ambitions had been rekindled out of nothing more than job-related boredom. The fact that he still remembers monologues from some five years ago suggests that he really is some sort of proper thesp. "At any rate, I've just remembered the main happening from last night..."

Ah yes: the happening. It was a 'happening' in the same kind of way that WWII was a 'happening'. And I say that because I gather both share similar degrees of moral blurriness and social devastation.

"...You and a young lady from this house having a bit of a smooch," he continued. His face had that childish but infectious 'wink-wink nudge-nudge' look about it that has the uncanny ability to make even grown men think they've done something a bit naughty, and shrink down inside themselves accordingly.

If, dear reader, you refer back to my scratchy descriptions of Saturday night, you'll remember that to me it was slightly more than just a 'smooch', but instead of telling Tim that I fancy the proverbial and literal pants off of May, I felt it was probably wise to keep my cool.

"Yeah... That happened," I said, the words falling out of my dry, hoarse mouth like feathers. "I didn't stay in her room though."

"Shame."

"No I'm glad actually. Makes things less complicated."

"Complicated my arse," Tim offered, eloquently. "You know mate, she's said to me and Jenny before that she likes you."

However old you are and no matter what the

circumstance, that is a really exceptional thing to hear. It massages the ego no end. When I was 14 someone told me that a girl I fancied felt the same way, and it had such a pleasantly numbing effect on me that I got run over by a VW Golf while looking at some clouds. Cars are hard to spot when you're riding high on the coattails of teenage infatuation.

"Really?" I asked, trying ever so hard to not smile like an idiot.

"Yeah man. Have you seen her today? How are you going to play it?"

How am I going to play it, he asks? It's such a sorry state of affairs that a romantic encounter with a girl - a fellow human animal - needs to be 'played'. Should (as a stereotypically patriarchal view would suggest) I play it 'cool'? Should I act aloof and pretend nothing had happened, or try and make a go of things?

"I don't really know," was what I said - and it was the truth.

"You mean you haven't thought what you're gonna do? You must have," was what he said.

Now, assessing these two statements results in the perfect example of where to 'assume' is to make an 'ass out of u and me':

My saying I didn't know by no means suggested that I hadn't given it any thought. I found it odd that Tim - who's known me for about nine years – thinks

I'm the kind of person that can go around kissing girls and not worry about the consequences.

I am the kind of person who kisses girls and then wonders what colour the wallpaper in our marital bedroom will be.

You know what? I think there is a real lack of fiction either written or portrayed on screen that deals with romance from the male's point of view. Or at least not the real, everyday, sensible male point of view. I think this is particularly strange because contrary to all the Bridget Jones-esque female liberation going on in the media, men are still the ones that have to do most of the chasing.

The honest truth about men in the twenty-first century is this: Unless a man is some sort of woman shuffling whore, any romantic clinch will send him on such an emotional mental journey that he'll be unable to fully enjoy it for at least the first 30 seconds. Usually it's worry. Pure worry. But in the very first instance we are taken back to that shy, unsure thirteen-year old boy who harbours both huge insecurities about ever actually meeting a woman, and ludicrously disciplined masturbatory habits. Following this flashback we worry about our looks, our smells, our breath, how we kiss, how we stand, where our hands are at and a myriad other things. In most cases the worrying will extend to whether this girl is 'the one', or just a random pit-stop on our journey towards finding biblical happiness with a member of the opposite sex. I think this is what women would find the most surprising: the fact that men actually deeply care about the opportunity for long term love. I know I probably lack the mental capacity to understand the thoughts of the entire world's population of men, but I can't imagine that many of my similarly-gendered brethren would disagree with me. Save for the mentals.

In short: men these days are not the men of yore. I fail to see how any man with rational thought can overcome this natural and unnerving thought process. The manly men on old film posters must have just been better at hiding it behind a solid wall of machismo than I am. Either way, if you're a woman with an opinion of men that we're nothing but misogynistic animals with one thing on the mind, you're probably hanging around with the few left that are. And they're probably partial to the odd bout of football hooliganism and mindless violence.

Tim doesn't know that I'm about to quietly shuffle off my mortal coil, but that obviously adds a massive amount of weight to my thoughts on the whole kissing girls fiasco - seeing as I think I really genuinely like May.

Actually I *know* I really genuinely like May. Quite a bit. Which makes things a lot harder for my poor brain to digest.

At any rate, I suppose that from now on you can use

my experiences with May as that much-needed male-centric romantic narrative; that literary insight into a man's side of all modern amorous goings on.

Off we go then: onwards with our bittersweet not-so fairytale romance.

The conversation with Tim about May petered out a bit after I told him that I had, in fact, put some thought towards things, albeit with little or no result. I didn't particularly want to go any further down that road with him because, frankly, it was unnecessarily stressful, so I slugged (that's not a word, but if it was it'd be a verb) into my room to write the chapter before the one you're currently reading.

May and Jenny had somehow been able to get up and act as normal human beings without any real sign of a hangover. In accordance with this, they had gone to Oxford Street to go shopping. I've honestly got no idea what would compel a semi-hungover person to go to one of the busiest and people-ridden streets in the world for pleasure, and I've also got literally no idea how they were only semi-hungover, seeing as by all accounts everyone out on Saturday was suitably brain-dead from booze.

The slightest reason to celebrate does bad things to the sensibilities of 'living for the weekend' types.

I got the following text from Jenny at about eight in the evening, which I can faithfully transcribe because I moved it to the 'saved' folder in my phone out of girly sentimentality:

"Alan, Alan, Alan... She's wondering when you're going to ask her out on a date."

This had two effects: The first was that it scared the bejesus out of me, the second was that I thought it was so staggeringly brilliant that I had to move it to the aforementioned folder.

The thought did cross my mind that it was just Jenny's way of trying to do some ill-informed matchmaking - wildly twisting something May had actually said to suit her evangelical aims. What if, for instance, what May had *actually* said was something along the lines of: "God I can't believe I let that horrible boy kiss me... I'm just counting down the minutes before he asks me out on some kind of date."

Extreme as that is, things have taken a similar route with my amorous endeavours before. The likelihood of Jenny's text being based *entirely* on fact was minimal, but enough probably *was* true to make me worry that - combined with what Tim had said - it seems as though this has all been a long time in the making. And all without my knowing.

True enough, I'd *tried* to resist fanciful feelings towards the girl, but now enough rumour and speculation had suddenly come out of the woodwork to make things look set in the stars. Or at least set in the woodchip on the lounge ceiling.

I'll tell you now, dear reader: things all went downhill from the moment the above bullshit set in my head. You'll probably be able to mark this moment down as the point where it all went wrong.

In the short time I have known May, she has become one of my best ever friends, simply because spending time with her is so very easy. As such, the nucleus of an idea in which I could spend a lot of addictive time with her whilst fulfilling whatever plans my overjoyed libido had at the same time began to form. And it shouldn't. It all became too much for my brain to focus on and so, in reaching for my phone, the tiny fact that I have slightly less than a year to live was instantly pushed out and neglected in favour of idiotic boyhood fantasies of love. My brain appears to operate on a strict one-in, one-out system.

The text I sent to May at 9:13pm, May 17th, read:

"Hi. Do you fancy some drinks one evening this week?"

I had that horrible sense of remorse as soon as I'd pressed 'send' - that dread at the realisation of what you've done. The worst moment is when the blasted screen lingers on the word 'sending', where you worry that if you were to press the 'cancel' button you'd have no idea if you'd done it in time and no idea whether it had sent or not. In the end, what you do is move the phone away from yourself and then try to chase it with your head - as if you are trying to chase the message back into some semblance of your control.

It never works, so you just throw the phone away from touching distance and try and sink into the bedding.

I came to from that overlong moment of self-loathing and disbelief only to launch an effort to make myself physically disappear into a cloud of idiocy. Rather predictably, this didn't work either, so I just decided the best thing to do was to eat something and wait for the inevitable tsunami of awkwardness my actions would have just unleashed.

3. JUNE

Shopping:

Baked Beans
Bread
Non-descript soft drink
More fruit
Some kind of vegetable (many)
Beer / cider
Frozen meat; two of every animal
You've run out of gin
Anything that doesn't resemble a takeaway pizza

Things learned:

- It's dangerously hard to keep secrets when drunk

- If you're the kind of person that's always worn a cravat, you can get away with it. If you've never worn one before and then one day decide to put one on, everyone will make fun of you. In some extreme cases it'll garner you the moniker 'cravat-boy'.

- Flat-pack furniture's sole job it to frustrate, humiliate and physically hurt human beings. 90% of the UK's alcoholics were turned to drink by a wayward chest of drawers. FACT.

Favourite Text:

May: "Drinks would be lovely."

i) Facts about Brazil and other lies

So as it turns out, 'drinks' was an idea that appealed to May also. This might sound like a good thing (and I don't want to appear like a man who'll never be happy with his lot), but it obviously then meant that I had to follow through and make real plans to go on a real date with a real live girl. This is arguably worse than if she'd said 'no'.

I arranged to meet her after work on Wednesday, (yesterday) and made sure I was busy enough until then that I didn't have to see her in any real capacity beforehand, thus neatly avoiding any pesky awkwardness. Not seeing someone you live with for two days is quite an easy thing to do when you know their exact routine. May goes to work (like a normal person) five days out of the week (like a normal person) and the gym on Tuesdays and Thursdays (like a person who wants to be better than normal people). I do precisely nothing but contemplate life, drink and write in this book, which means that I'm able to go out and about when she comes home from work.

Some might call this cowardice. I call it providing a service; nobody likes the gauche nervousness between organising a date and actually going on it. At any rate, I neatly avoided May until Wednesday, which was when I met her at Leicester Square dressed in the dictionary definition of smart casual.

If you, dear reader, happen to find yourself as a woman (physically), I think you might be quite interested and surprised to learn that men worry about what to wear on dates as much, if not more than yourselves. The 'outfits' I tried on are as follows:

- Dark blue Jeans, white shirt, grey jumper

- Dark blue jeans, black shirt, tweed jacket

- Light blue jeans, white T-shirt, tweed jacket

- Grey cords, white shirt, gormless expression

I conceded that whenever your apparel *really* matters it becomes blindingly obvious that you hate everything you own, and that you must have been recklessly drunk when you bought it all. Such a revelation usually leads me to operate under the assumption that my first choice must be the least offensive combination if I'd chosen it first so I reverted to the white shirt/grey jumper combination I had on in the first place, adding the gormless expression for good measure.

A dying man should not have to worry about outfits.

Actually, a dying man probably shouldn't be going on a bloody date, but that's beside the point.

May had come from work but still somehow managed to look rather special. She was wearing skinny jeans, a dark green jumper and a beanie hat of the same hue that let two sheets of black hair fall around her face and past her smiling eyes. She made me smile back like a fool.

"Where do you want to go then?" I asked, blurtily. It was a rather forceful attempt to inject conversation into what I thought had been too long a silence, when it was probably only about three seconds.

"I don't mind. You?"

I've read on many separate occasions that women much prefer to be told where they are going than to be part of the decision making process, as it makes them feel like they are in the presence of a real man and, ergo, their perceived ladyness gets a boost. This is fairly simple in theory, but I'm not that good at organising things (as in, I physically lack the capacity to do so beyond the digital nudge of 'drinks') and I'm also very much too polite for my own good. Being polite in a chivalrous way strikes me as a conflicting practice to ordering women about, and so - if pushed - nine times out of ten I'll just say "I don't mind," and perpetuate the indecisiveness. Because I am entirely rubbish.

The 'I don't mind' dance continued its futile existence for a few more rounds before we blinked and were suddenly in a Brazilian bar in Soho. Here we sat and drank Brazilian beer, as is the done thing.

"Did you know," she said, "that nine out of every ten Brazilians are gay?"

"Really?" I answered glibly, having seen the joke form and jump around in her eyes before she'd released it.

"Yep." She nodded cheekily. "And that seven of those gay men will actually be girls."

I laughed. She's very addictive, May. I find it very easy to talk to her because she appreciates, and in turn produces, my specific breed of nonsense. Thinking about it, I'd say that the vast majority of our conversations are based on three principle themes:

- Trying to understand tricky concepts (such as fire)

- Starting sentences out of fidgety boredom that we can't finish because they weren't about anything in the first place

- Spurious (read: completely made up) facts

This is exactly what I like to do with my power to converse; I like to talk nonsense with people. Of course there's a time and a place for being serious and embarking on very deep and profound conversation topics, but I feel its hugely important that most of the time people just forget themselves and talk a load of old bollocks.

"You wanna hear a fact?" I asked.

"Go on," she said, smiling in jovial anticipation.

"I've heard... well I read once... somewhere... that only one Brazilian person out of every ten is straight." That won me a giggle. It was a completely excellent giggle.

I've come to the conclusion that the very fact that 'drinks' (i.e. Alcoholic) is enough of a basis for an entire date highlights people's inherent need for booze to loosen themselves up. There's a limit to what's acceptable, of course (denoted by the amount your partner consumes, themselves), but generally I think its safe to say that the human race would be socially lost without its precious alcohol. When I moved to university for example, everybody was continuously drunk for at least the first fourteen days and at most the entire three years. This wasn't just because drinking during fresher's is the done thing though; it was because you had to meet and befriend a whole host of new people and that's a much harder thing to do while sober. It was as effective a tactic as you'd expect; after the hangover inevitably wore off you realised that you were suddenly bestest friends with about 80 people you didn't know existed some days earlier.

Similarly (albeit unfortunately), the boozing on a date can't very well go on forever, so we left the bar in order to get sustenance. Unbeknownst to May, I would be paying for the meal - because that's what a gentleman does.

A gentleman says "I don't mind" enough times to wind up in an unfortunately fancy place and then eschews any feminine equality hitherto built up by paying for the whole thing. With money the bank accidentally paid him.

How times have changed.

The meal portion of a date is the literal and metaphorical meat of it, but I don't really understand why. It bludgeons its way into the proceedings under the guise of sophistication and then forces you to sit opposite each other masticating and going "Mmmmm". This isn't to say that I had a bad time, of course - far from it. In fact I had a wonderful time; May continued to wow me with 'facts' and I did that thing where you hold a fork behind a napkin to make it look possessed (that thing that nobody does after the age of twelve, but that my very own date May Cooper laughed at with her beautiful wide eyes). ...It's just that eating isn't a particularly attractive thing to witness. It seems bizarre that it features so heavily in courtship rituals.

In fairness, the restaurant was very nice and helped the atmosphere no end. It had the kind of aesthetically romantic look that I didn't actually think existed in the real world. The warmest shade of cream – almost bordering on gold – filled the air from the walls and morphed into a descending, darkened glow until it bounced off the candles, which were littered around the tables like a net of light. It was small too. Cosy. Her eyes sparkled throughout.

That, and joking (in what I suppose could be considered a casually racist manner) about the waiter's accent is all I can really remember. Not because of alcohol, mind, but through a kind of blinding, numbing enjoyment. When we left, our eyes were very happy.

What's this thing about eyes? It's a fascination that I've somehow developed and will continue to struggle to write about without wandering down an alleyway of awful clichés. I'm not about to say that they're 'the window to the soul', but I value them above any other part of someone's appearance because, in a very real way, they let me see who that person is. Eyes let you see how happy someone is, they let you see if they are good or nice. They genuinely let you see their 'being', in whatever capacity that renders itself in the human brain.

Sod it. They're the window to the soul. Whoever said that was a bloody clever chap.

***

I just looked it up, and apparently it's from the bible. Or something. ...I just scanned the website.

***

Anyway, May was happy and I was extremely happy. I was soaking up the addictive aura that Miss Cooper gave off all the way to the tube, during which time we held hands and kissed a ruffled, warm and quick kiss just as we passed through Leicester Square. It was our first whilst (fairly) sober. Fairly sober was more than good enough.

On the way home we did little but sit and contently hold hands, as if in triumph of a date well done; the tube was fleetingly busy, with enough people to stop us from kissing. Public displays of affection are an odd beast. Nobody likes to watch them, and yet if you're the person partaking there is little you care less about than the outside world's opinion. Regardless of our candid contact, I'd like to think that the few people who did glance over at us presumed we were happy. The few people we glanced back at were mostly harmless, except from an elderly blonde woman with long, scraggly hair, whom May wrote this about on my phone:

"Hello, I'm the blonde woman across the tube from you. Do you have any change so that I can go buy some crack? It's for my kids. My ears hurt."

It made me laugh so much that I thought the elderly blonde woman was genuinely going to murder us both. In a very painful fashion.

She didn't, as you can probably tell, which is just as well seeing as I'm dying anyway and don't really think I deserve to not finish this book to the extent a year allows. Not now that I've started it. Not to dwell on how much of a bastard I'm apparently capable of being, but I wouldn't be painting myself a very good public image if I ended the book sharply with the announcement of a date with a poor young girl that doesn't know I'm about to die. At least this way I've got time to redeem my deceiving self.

The walk home was quiet. It was quiet because we had entered the stage of a date where the girl knows exactly how it will end and the boy doesn't, and that rift and upheaval of power is scary. I became deeply wrapped up in thought, as I suppose May was also – both about each other, both about morals. Both for very different reasons.

May is a very honest and *good* girl - you can tell that from half an hour in her company. She's the kind of girl your family would love to welcome for Christmas. She'd told me previously, and in less romantically-weighted circumstances, that she had never been the girl at school or university that had a gaggle of boys to switch between, nor has she ever gone out to a club specifically to 'pull'. This is an admirable quality in a society obsessed with frivolity, pace and STDs - and it's part of the reason I find her attractive. It's because she has substance; she's not an empty thing waiting loosely to be filled, she's a real and beautiful package of a person. As pure an interest as I think my brain's met. She's restrained without being dull. Far from it.

That said, there are obvious limits to chastity. We've both had partners before, are both (mid-to-)late twenties, and both have the same primal needs as any animal of a similar disposition.

What I mean to say is this: the door shut, and youthful, shining eyes flitted about wildly under lamplight as clothes fell to the floor. Revealed were two figures of tangible warmth that performed a dance together so right that it made heat swell throughout the room. Ripe sheets folded through creased fingers and slatted moonlight. It writhed around us and buried into our skin like magic. It made our skins translucent and stuck them together, fast. Heat caressed us, kissed us, and loved us both as we did one another. For *at least* four minutes.

Dear reader, I make no claims to be a saint. I can't pretend that doing this to a girl - let alone a girl I already regard so highly as something fragile and special – is right. Knowing I'm dying and not telling anyone is not 'right', but then last night I did the thing that my heart and mind told me felt 'right'. I don't think I really know how to tell the difference between the social, moral and personal 'right' anymore - or more to the point, which one takes priority. Dying has the result of making you very disconnected from everything trivial that the rest of the world is thickly stuck in. I suppose the best I can do is to say that at least last night is something interesting to write about for this book.

As much of a conniving, heartless bastard as that makes me.

ii) Garbled, clunky analogies

I've long since come to terms with the fact that I have absolutely no idea what sperm is… nor will I ever. After the best part of twelve years thinking, all I can do is safely rule out the possibility of it being either mineral or vegetable. This obviously leaves animal, but then I don't really think sperm *can* be an animal due to its involvement in making other animals. It's an animal ingredient. …Like fur.

If Darwin's theory is to be believed, we all trudged out of the sea and grew fur and, for whatever reason, started having sex instead of laying eggs. I've always understood this to be the result of a lengthy and boring spell of evolution, which lasted millions upon millions of years. That doesn't wash though, because presumably at some point there weren't any animals on earth that used the sperm/egg process and then suddenly one day there was. I can't envision a middle point where sperm kind-of existed (if only as an abstract notion), so presumably at some point in history one unlucky bastard of an animal was born that began feeling urges to penetrate everything around him, whereas everyone else just casually laid their eggs and passed judgemental looks.

As stupid as that all sounds, I just can't get my tiny brain around the idea that this massive shift - from spraying pre-laid eggs with fertiliser to having sex and birthing live young - happened in droves. It must have happened on a singular basis that spread by... peer pressure, or something.

But then, I have no idea what I'm talking about; quite clearly I understand scarily little about the world at large. Least of all anthropology.

At any rate, I think I'm trying to get to the point that the whole complex and multi-layered system of life and reproduction on earth boils down nothing but a seemingly neatly organised, but ultimately messy and dirty old pile of sex. Animals, without actually having a conscious train of thought, know that they need to have sex. They know that they don't really have anything to do all day other than lay about looking bored, and as such their one directive in life is to shag something that looks like they do and hope that, after a variable amount of time, a smaller thing that also looks like they do will pop out; equally as horny. Then they can die.

It's an undoubtedly good system. However, that's quite a realist way of looking at something that, in certain circumstances, can be the best thing two people can experience. I think the problem lies in trying to explain two very different things that stem from the same, err… sex plant.

Sex is not the same thing as love by any means, but it *can* compliment it. Things have probably always been the same but, at least since I've been old enough to realise it, sex has dominated almost every aspect of modern life. Human beings like to pretend that we're better than animals because we have central heating, wind up radios and seventeen different types of cooking oil, but when push comes to shove (as apt an expression as probably exists) we're just a bunch of sex-mad hairless chimps.

If you think about it, the average day normally starts with: getting up, getting dressed nicely, doing your hair and/or applying make up. This is all a tactic to look appealing to the opposite sex; similar to the peacock with its overtly flamboyant feathers. A journey to work could then see you take in a variety of adverts that use sex to sell products that are themselves designed to boost your sex appeal or net yourself a partner. You might be listening to some love songs on the way home (let's be honest, nearly every song ever written is in some way about the relationship between man and woman – the relationship that eventually leads to them getting, as Olivia Newton John put it, 'physical'), or maybe on your way to the cinema to see a film that at some juncture will have the male protagonist get down to business with a female love interest. Or the other way round, of course; Girl Power, and all that.

The fact remains: I don't think I have ever seen a film that doesn't at some point concern itself with sex.

None of this is very surprising. Nor is it very surprising that a lot of the best things we can experience as people are compared to sex. Indeed, things that are 'better than sex' are few and far between, because if you ask any adult who has actually had good, consensual sex, they'll tell you it really is a lot of bloody good fun.

Fun things in life - such as the cinema - are distractions that we enjoy because they make us forget about the rest of our lives. When it comes down to it, we're pretty easily pleased. All we really need to keep us chirpy are a few events, games, activities or shows that merge bright colours, loud noises and the right amount of endorphins exploding in our heads to stop everyone from killing themselves.

The problem is, most of these things cost money. I hate to keep sticking to the same tired examples, but at the time of writing going to the cinema will set you back about twelve or thirteen pounds (assuming you wish to gorge on popcorn). That's a lot of money to spend just to sit and watch Actor X and Actress Y skirt around a shag for two hours. Sex though, aside from the small cost of keeping it safe (which is legally speaking optional, socially speaking mandatory), is absolutely, magnificently and thankfully free. If you manage to find it, sex is like some sort of marvellous free hobby.

Christians think that the reason it's so good is because it's a sort of gift from God, the pagans thought that an orgasm was the closest you could get to him while still stitched into your mortal pyjamas. I appreciate the truth: sex feels so good because nature wants each species to partake in it, so that they don't die out. The happy madness of sexual climax is the reward for continuing the species. Nature didn't really bank on us inventing condoms though, and in doing so, we've nicely cheated the system.

While sex is all very nice when done properly, the real reason most people seek out a partner of the opposite sex is to experience love. Love is a tricky concept to understand - let alone describe in an informed manner - so I'm quite inclined to give up before I even start. I gather that songs, poems, stories and films have been written on the subject ever since civilised thought sprung into existence, but (despite other writers' efforts being infinitely more accomplished than whatever I'm about to cobble together) I doubt that all of it combined really does the subject any justice. For most of the world, love is the most confusing, prevalent, magical and often painful thing that we know. It's a universal truth.

I think it's fair to say that, in most cases, people don't actively look for love from the off. Normally it finds us, awakens us to its powers and then disappears suddenly, leaving us heartbroken but - crucially - aware that it exists. Like a surprise dinosaur attack. From the first time we experience love we want it more than anything else. Even if at times you forget about it or organise your priorities differently, deep down inside us there remains a primal and all-conquering need for it.

The bad news is this: there's no scientific proof whatsoever to say that what we think of as love is anything but a series of exciting chemical reactions that go off in our heads. Getting as enamoured with one person as is possible could link that specific mix of lovely endorphins solely to them, making you think you're in love, but thankfully science keeps its beak out enough for 'love' in the typical sense to remain a pretty abstract notion. And of course, that's not what anybody who's truly been in love would tell you, anyway. Anyone who's experienced being in love will know that it is a very real, very palpable force - in turn stunningly beautiful and enormously painful. It can rip you apart from the very centre of your heart, or lift you up with such pure glee that you feel genuinely invincible.

Having read over that last paragraph, I think it'd be wise of me not to carry on with garbled, clunky analogies and descriptions… such floweriness is hard to pull off without sounding like an absolute prat. Not only that, but so many have explained love better than I think my brain's ropey thoughts are entirely capable of. What I *can* say about love with a degree of confidence is this: it's a bloody scary thing.

I suppose that since most of us seem to spend our entire lives looking for the blasted thing, there's some argument in saying that love is the meaning of, or purpose to, life. The feeling of love could very well just be key to nature's clever tactic to keep us shagging and making babies, but then, with the gift of civilised thought, sex and love can be seen as two very different things. You can have sex with someone you never intend on seeing again, but when you do find somebody whom you absolutely adore, love forbids you from forgetting them, forbids you from hurting them and forbids you from doing anything other than making sure they're always perfectly safe and happy, even if that means putting yourself in harms way.

Surely that kind of selflessness goes against nature's will? Self preservation is normally a high priority in the base instincts of most living things, but the fact that someone would willingly take a bullet for their most loved one transcends that. It boosts love out of abstract territory and shifts it to something altogether more real. Something, I suppose, bordering on the spiritual. It goes directly against your primal directives and programming.

My name is Alan Bell and I like to think of myself as a writer. I write because I just about know how to type and because I have a compulsion to get all the stupid things in my head out in a way that can be considered ordered. I find it a lot easier than talking. I'm not, however, an exceptionally clever man. Many, many people have written about the things I try to describe with much more aplomb, confidence and genuine wisdom than I ever could. My lack of knowledge and literary technique notwithstanding, here I've written about 2000 very rubbish words in an effort to try and get one point across: whilst sex is amazing, special, rewarding and necessary, love is so, so much more so. Love is that thing that makes you willing and wanting to let your guard down and share your entire life with someone, despite knowing that the best possible outcome will be death ripping the two of you apart years down the line. Love is gambling that terrible fear against all of the astounding highs that come with it, while clinging on to the selfish but truly sincere hope that when that does happen, you'll be the one to go first.

Thankfully, in my case, I think I will be.

iii) Passing wind with lovers

I have just realised the full extent of what I'm doing to this poor girl.

When first seeing someone, it's not generally advisable to think about things as if you intend to spend the rest of your life with that person for reasons owing to your mental health. I've always struggled to stop myself from doing this though, because my romantic mindset runs under instruction from the basic knowledge that in natural human behaviour the ideal is to meet someone and stay with them forever. I suppose it takes a different type of person from myself to be happy with endless one-night-stands with endless partners, but as it is I've always suffered from a debilitating defect that forbids me to fancy someone unless I can picture a long and happy life with them - culminating with kids, dogs and tracker mortgages.

This way of functioning has a strange effect on a young man's ability to meet women. In the first instance, any given girl whom to most would be seem as quite stunningly gorgeous can appear to me ugly and uninteresting if she doesn't have the right personality. It's not that I'm fussy, it's just that men and women are inherently very different (with different needs, interests and tastes), meaning finding a common personality imbued in a member of both sexes is frustratingly hard. This is especially so when you factor in the knowledge that most people won't actually get to meet *every* single member of the opposite sex in the entire world. Or anything close.

Obviously you can (and should) do as much as you can in life to meet as many people as possible, but chances are there's only quite a limited number of people who are actually willing to be your friend anyway. Therefore, the person you end up with (if you're so lucky) will inevitably be your best possible match from the pool of, say, 1000 people you meet in your lifetime. (Facebook tells me I've got over 100 as it stands, but since I'm being denied about 50 years of life I think I'm a special case).

To me, this makes one-night-stands seem a bit pointless. At least adopting the kind of rigorous future planning I undertake has the added benefit that you can at least tick potential life partners off as you go along. What I'm trying to say is that I find it impossible to start any romantic endeavour with a girl unless I see a real future in it. As naïve as may be, every girl I have ever kissed has at one point in my life been 'the one'.

I can only hope, dear reader, that this goes some way to explaining my recent actions with May. I am not a habitually callous man. I'm not a user or a natural deceiver, or indeed anything that I have been brought up specifically not to be. What I am is a man in love with a woman. I am a man in love with a woman whom - through optimistic naivety and romantic ideology - I now want to spend the rest of my life with.

But I can't.

Well I could, but the problem is that 'the rest of my life' is considerably shorter an amount of time than that phrase usually amounts to. And now I just don't know what to do because, while this situation should be making me overrun with guilt and sadness, I'm actually happier than I've been in a long time.

***

It's been a little over a week since I wrote what lies just above those three asterisks. A little over a week since May and I first went out to dinner. In that time our friendship has morphed rapidly into a relationship. The house that I moved into expecting to re-experience the joys of student-hood has matured suddenly into a house of two happy couples; the four of us sit and laugh and watch films and drink red wine and do all the things that grown up couples do, and I can't believe how right everything in my life is. The Very Contented Death of Alan Bell.

...But then I know that all of this means absolutely nothing because the happy and warm and electric relationship I've stumbled into only has a shelf life of eleven months. And it's all based on one big bollocking lie.

I've been told by various people throughout the years that relationships go through several key stages depending on how long they last. My personal experience is that relationships go through several stages depending on how soon things will be over, but nonetheless, I'll talk us through the most commonly perceived ones now, because doing so helps me forget about being a complete bastard.

(I've decided to name the stages myself because I don't know what they're actually called.)

Exciting times

Exciting times is the very first stage of a relationship, existing perhaps even before either party is willing to acknowledge it as a 'relationship' at all. It's the umbrella term under which exists those first sparkling kisses, the warmth of holding hands and the first time that each sees the other sans clothing. 'Exciting times' are perhaps some of the absolute best moments in life.

Honeymoon period

While still an enormously happy time, there is still a near-indistinguishable line drawn between Exciting times and the Honeymoon period that keeps them apart. The Honeymoon period can last for a completely varying amount of time and is when a couple are still enamoured totally and exclusively with each other, but begin to find out little facts and habits about their partners that their loved-up brains skew to seem endearing. Even if they'd probably seem weird under different circumstances. It's also the time that you realise exactly how much time you feel you *need* to spend with your partner. Phone bills usually rise.

Comfort period

The Comfort period is just fucking brilliant from the male point of view. It kicks into gear at an immeasurable moment in a relationship (although at least a few months in) and brings down any walls that shyness and bravado had built up to protect the young love at stake. What this essentially means is three key changes come into effect:

A) You're allowed to stop worrying about what you wear and how your hair looks.

B) You're allowed to pass wind around each other.

C) With the looming risk of getting enormously fat understood by both parties, you're allowed to eat an exorbitant amount of takeaways and ice cream.

At this stage a couple can even start to subconsciously

mirror each other's positions whilst seated or in bed, just as animal partners do. People tend to reason that these shifting practices are a bad thing, but - so long as the love is still there – I think being definitively comfortable around a partner is probably the most 'themselves' one person can be around another.

Really very comfortable period

Things start to go bad when a couple begin to decline into this last stage. Not all relationships get here and the aim is to steer well clear of it, since the 'Really very comfortable period' is basically identical to the 'Comfortable period' except with the absence of love. Without love, the level of comfort can decline into a state of apathy that eventually leads to each person detesting those little actions and habits learnt about each other during the Honeymoon period. At this point in a relationship, being too lazy, full of ice cream or too stuck in a reluctantly co-dependant home structure to do anything about it causes tension and breeds hatred. In short: not good.

I think that May and myself have taken a swift route through stage one, and are somehow now safely in our Honeymoon period. I'm lead to believe this because last night I found out that - due to some form of mild OCD - she can only hold a mug with her right hand, and I've spent most of today thinking about how funny and sweet that is. I guess things move quickly when you live together.

I think Tim and Jenny are somewhere between the Honeymoon period and the Comfort period, despite having been a couple now for the best part of a million years. I say that because, while they got together the same way that most couples do at university (drunken fumblings at a student night), there are some extraneous complications that Jenny still doesn't know about. There are still some secrets.

Tim lived down the hall from me in our halls of residence. I still to this day wonder about the strength of the University's legal right to call what was clearly an ex-prison a 'halls of residence', but nonetheless there we lived. Our flat had three boys and three girls, none of whom (apart from Tim) I still keep in touch with. As such I don't think it's a very productive use of ink or finger strength to write about them, except to say that one of them collected photographs of himself and another told everyone her name was 'Baby', and continued to do so even after we found out it was actually Sarah.

Probably the only other person worth talking about from halls - out of the entire cast of characters I met there - is Jenny.

Jenny lived in the flat above us, and as the two floors melted into one continuous hedonistic grog-fest it soon became apparent that Tim had a thing for her. In fairness, Jenny is a very attractive woman. She has shoulder length mousy hair that envelops her symmetrically angular face, all sitting atop a slender-yet-curvaceous figure. She looks no different now to when we met at the age of 18.

"I tell you what..." Tim slurred to me one night. It was early on in our Uni career; he could only just manage to lift his head above a city of empty bottles.

"What?"

"I'd love to do things to Jenny. Naughty things."

Obviously, this candid revelation wasn't my first inkling about who it was that a young (but still hairy) Tim had is eye on, nor was it the first time I'd heard him utter that particular turn of phrase. The problem for Tim though, was that when we first started Uni he was engaged.

I'm not suggesting that (usually self-obsessed) 18 year-old kids have the wherewithal to truly know what it means to know another person fully, but I think that in that first month at university Tim and Jenny came as close as they possibly could. We all spent time as a group of course; the best part of 15 people were always out together, always annoying bar staff and tormenting the halls security team, but Tim and Jenny were quietly inseparable in the midst of it all. They were happy with the fact that the sudden closeness of such a large ensemble allowed them to get away with being together at all times.

The two of them simply clicked; they got on in a way that I still lack the ability to explain convincingly, as my vague ramblings about May and myself have probably made clear.

Of course, this would be all well and good if it

weren't for the fact that the *other* time I'd heard Tim suggest that he'd like to 'do naughty things' to someone was when he was on the phone to his fiancé.

I'm sure I'm making it sound as if Tim is a bad man. Let me please make it perfectly clear that he isn't. Timothy Lee Osmond (Esquire) is one of the most genuinely nice people I have ever met. The fact that I'm currently deceiving everyone I know might take away my right to correctly judge anyone's character, but I know for a fact that the situation he found himself in with Jenny put him in real emotional turmoil. Tim, being the gent that he is, wouldn't allow himself to cheat on Amy - his long standing girlfriend turned wife-to-be - despite the fact that he had fallen obviously in love with Jenny. Jenny didn't even know that he was seeing somebody, and I understood from our friend's gossiping that she found Tim's fruitless flirting at the time quite upsetting.

"What can I do, mate?" he'd asked me one night. "I can't end four years with Amy for this girl that I've only just met. …Much as I'd like to."

I'm not sure if it makes me a bad person, but I've always pushed for those around me to take risks. It may well be a mere disregard for their overall wellbeing or a lack of appreciation for real world repercussions, but there's a part of me deep down that hopes my insistence in seizing opportunities merely stems from not wanting anyone I know to end up regretting anything. It's long been my opinion that no matter how bad the consequences, it's far better to regret doing something than to regret not. Omission is worse than commission.

I don't waste time pretending that I'm the reason Tim and Jenny got together, nor do I wish to take credit in any way for the happiness they've found since. All I know is that at some point after my reply to Tim's (probably rhetorical) question, he had made perhaps the biggest decision of his life.

I don't think he regrets it though; now he can pass wind whenever he wants.

iv) Other things that happen in the month of June

Today I'm that yuppie in Starbucks with a laptop. I thought I'd get out of the house because I could hear the couple I spent most of the last chapter describing as 'infinitely happy' having an argument. I can't tell them that they've now made me sound foolish because of the nature of both the book and the state of my current health, but I hope that deep down they felt a twang of guilt when I left the house. They should; now you probably think I'm just an idealistic liar.

Tim has got himself a part in a play that will be going to the Edinburgh Fringe Festival. I would tell you what it's about but I'm not really sure, and more to the point I'm not sure he is either. When I asked he replied by saying:

"Something weird about the passage of time," which by anyone's standards sounds a bit too ambitious a topic to be ably covered by a troupe of three in just eighty minutes - unless they plan to downplay the 'passage of time' bit and seriously up-play the 'weird'. I've every faith that our Tim will pull his weight, though.

Whilst this may sound like reason to celebrate, tensions have been rising about the fact that Jenny works a lot and Tim doesn't. I've every sympathy for her. Jenny's caught between the pride associated with her boyfriend finally doing something he actually wants to do and the realisation that she's paying the lion-share of their rent. To that end, Tim has been working for little over a week at a bar in Soho, which is good news for the opportunistic friend who has nowhere to be and plenty of thirst. Apparently this hasn't appeased things too much though, as their squabbling can duly attest.

Coffee shops are curious places. They seemed to have sprung up over night in droves a few years ago, filling a gap in the market that nobody thought was actually there. As the 11 other patrons in here with me will probably confirm though, they're now a wholly necessary part of modern living and we'd probably all be dead without them. In fairness, whereas the American branding of coffee houses is a pretty new development, they have been around for hundreds of years. King Charles II actually ordered that they all be shut down during his reign because he thought they were just places for people to sit and conspire against him, which can only be described as a level of paranoia bordering on the impressive.

I think the only purpose they serve today is making

people feel slightly more cosmopolitan, swish and important than a baker's or greasy spoon café would. Come to think of it, if you want a sandwich you go to a bakers and if you want a coffee you go to a café; the only unique thing I can see that coffee shops offer anyone is a comfier range of seats for those wanting to sit and write. And free Wi-Fi. With that in mind, the fact that I'm the only one here with a laptop, notepad, pen or even conscious facial expression makes me wonder what all these other people are actually doing here. Maybe they've all bought shares.

I justify my decision to stay on the grounds that I'm sitting on a particularly comfy brown leather sofa.

At any rate, I'll be the first to admit that Jenny's looked a bit run down of late. The fact that she's an enormous hypochondriac not withstanding, I've big respect for her for supporting Tim's career upheaval, just as I have for her agreeing to stumble out of their little bubble and move in with May and myself.

May, by the way, is at home in Bristol visiting her family. This is probably for the best seeing as I've been veering closer and closer to blurting out "I love you" every night. That is by far the worst of what's now building into a compendium of stalker-esque, amorous ramblings swirling round my head, some of which occasionally pop out in an effort to make me sound mental. Two nights ago for instance, we were lying in bed joking that I was going to beat her up. I then said I wouldn't beat her up but I would still hurt her, and when asked how I replied (and this is honestly what I said):

"By over kissing."

Now, not only is this sickly beyond belief but - when followed by the barrage of kisses I then planted about her face - it means I've somehow turned into a kind of Cary Grant character from a 50's romantic comedy. I don't think that kind of faux suavity washes very well with today's modern woman. Especially as Cary Grant was gay.

As overzealously romantic a man as I apparently am, I agree that it's far from time to meet her parents. From her point of view it's because we've only been seeing each other for a couple of weeks, but from mine it's because I don't much fancy the idea of introducing myself to them while my brain goes: "Hi, I'm the chap that's started a relationship with your lovely daughter in spite of the fact that I've got a very short expiration date," over and over again. I might be stating the obvious (not to mention making light of the situation), but relationships are so much harder when you're dying and the other person doesn't know. In all honesty, dear reader, I've no idea what I'm going to do about this whole thing. I can't physically bring myself to tear away from such a wonderful human being. None of this was really part of my big plan for this last year.

Oh well. She's away at the moment, meaning the only people in my life of any relevance at this very moment in time are the (now seven) other people in this coffee shop.

In lighter news, I received a letter this morning very politely informing me that I've been fired from work. I haven't turned up in a month, but I've been paid for that time's not-so hard graft. I spent a sizeable chunk of my life stuffed into that giant tin box and most days worried if I was doing a good enough job. Turns out my best efforts were about the same as a month of sitting on my arse at home.

The working world is a joke. Fact.

4. JULY

<u>Shopping:</u>

Baked Beans
Tea
Milk
Bread
More fruit. Go with Apples.
Some kind of vegetable (many)
Red wine & Cheese - at least 3 kinds
Frozen meat; two of every animal
You've run out of gin

<u>Things learned:</u>

- There's no point in looking forward to summer
when you're a grown-up. It's ingrained in us as youths
to count down the days until heat finally arrives,
because when it does you get a shed-load of time off
to hang around outside shops and such like. That
longstanding habit stays with you. The tubes become
unbearably hot and you still have to go to work. The
summer is wasted. This summer I'm going to drink
cider in the garden. Sorry.

- Having questioned Jenny about the fact that I'd seen
nary a pinnie in the kitchen since we'd moved in
together, she told me that Tim had chucked them out
after I made fun of him. I might buy him a new,
girlier one by way of apology.

<u>Favourite Text:</u>

May: "Home's a bit boring; not much going on. Mum's asking about you. ...I told her you were very lovely. ;) How's the writing going? xx"

i) We could be heroes

At which point in history did everybody start working off the same calendar? I understand that most countries who count Christianity as their main religion go off the date that Jesus first showed his face, but today is Sunday the 4th of July and I'm fairly certain that I could fly anywhere in the world to find that it would still be round about Sunday the 4th of July. Presumably, in the times when an ocean might as well have meant the edge of the world, every country had its own system for tallying up the days, months and years – but when and why did it all flick over to the system we're on now? Was it something to do with the stock market? A more important question would probably be who on Earth it was with such an arrogantly persuasive manner that he was able to visit a foreign land and convince its entire populous that it wasn't in fact schmorgeday (or whatever they would have called it) morning; it was actually Friday evening? Whomever it was, I can't help but think that he could have probably made millions if he'd only taken the gravitas and enthusiasm he had in his evangelical time-telling mission and transferred it to the world of business.

The reason I'm so worried about dates is because two days ago it was my 27th birthday. Birthdays stop being fun once you realise that 30 is in sight, but it's a different matter entirely when it reminds you so brazenly of your own imminent death. I was 26 when I had that fateful talk with my doctor. I was told I'd not die until I was 27. This seemed like a while away, in the same naïve fashion that a second year university student doesn't have to think about his future because graduating seems like 'a while away', before every possible flavour of responsibility lands squarely in his lap. Time always flies by when you least want it to.

So I'm going to die, and I'm going to be this age when it happens. Good. As if that's not too much of a complete head fuck, it might be worth mentioning that I had to come to terms with it all whilst bounding round central London dressed as Batman.

The last time I'd been out with a big bunch of friends I'd spent the whole night drunkenly wrestling with the idea of letting everyone know about this book and my health. Unless you lost faith in my storytelling abilities and buggered off to the next chapter, you'll remember that all that mental turmoil was neatly stopped when I became distracted with romantic endeavours. This time, the thought of telling people about anything even remotely serious was put to bed merely by the fact that I was parading about amongst a team of shoddily-dressed superheroes.

It was May's idea. Without my knowing she'd organised for everyone to dress up as comic book heroes, and that they'd all chip in and get me a Batman costume because it was common knowledge amongst friends that if could have any job in the world (other than terminally-ill author) it would definitely be defending Gotham city by beating people up in a PVC gimp suit.

"I know someone who's got a birthday today," she said as we lay in bed. She'd booked the day off work for it specially.

"Oh yeah? Who's that?"

"Umm... Sedrick," she reeled off slowly, adopting the childlike voice she turns to when making things up on the spot. It's in turn brilliantly funny and achingly cute - and so hard to explain in writing.

"Sedrick who?"

"No it's not really Sedrick. It's Alan."

"Well that's me, isn't it?" I said. I was enjoying her playful smile and didn't want it to go away, so I happily perpetuated the nonsense.

Among my presents were books, clothes, toiletries and booze. My expectant hope for each wrapped box diminished more and more as every one I opened proved not to contain toys. Why don't people buy me toys anymore? If it's because they think I'm too old then I'll put it here in writing: that's bollocks. Quite clearly it's a self-perpetuating problem, because if they bought me toys I'd bloody well play with them. This would undoubtedly lead to more toys next year and...

...Well. Next year in theory. I'm not going to get another birthday. It has only just occurred to me that, age aside, this was my last ever birthday. That's just very depressing.

I finished opening my presents with the kind of speed usually reserved for military aircraft (in terms of their general speed, not how well they unwrap presents) and May thrust me a gift bag that wore a blue bow as a hat. It was about the size of an upturned laptop, and six inches wide at the base. The only reason I say as such is because she <u>literally</u> pulled it from nowhere - like how cartoon character pulls a giant mallet from their pocket. It was so amazing that I made a point of asking her how she did it.

"Magic," she replied. "Birthday magic."

"No, seriously. That was mental," I said. "Was it under the duvet all night or something?"

"I'll tell you which shop I got the bloody bow from if you tell me what your book's about," she replied. There was a hint of annoyance in her voice.

It wasn't the first time May had asked about this

book, and I hate it when she does. Every time she does it sends me down the same depressing line of thought that begins with me acknowledging that a man's girlfriend probably has the right to know what her boyfriend's book is about, and ends with me realising that I'm in a relationship that has no future. And that I'm a deceiving bastard.

"Honestly, I'm really sorry," I replied, as softly as I could. "I just want to keep it a secret. If I decide to tell anyone, you'll be first. Promise."

"Ok, whatever. Just open your bloody present!"

She seemed more excited about all this than I was, which helped lift my mood again. The bag was done up with more tape than any normal person knows how to manage, and when I finally did get in I was confronted with a sheet of deep black, perforated with blocks of yellow. It was the costume. I pulled it out and held it in front of me, very aware that when receiving presents one should adopt a face that's a lot more grateful than the one I was actually wearing, but unable to do much about it. I held the costume aloft and stared at it intently like it was a magic-eye picture, moving back and forth in the hope that it would reveal the right thing to say.

I love Batman. I think he's very cool. I've never thought of his skin-tight costume as being in least bit homo-erotic, submissive, or embarrassing. That said, the thought that my birthday's destiny involved dressing as my bat-powered hero didn't make me happy. It didn't make me happy for two very important reasons:

1. I don't have the muscular figure Bruce Wayne's blessed with.

2. Costume shop costumes are invariably shite in the most humiliating of ways.

This costume in particular was a brave new world of shite, to such a degree that made me assume it could only have been designed to meet a stringent brief of making the wearer look like as big a tit as one item of apparel physically could, without just being a giant tit costume. I should say now that if you're reading this and were in any way involved in the making, buying or selling of that specific costume, I thank you and hope you realise that I *am* grateful for both the thought and the excellent night that followed... but my god was it an unflattering bundle of bad.

Hang on: I've jumped ahead. I took the costume out of the bag, held it aloft, stared at it for a while and - with questionable gratitude - said at last: "Ah, that's amazing, thanks!" to May. I was still moving it backwards and forwards in an effort to change it into something else with the power of my brain.

"It's from all of us," she said, and all of a sudden I had a list of people to kill. "Bet you can't guess tonight's theme?" she continued, and I breathed a tremendous sigh of relief: there was a theme. I wouldn't be the only one dressed as a giant tit.

I put the batman suit to one side and delved back into the exciting and unknown world of the gift bag's innards. There were two items, both wrapped in red tissue paper and both brimming with the potential for being toys; I ripped the first open.

Beneath the tissue paper was a notebook – a handmade, leather-bound notebook. The second, smaller parcel contained a pen, which I can only assume is a very expensive pen. May had bought me a notebook and a pen with which I could continue to write the book about how I'm misleading and conning her. There's a can of emotionally charged worms right there. Looking back, I can only hope that I managed to hide the horrific pangs of guilt and shame crashing around me behind something at least *resembling* gratitude.

I thanked her profusely, told her she shouldn't have spent any money on me (as is customary) and went about the rest of the day with a very calm and relaxed face affixed to my subversively unwell head.

Come evening time, a gaggle of friends had assembled at our house. Laughter seemed to fall out of a lot of the rooms as people got changed into their costumes, fell over putting legs into leg holes and tried desperately to conceal their various bulges. Among our number were the following:

• Batman (That would be me)

• Wonder Woman (May)

- Spiderman

- Joker

- Poison Ivy (Jenny)

- Cat woman

- A Teenage Mutant Ninja Turtle

- Buffy the Vampire Slayer (who I hadn't realised had super powers)

- Clark Kent (apparently, although it was really just Tim with a superman t-shirt on under his shirt)

- V (from V for Vendetta)

- Incredibles woman (from the Disney film)

- Drink-Man (A creation of Ross', and one that looked uncannily like Ross save for a St Patrick's Day hat, a picture of a pint on his shirt and a pair of shamrock pants over his trousers.)

We all knew, as an unspoken rule, that it was vitally important for all involved to hit a certain level of drunkenness before the notion of leaving the house in such a state was even considered as a feasible plan of action. If ever there was a reason for feeling self-conscious in public, it's when the parts of you that should normally remain undefined are being proudly framed by lycra.

The idea of fancy dress is, I'm sure, a female invention. I say this because I have never been involved in a fancy dress party where the male participants look good. I'd go as far as to say that it's nigh on impossible to be a man in fancy dress and look anything but completely fucking ridiculous. Women, on the other hand, are able to twist any possible theme into a way to dress up in an extremely sexy manner.

This duality isn't necessarily a bad thing, since men can laugh about how stupid they look whilst ogling scantily clad women, but it's a shame sometimes because any attempt on behalf of the men to look even remotely cool or handsome will be lambasted, and their efforts labelled as boring.

As it was, my costume was pants. The black was almost grey under artificial light, the head part was floppy and uncomfortable and the whole thing was made out of that kind of mystery stretchy tissue paper, which I'm sure is a joint discovery by the costume industry and NASA. It was ill-fitting, compounded by the fact that I was wearing trousers and a shirt underneath, giving me bulges where there shouldn't be any and keeping me unfortunately bulge-free wherever my physique could have done with one. In short: I looked like a tit.

My friends and I bounded towards SoHo via the tube, all dressed as a differing breeds of mental patient, while strangers stared and onlookers looked on. Oddly enough, for however much of a loon I looked, it actually felt safe to be hidden under a mask. Nobody from the outside world could see me but I could see them, and that kind of anonymity gives you massive amounts artificial confidence.

As does a massive amount of alcohol.

Anonymity, as it turns out though, is a concept that works best when you're not dressed as an easily recognisable character. The oddest thing was that, while by anyone's standard I was a poorly attired Batman, to the (drunken) people of London, I actually *was* the caped crusader.

I've never known celebrity before, but it's a very addictive thing. People kept coming up to me wanting photographs with me, or to buy me drinks, or - bizarrely - even just to shake my hand. It seems that despite his controversial reputation in Gotham City, Batman is a very popular fellow round these parts. The best part for me was that underneath the costume of a superhero stood a man at the weakest he's ever been. It gifted the whole thing a wonderful sense of irony.

The evening took us from bar to bar until we settled in the same place we'd been in the night May and I had first kissed. Drink flowed and laughter ensued in the way that only alcohol and its wonderful reckless abandon can bring. May was with Jenny a lot of the night. I made myself busy with the boys. It's probably just paranoia, but I'm sure there was a time where – for a while – May kept herself very distant from me, and I don't know why. I'm sure it's just paranoia.

Since this was my last ever birthday I suppose I'd best evaluate how much I enjoyed it. Just for something to do. I certainly had a fun day, but one has to question whether that means I made the most of it. I reckon it's the same with most birthdays: the problem with days that are built up or supposed to be a big deal is that it usually becomes impossible for them to live up to their own hype. This disappointment, coupled with the fact that a birthday signifies the process of ageing, is probably why people tend to make less and less of an effort each year. This one certainly wasn't the best birthday anyone's ever had, but it *was* my last. I was surrounded by enough loved ones for me not to dwell on its shortcomings for what I've got left of my life, and that's more than good enough for me.

***

I think there's a lot to be said for the phrase 'appearances can be deceiving'. We often reach for it when things turn out to be worse than we'd imagined they would. A plate of food can look like the most gorgeous culinary delight ever created, and then have you cradling the toilet bowl for hours afterwards. A member of the opposite sex can seem like the sexiest human being ever sculpted until they give you the clap. Likewise, what appears to be a footloose gang of friends dressed as superheroes (fronted by the seemingly happy partnership of Batman and Wonder Woman) is often just as likely to be a band of embarrassingly drunken late-twenty-somethings ,fronted by a dying man. A dying man with an awkwardly distant girlfriend and a sweaty neck.

Happy birthday to me.

ii) Out of the mouths of babes

There is something dangerously and seriously wrong in the brains of womankind. I'm so worried about it that if I had more time on Earth I would probably devote the remainder of my entire life to fixing it.

Racists often start offensive sentences by saying "I'm not a racist, but…" and, whilst I recognise this as just a ploy to cushion hateful slander, I should warn you that I'm about to start the following sentence by employing this obviously ineffective tactic myself. You've been warned.

I'm not sexist, but… it strikes me that women in general lack the ability to say what they're thinking. There obviously has to be a link betwixt their brains and their mouths, but somewhere along the line lives a wholly unnecessary filtering system that takes the raw and uncensored thought, mangles it about and spurts it out the other end in code that can only be correctly deciphered if you're:

A) Another woman

Or

B) Clinically insane

I've no doubt just lost the female readership. In fairness though, everything in this book thus far has probably acted as nothing but an exercise in stripping away demographics so that the only person left (that's you, dear reader) is someone who thinks and acts (and quite possibly looks) a lot like myself. That's the problem with honesty; the only people who can stand it are usually the ones who agree.

No big loss. At least now I'm quite sure that you and I share similar views. I'll probably just write whatever gibberish I like for the rest of the book and draw little doodles, safe in the knowledge that I'm writing for a mid-to-late twenties male audience with a penchant for offending women and a lack of allegiance to the tropes found in, and expected of, typical literature. I'd like to buy you a pint if I weren't quite so dead.

Where was I? Oh yes; the complete inability in a woman's being to express what she's actually thinking. Now, I of course realise that men are far from perfect creatures. If they were I would probably be gay. Having said that, one thing you can bet on in most cases is the fact that when you talk to a man he'll at least tell you exactly what he thinks - regardless of how stupid, irrelevant, unsympathetic, hurtful, inappropriate, slanderous or bamboozling that thought might be.

In an effort to stop skirting around the issue I should probably just come out and say that things have hit the rocks. May's been giving me a cold shoulder. Things have gone mental.

When 'things' started, we agreed that to stop us from moving too swiftly into a fully blown cohabitating couple we would only sleep in the same bed a few nights a week. That's fair enough - we each need space - but I've not been allowed to sleep in the same room as her for four days now. And she won't tell me why.

"My best guess is that she's feeling that this is all too sudden," Jenny said.

"Well if that's the case she should bloody well tell me so," I replied. We were sat in the lounge. Jenny had been watching Eastenders until she'd gotten annoyed at my sighing and forlorn looks. I imagine it didn't help that I was slugging it on the pile of cushions; its sunken, floppy consistency would make a pharaoh look like a melancholic slave-child.

"Yeah perhaps."

"Perhaps?" I reposted. "If I'm posing some sort of problem to her, I won't go away just because she's ignoring me. Problems don't work like that. That's quite clearly the problem-solving tactic of a complete mental."

"Yes," said Jenny. "But you've got to understand, Alan, that going from not even knowing someone existed to romantically cohabiting in such a short space of time is a pretty drastic thing to have to deal with." Apparently, despite the clearly-stated precautions May and I had taken to prevent ourselves from jumping into couple-hood, it had happened anyway. The problem is that I don't really mind and May does. But then, since I'm nearing the end of my life, it is probably for the best.

This is a bit of a mess I've got myself into. Why didn't you warn me, reader? Things'd be so much simpler if I weren't quite so hopelessly in love with the girl. Or dying.

Or an utterly deceiving prick.

iii) The whites of my eyes

May continues to avoid me. She claims that its due to stress at work; her company takes on contracts to outfit people for TV shows on the BBC and they've just taken on the mother of all period drama deals, but even so she's abnormally distant. We shared a bed last night, but there was no tom-foolery. Nor was there any attempt on her part to return the affection I was trying to give.

It's making me deeply sad and afraid.

There are well over 19 different species of animal on Earth. Of which the stupid, needy and emotionally-fragile human being is one.

I would disclose the exact amount but, since new species of animal are becoming extinct or being discovered daily, any amount I write would probably be false about five seconds thereafter. Thus, I think it's best if we work from the approximation that there are at least 19 and at most 'lots', and carry on safe in the knowledge that this body of work remains immaculately, factually correct.

Never let it be said that Alan Bell was a charlatan. ...Well, apart from the whole dying and lying thing.

In the post-Big Bang free-for-all, once enough celestial crumbs had clumped together and cooled down, Earth was formed. In celebration, water was invited to splodge into all the troughs; a happy accident of which being that the place became nice and hospitable for life. In a move that could best be described as beautifully-timed, opportunistic industrialism, bacteria and other single-celled organisms moved in and soon began to flourish in the soggy goodness.

Sometime later - presumably out of boredom - Bacteria evolved into fish, squid, jellyfish, snails and all manner of other slimy creatures until the sea was teeming with life. So full was the sea in fact, that it became over-crowded and things began flinging themselves out onto the land in search of elbow room. Thanks to evolution/God (delete as appropriate), this mass marooning drove everything down the following route:

Fish > fish with legs > legs without much fish > lizard (with legs) > dinosaur > alarmingly big meteor > dead dinosaur > mammal > chimp > chimp that smokes cigars > human.

Note: *This might not be exactly accurate, but it's good enough. Regrettably, my knowledge of evolution has been built less from Darwin and a lot more from Pokemon than it perhaps should be. Also, I'm not sure where things are going to go from here, but I did see a documentary once that suggested cats will learn how to fly. Humans, on the other hand, will probably either get bigger brains or just grow enormously fat. Isn't learning fun?*

By way of a quick zoological lesson, reptiles are the scaly ones that lay eggs (not to be confused with birds), and mammals are the flabbier, hairier ones that squeeze out smaller, more demanding, living versions of themselves. Just so you know. Move on several hundred years or so (probably more), and the smattering of animals on earth remains mostly the same. Mankind dominates all the other animals (Otters, for example) because we have opposable thumbs and the brain capacity to make things that let us use them. Like Tetris. …which Otters are inherently rubbish at.

Proof - if it were needed - of this thumb-founded supremacy can be found in the Dolphin. Dolphins have a brain one and a half times the size of our own and have been proven to be one of the most intelligent creatures on the planet. And yet, despite all this brainpower, Dolphins have failed spectacularly to create anything even resembling a habitable building - much less Tetris. Where we have Playstations, they push balls around with their noses. Where we have aeroplanes, they're content to lunge a couple of metres above sea level. Where we have comfy (but hard-gotten) IKEA beds, they sleep with one eye open in the dangerous ocean – and it's all because their thumb-less fins have scuppered their chance of ever being Earth's big cheese.

They also don't have any legs, come to think of it, which can't have helped. Legs and thumbs, dear reader: a recipe for success.

My point is this: one way or another we've become the dominant species. However - and it's a big 'however' - the superior position we hold over other animals does come with its downsides. As part of the inbuilt and very basic need to survive, all creatures are predisposed to fear certain things. It's as simple as knowing that if you get too near to something with pointier teeth than yours, it'll kill you. Your brain drives you away from that thing by using fear. It's based on primal endurance. Humans, on the other hand, can be scared of any number of bizarre and inanimate things (like buttons, for example). We are also afraid of things that can't be seen or felt.

I am afraid that May will leave me. I am afraid of it. It's not a worry of mine, or a concern. It is a fear. I am scared on a primal level that the girl I am in love with will soon no longer want to be part of that arrangement. My veins seem to run hot when I think about it. My head becomes flushed.

It's an animalistic reaction to a uniquely human

situation. Just like my health, it's a situation that's now well out of my control. Just like an animal, I'm doing everything in my power to stop my fear from hurting me. It doesn't seem to be working; every arm I try and wrap over her and every kiss I try and give is unmet and unrequited.

It's all only making me more terrified.

iv) This is still a book

She put her dressing gown on - that's what I remember the most.

Quite rightly, you might be getting annoyed at my inability to remember things that would make this book a considerably easier read. There's a severe lack of written dialogue because I can't recall very much of what people say to me, and there's not much in the way of description because I can't often draw upon what a given room or scene looked like once a day has passed. I fill most of this book with the inane and spurious notions that I pull from my head because without them there wouldn't be much else. But what I *can* remember vividly is that May got up, walked over to her bedroom door and sheepishly peeled her dressing gown from its hook, before shamefully wrapping herself inside it.

I was on the bed, worrying about her sudden unwillingness to show me her body.

This is still a book more than it is a diary - I want that intention made clear.

In filling it with passages about how I see the world at large and not just daily occurrences, I've clearly made a decision that this is going to be an entertaining and informative read, with something to make the endless pages worth trudging though. I suppose that this ill-fated love story has injected some kind of narrative to the proceedings, but the problem is that - in my logical, over-thinking way - I've never been very proficient at writing romance, despite claiming to be a romantic.

When I was at university I took a bit of an invested interest in stealing an education from a friend who was studying English Literature - probably more of an invested interest than I shoved into my own course, if anything. I remember him being told that for a story to work it needs a beginning, middle and end, but it also needs a protagonist (which I suppose would be me) and an antagonist or challenge. The former should cross paths with the latter, and come out the other end either triumphant (comedy) or much worse off (tragedy).

Trouble is, I'm having a lot of trouble pinning down which specific challenge is my main one - and I think it needs sorting out in order for the rest of the book to have any kind of proper direction.

If we analyse the state of my life at the moment we can probably make a fairly safe bet that I'm not going to come out smiling at the end. My ill-health is, for lack of better terminology, a 'major problem' that I'm currently facing. It's an adversary that I'm quite clearly not going to beat. If that's the case then I'm going to, in the very first instance, suggest that the book is a tragedy.

Tragedy being tragedy we can all look forward to tears and upset heads at the end, but what I'm unsure of at the moment is whether this whole May business is just a sub plot in my life tragedy, or whether it's the main element of a gripping romantic tragedy. It's confusing. One of the most famous romantic tragedies ever written is Romeo and Juliet, which begins by telling the audience that the two lovers don't make it through with hearts intact, and then shows why. If that dramatic irony was the key to Shakespeare's success, then I'll just jump on the literary bandwagon and tell you – *before* divulging how - that May and I have broken up, and it happened when she put on her dressing gown.

If I'm honest with myself, things had broken down some days before that and I'd been desperately trying to ignore it. Following from her distance at my birthday party and several days of doing her upmost to ignore my existence, May and I had had an argument. A proper argument. It seemed to come out of nothing but quickly built into everything, and that scared me no end. All this honeymoon period bunkum that I'd previously been spouting fell apart and all that'd been left were two people much further apart than the metre of cold air allowed.

As small and as stupid an argument it had been, things weren't the same after. Maybe I was to blame, but in my heart it didn't feel like I was. I'd ended up apologising to keep the peace. I apologised, it was accepted, and then we'd gone to bed facing opposite directions, which really didn't feel like much of a denouement.

Since then we've been spooning. Spooning in a wanky, metaphorical sense, I mean. I've been trying incredibly hard to make everything seem happy and loving, but she's been facing away, with my proverbial arm trying to latch on and keep her close. It's done nothing but given me that sickly pain you get between your heart and your throat when the part of you that loves things gets hurt. It feels like someone's standing on your neck, forcing all the blood in your head to stay there and warm up.

"Mate, I'm not trying to upset you or anything, but I think maybe she wanted that argument to happen," Tim said. He was supping his pint as I stared down at the table.

"Perhaps. She's just been ignoring me; shirking me off when I try and kiss her, and acting like it's a chore to have my arm round her."

"Women are mental. I've always said that."

It was true; Tim had always jumped on any opportunity to let that catchphrase escape his stupid, hairy face. In fairness, it's a great phrase to claim ownership of. It's something that can only be said around other men and, seeing as it's usually not unprovoked, it's safe to say that whoever Tim finds himself using it to comfort is often very inclined to agree with him. It's like suggesting to Hitler that some races are somewhat inferior; Tim was preaching to the choir. A choir that really doesn't understand women. I bet he'd trademark those three words if he could figure out how.

At the time, I was very, very inclined to agree with him. I couldn't (read: can't) understand how things had gone from exceedingly happy to awkward and tense just as the result of one argument - especially one that I can't remember the subject of.

"Women are mental," I replied, glumly.

On the dressing gown night we were in her bedroom watching a film. It was the first thing we'd done as just the two of us for three days. The film was a comedy, but neither one of us were laughing. We sat there for its entire duration in a painfully awkward silence. I spent a long time both trying to think of something to say and praying for the thing to end. It was impossible. The situation was impossible because the only thing I wanted to say was that things between us were clearly strained, and also impossible because the words were stuck behind that clingy widget of love-sickness that pushes against the very front of your vocal cords. In the face of such a wall of silence there was nothing I could think of to say that wouldn't sound like a feeble attempt at small talk, apart from one very obvious thing. So I said that instead.

"What's wrong with this relationship at the moment?"

She turned to look at me, and there was a face of such cowardly reluctance spread across her brow that it makes me angry to remember it.

"There isn't anyth-"

"There is."

There was a long and terrifying pause before she got up, walked over to her door and put on that bloody dressing gown.

She hadn't even been naked. She'd been wearing a green vest top and pyjama shorts, but the thought of this climatic conversation had obviously made her acutely aware that she had flesh on display that I now wasn't allowed to see. She'd decided there and then that our relationship was over, and as such I'd instantly lost all those rights and privileges that boyfriends are privy to. The rest of our talk would just be the two of us going through the motions, filling the harsh space with pointless words.

"It's just," she started. "It's just that I've been finding this all very hard."

"Finding what all very hard? Everything's been amazing, and then we have one argument and things haven't been the same."

She looked at the floor. When she talked the words were littered with tiny, sparse glances back at my eyes. I felt like she was only doing me the courtesy of looking at me because she felt she needed to do so a certain number of times. Every time she did it caused her obvious trauma.

"A month ago I didn't even know you, Alan, and now we're this little happy co-habiting couple. I just don't think I can carry on with it at the moment. Do… do you understand? I think we need to have time in this house as just friends."

My brain was swimming in blood. By turns I was reeling and feeling sick all over - even if I knew that, if there was one thing a terminally ill man shouldn't participate in, it's a relationship. Everything was wrong in that room. The afternoon sun spilling onto May's bed, which had often made us feel safe and snug, was falling through her bay window as a thick wall and trapping us in a horribly claustrophobic atmosphere. I needed to get out and away from it.

"OK."

"OK what?" she asked.

She didn't know the right words to say any more than I did, but she knew what she wanted out of the situation. I just wanted to be out of it as soon as possible, so I tried to push myself over to her point of view. Quite clearly, she didn't love me, or at least not as much as I did her. To May, we'd just been a couple of people who'd met and gone out for a few weeks. Things had gotten too heavy too fast for her and - although ending our young relationship was the last thing I wanted to do - I could see that I had no right to try and convince her otherwise. I had to go along with it, as sickening as that was.

"OK. We'll end things."

Pauses, heavy breathing and a quivering lip.

"I'm so sorry, Alan." I still don't know if she was or not. "I just don't think I want to be in a relationship at the moment, you know?"

I think that most adults with any kind of romantic history will have heard this heart-rending phrase at some point. It's terrible. It's never something that's met with agreement and, much like 'lets still be friends', it does nothing to soothe the pain or seal the cracks that the conversation it's buried inside manages to cause.

"OK," I repeated. "It's OK; we'll just go |

how it was before."

That was basically it. We hugged, I resisted the strong urge to strangle her and then I left her room as quickly as I possibly could. I walked into mine, closed the door and dived onto the bed. I stayed there for about an hour, until I pulled out the notebook she'd bought me, scrawled the word 'Fuck' in big letters (after a lengthy pause) and then finally went to sleep.

When I woke, I sat in front of my computer screen trying to work out how best to write down what had happened. The reason I'm only attempting to write this now - a day later - is because it became quite apparent yesterday that, had I managed it, I would probably be the first man in history to eloquently write down how it feels to have a broken heart. That's what it is, too. I've only known this girl for a month but there's nothing in this world that could convince me I wasn't actually in love with her. I am in love with May Cooper, and now I can't have her because she doesn't want me. It's that bloody simple, and that bloody complicated.

...Only it's not really, is it? There's a strong argument for saying that this needed to happen. Seeing as I would at some point need to break her heart had she not done mine in, logic would dictate that the sooner such a doomed relationship ended, the better. Problem is that logic doesn't often get a look in where relationships are concerned.

I'm at a bit of a loss about the whole thing, dear reader.

I would so desperately like to be a lot better at all this than I am, you know. I can't describe scenes, dialogue always seems forced and unnatural when written down and I loathe describing feelings. I truly hope, however, that on at least some level you understand how I'm feeling because I'm sure that you've been there too. I'm dead so any empathy you have is wasted, but I've written this down as record that today - just a few days after my 27th birthday - I have just been cast aside by the woman I love. My heart is lodged in my throat, my home feels a sickening place to be and, for the first time since I found out I was ill, there are hot tears closing in around my eyes.

All I can think about, replayed over and over in my head, is May donning that dressing gown - in doing so hiding herself from me forever. At this moment it hurts more than I think any kind of death possibly could.

v) Love is a Dog

Love is a dog.

It creates excitement,

fills rooms with an addictive and breathtaking energy,

misbehaves

and then dies.

vi) A ramble, a list and a some deleted notes

I'm not best pleased with anything.

I'm sitting in Tim's pub while he busies himself cleaning glasses. The sporadic flow of punters is putting me off both writing and drinking. Apparently, today I've got the type of elbows that people like to bump theirs against. I've not really spoken any more than a few words (and decidedly serious texts) to May all week, and the lack of contact is just making everything harder because my instinct is to dramatise what was only a month-long relationship so as to make it seem like there is something to really get upset about.

Actually, fuck that: there definitely is.

"Same again?" Tim asked, making that mouth-adjacent, wrist-flicking gesture that people use to indicate that they're talking about the act of drinking. Even when they actually *are* talking about the act of drinking.

"Please." I didn't feel it necessary to tell him that, since we're in a pub and the only finished thing near me that I could possibly want another of is my drink, the gesture was probably a bit redundant. Unless, of course, he thinks I'm the kind of person that would hear 'Same again?' and think they were being spoken to about the breath of air they just enjoyed.

I'd like the same again of both whilst I still can, at any rate.

Before you jump to any wild conclusions, dear reader; I'm not here drowning my sorrows, or seeking solace at the bottom of a bottle or any of that nonsense. I'm just here to seek some company and get out of the house. My mind is an unabridged cluster of confusion and has been for several days, because I've been desperately trying to get my head around a situation that I'm fairly sure I'm the only person in the world to have gone through. Let's deconstruct it on paper in ten decipherable points:

1/Alan finds out he's dying

2/Alan doesn't tell anyone that he's dying

3/Alan meets a girl that he lives with

4/Alan goes out with and subsequently falls in love with said girl

5/Alan feels ashamed that he's in a relationship with

said girl, since he's dying and she doesn't know

6/Alan can't bloody help himself

7/Relationship ends

8/Alan feels ashamed, still in love, angry, upset, a fool etc.

9/Alan should feel relieved

10/Alan drinks

I think I might have been a touch premature when I started spouting rubbish about how my dying has gifted an outside view of the world and the human experience. If anything it's just made everything ten times worse - ten times more closed in. In theory, I should be able to sit at this bar feeling like some kind of invincible god - laughing maniacally at all the silly little humans around me and their preoccupations with grooming and sex. Matters of the heart shouldn't really seep through my forcefield of detached smugness and I *should* be able to write in an intellectual and erudite manner about the subject, the situation and the entire phenomenon of life as a human.

The reality? Much like an emotionally crippled, fake ID-carrying teenager, I'm rounding off a night of listening to sad songs with a day of drinking. It seems I lack the mental innards to be able to understand

and decode the human experience in any profound way. Or even any simple way.

I suppose what I'm trying to say is that I should never have been involved with May in the first place, but now it's over and I should be relieved. I should be washed over and cleansed with the knowledge that I can get on with being a secretly dying man-child and author. Problem is, I've never been the type of person who's done what they *should* do. I've made that sound like I'm some James Dean, rebellious maverick, but in truth I've never done what I should do because I'm just incredibly stupid.

"It'll get better mate, maybe not straight away, but it'll get better. It's probably for the best, anyway."

That was the last thing I really remember Tim saying. I've had to ignore most of what I wrote in my notebook in the time after that point because it was either covered in beer, illegible, or shit. The fact is: Tim was right. It *is* for the best, and it *will* get better. I'll just have to bite my tongue, do whatever the mental equivalent is to my brain (clamp it?), and get on with what's left of life.

As it turns out though, I think I probably was at that pub to drown my sorrows.

5. AUGUST

<u>Shopping</u>:

Baked Beans
Tea/Milk
Sugar
Brown bread
More fruit. Apples?
Vitamins
Beer / cider
Red wine & Cheeses
Frozen meat; two of every animal
Soup
You've run out of gin

<u>Things learned</u>:

- Any comic book story in which the super hero is berated by the general public is based on fallacy. In real life, superheroes are superstars.

- Dying doesn't quite take you out of any human situation as much as you'd expect or like it to.

- Talking seriously about serious subject makes real people sound exactly like people do in TV dramas. You even repeat sentences for effect and emphasis. I'm yet to figure out if this is TV aping real life or real life being influenced by TV.

Favourite Text:

Tim: "Mate, if it makes you feel any better, I just fell over by accidentally trying to go up a down-escalator."

i) Getting stung

During a bit of a drunken conversation with Tim it occurred to me that I have never been stung by either a wasp or a bee. Today I sought to rectify this as one of the things I feel I should do before I can no longer do anything. Before you jump to any wild conclusions; this is not a clever metaphor about experimenting with Heroin or similar Class A drugs - I'm genuinely talking about wasps and bees. Perhaps a more adventurous dying man may do some wilder things, but I suppose this is what comes from having the mind of a child.

I did a bit of research in the morning and found that bees and wasps kill four people a year in the UK. I'm not sure if this is an average number or if four is some kind of special quota that they feel inclined to reach. I'm not sure because I basically read "four per year" and then checked my emails.

I didn't have any.

At any rate, it turns out that it's a lot harder to get

stung than I ever thought it was, which is annoying because I've spent the last twenty-seven years being absolutely bloody terrified of the things. I'd always assumed that wasps especially were evil little bastards. I've functioned thus far under the reasoning that if a bee stings you it dies and you theoretically win, whereas wasps can afford to be vicious because they've nothing to lose. On that score, even though the internet can tell me exactly what celebrity X or Y is up to at any given nanosecond, it still can't answer one of the eternal questions perplexing mankind: do bees know that they'll die if they sting you?

I can only imagine that they don't, otherwise they never would... unless something really, really pissed them off and they became so transfixed with rage that they lost the will to live. You'd have thought though, that at some point one bee would witness another bee perish (having stung some hapless barbecuer) and then tell the rest of the hive (and ergo the rest of bee-kind via word-of-mouth) the horrors he'd seen. The problem is that bees talk to each other through interpretive dance, which I suppose is a medium of communiqué that could easily be performed or translated wrongly - especially if said bee-witness was a bit shook up by what he'd seen. It's only logical (yes, logical) then, to suggest they might be able to avoid having any more deaths, *and* embark on lasting human/bee peacetime if only they'd change their fruity way of speaking. I chalk it all up to bad communication. It's the same reason why insects don't have any decent system of government and quite often bow to a dictatorship.

It's odd, but because I'm not long for this world (no, don't cry) I felt it was only right to adopt a sort of 'live and let live' attitude and go in search of a wasp. I say 'odd' firstly because no evangelist eco-warrior types were aware of what I was doing, and secondly because I don't *really* care either way. Maybe deep down I'm just an optimist – I just think give them some time and eventually word'll spread and render the bee sting/death practice a thing of the past. It took *us* thousands of years to develop proper language after all, and our brains are (at least) four times the size of a bee's.

It was a nice day today, so I decided to go to a place I thought wasps would congregate on nice days: Hyde Park. I've spoken about it before, but for those that haven't been there, it's a bloody great big park. Named Hyde. It's good to see that there are places like this that'll never get built or touched upon, both because London needs some green areas and also because it provides ample wasp supplies for people who are looking to get stung. Or at least it should.

Dying hasn't yet blessed me with the loving and serene attitude you might think it would: the truth is that wasps are cunning, conniving little shits. I can't see what it is they offer to the world around them because they don't make honey, but my biggest problem is that they're ever-present when you don't want them and absolutely nowhere to be seen when you try actively seeking one out.

I wandered around the park for a while, enjoying the warmth but sticking close to the edge of the paths and forever scanning the surrounding bushes for any hint of their yellow and black jackets.

I think there's a strong possibility I might have looked quite odd.

Tim is allergic to wasp stings; when we were talking he mentioned that one got him in the hand when he was eleven. He said it ballooned until it looked like a rubber glove inflated until it resembles a cow's udder. He then told me (and these are his words):

"If five wasps ever stung me at once, I would probably die."

Maybe I read into that wrong, but to me it was as if he was implying that wasps act with an organised team attitude - that they know how to work together to get a job done. The sentiment only strengthens my aforementioned theory that, for whatever reason, they have an annual death quota that needs filling.

I've no idea who issues this quota but I can only assume it's the Devil himself. He seems the logical choice.

All this allergy talk was buzzing (pun definitely intended) round my head and rammed the fear of God into me. By this point the elusiveness of the winged beasts was making me worried that I might somehow need to seek out an entire nest, aggravating them just enough so that no more than four felt the need to sting me. I had no reason to believe I'm susceptible to anaphylaxis, but I didn't want to run the risk of spending any more of my last year in a hospital bed than I particularly need to. I pushed on regardless, hoping they weren't secretly watching with designs on making me one of their ill-fated four for this year. I took solace in the notion that they may be able to sense that I was dying anyway and save themselves the energy. As if I wouldn't count.

At about one in the afternoon I veered off the beaten track and finally clocked a little wasp, busily doing whatever it is they pretend to do during the day. He was fooling nobody. It was flitting madly around some plants that were amidst waist-high grass in an unkempt field off the back of the Serpentine. I watched it with my heart in my throat as it kept threatening to fly off; every time it lifted above the greenery something else would catch its attention and it would drop back down to investigate. God knows what it was up to - they don't have any business with flowers. You know that, I know that.

I decided to call it Neville. Unlike his waspy brethren I'd met in the past, Neville and I would not be enemies; I decided we were to put our lifelong differences aside and become comrades. A torrid emotional allegiance would bind us as he unwittingly and unwilling did my bidding. With that decision made - and understood at least on my part if not Neville's - I checked that nobody was watching, took a deep breath and charged like a flaming lunatic towards him; my arms flailing skyward like a mental. I may have also been shouting the words "Neville you bastard!" but I can't be completely sure due to the intensity of the situation.

Contrary to my entire (obviously ill-informed) wasp-belief system, he flew off. Rather nonchalantly, I might add. I was waving around and trying desperately to make him angry but Neville the peaceful wasp was having none of it. I hoped he wasn't going off to get the rest of the nest (or at least four of his friends), but that never happened. He just disappeared. Finding the least temperamental wasp in the world was disappointing and wearying, so I laid down in the thick grass and went to sleep.

I woke up feeling a lot more relaxed. Neville's departure had led me to reason that I probably should have brought food. It's been my experience that wasps are generally very hungry creatures. I'm not sure if this is because they're malnourished or just greedy by nature, but they are definitely invariably hungry nonetheless. I had nothing to offer. All wasn't lost, though: it was now very hot. The enveloping heat pushed me up to my feet and imbued me with a powerful sense of optimism. Something that I'd been warned about on several occasions was that wasps are adverse to heat - it makes them dozy and angry. Surely the influence of such motiveless anger would boost my chances of getting stung?

Logical nous like this is the kind of stuff that solves

mysteries and completes difficult missions, so I knew it would get me through mine. I felt as though I was learning more about the wasp psyche than anyone in human history - like I was getting inside their fucking minds, man.

That said, I kept walking and wasps kept flying away. All this dozy/angry/senseless-violence bunkum fell apart when I realised that, through no specific acts of avoidance on my part, in 27 years I've never been stung - meaning it must be down to nothing but plain old bad luck for anyone who *has* run into a wasp with an agenda. Then, as I got so far out that I wasn't really sure if I was technically still in the park itself, one of the little buggers actually started to buzz around me rather aggressively. Given the circumstances, I think it was a perfectly natural response to do the following:

A) Wave manically in self defence.

B) Act under the false pretence that it was Neville, and greet him verbally as such.

Once I realised that I wasn't making him quite angry enough, I stood still for a second and waited for him to grant me the same courtesy. After some frenzied buzzing the new Neville sat on a blade of grass, leaving us biding our time a few yards apart like boxers taking our corners. With excited (read: panicked) whispers of "okay, okay," I edged closer to him and, after a shared respectful glance, snatched him from his leafy base and locked him firmly in my clasped hands.

It was at precisely this moment that I realised how stupid an idea getting stung on purpose was and what a ridiculous farce it was I'd gotten myself into – one that I would have to somehow explain to my housemates. I suspect that this kind of behaviour falls into the '*not very well*' bracket of the '*how's he coping with the breakup?*' spectrum.

Neville scurried around my closed palms for an agonising <u>twelve</u> seconds, during which time I did little but count (to twelve) and hope against hope that I wasn't allergic to wasps. He had free reign with both of my hands, after all, and I really didn't want two inflated rubber-glove mitts hampering my otherwise promising Playstation career. Not to mention that fact that if he somehow managed to sting me five times in a row there's every possibility I could die. Eventually, the peace-loving Neville had a crisis of faith and reluctantly did his business. His stinger stabbed at the inside of my left hand just below the thumb, which hurt. It hurt very much.

I swore at poor Neville, who to be fair had had very little say in the whole fiasco. At this point he flew off – probably crying – never to be seen again. It was just as well, because after what I'd just forced him to do it would probably have been exceedingly difficult for me to get along with him. Bottom line is this: he stung me and flew away.

And now it hurts to type.

I suppose the point of all this was that there are a lot of things that people feel they should do before they push up the proverbial daisies, but that list might exclude them from other equally important things. I guess I'm just not sure how you can rate one human experience over another when, at the end of the day, all any of them do is produce slightly different chemical reactions in your brain. A wasp sting, as it turns out, really hurts. Eating your favourite meal doesn't, but either way that reaction still comes from the same place. This may well be the most unnatural way I've ever seen a moral shoehorned into a passage of text, but that chemical reaction - *regardless* of its source - still reminds you that you're alive, which is something I should probably appreciate more now than ever.

I'm sure Neville does, after all.

ii) Poem from Hyde Park

Indigo shoots from grass-green roots,
to nudge the deepest blue -
adorning pests that cling to nests,
policed by morning dew.

Kissed by sun once water's run -
tangled grass and reed
reach upwards now from deepest plough
and spread the season's seed.

Down to hills the greenest frills
unfold and soften ground,
until the years uncurl their ears
to hear the waters sound.

And blue, that mirrors upwards view,
stretches far from sight.
And fish and hare, the banks they share,
sleep sound till new sunlight.

iii) **A man named Monty**

I began my day yesterday by nursing an overwhelming desire to leave the country in an urgent fashion.

The only clue I've got as to why I would want to do this isn't one I'd openly admit to, though I'm sure that if you've been following recent events then you can probably hazard a reasonable guess. I awoke at 07.57, packed a change of clothes, a toothbrush, my passport and my notebook and jumped on the tube for Heathrow.

On the way I was required to do two usually mundane things. These two things are not normally seen as noteworthy activities, but I wouldn't waste time writing about them had the actions involved not got me thinking about fascinating aspects of the human condition. These two things were to get out some cash, and to change trains. Let me explain:

Near our house, on the way to the tube, there's a bank of four cash points that's perpetually busy. No matter how close to that ever-elusive payday it is, the four machines always enjoy a healthy flow of business. I needed food (ergo needed cash, ergo needed to use the machines) so I joined the queue. The beautiful thing about queues is that if you're in one long enough – no matter what it's for – you become privy to nuances of human activity that you won't see in any other situation. People reveal themselves and, if you're self-aware enough, you can learn a lot about yourself.

In society we're bound by a lot of unwritten rules ,most of which stem from British manners, good graces and the desire to be civilised. A queue, for instance, exists to stop us from either fighting to the death to get to something or from actually entering into contact with strangers through unnecessary hustle and bustle. In a lot of ways queuing is what separates us from the animals.

Problems arise when grey areas show themselves and the lack of concrete, tangible rules becomes apparent. I'll get to the point: this is a row of four cash machines and, depending on the type of person that majorities the queues, there will either be one long line or four short lines.

I'll say that again like the epiphany it was to me: one long line, or four short lines.

I find this variation really, really captivating to behold because it unknowingly shows the strength of everyone's resolve like a flashing beacon.

Queuing is a basic activity with a linear rule set that doesn't need explaining here but in this case Joe

Public is thrown a choice and it turns the whole system on its head. A very fundamental shade of someone's personality can be glimpsed by observing the action or choice they take, since it shows whether their desire to use the cash point outweighs their hesitance of confrontation. Simply put: if they queue in the long line they're safe but weak, whereas if they see that the other machines are nearly free and move to wait behind the current user (thus beginning a separate line) they are clearly prepared and willing to face a backlash from the rest of the people waiting.

It's a choice that most people won't even realise they're making, but it's so candid an exposé that I couldn't stop thinking about it. I couldn't stop thinking about this display of civilised beauty. I couldn't stop thinking about it all the way until I got to King's Cross St Pancras on the tube, where I needed to change trains. This is where the second of my seemingly mundane activities (that turned out to be quite thought provoking) took place.

There is a part of Kings Cross - where the herd is funnelled down one half of a wide corridor - that changed a very small part of me inside.

This corridor runs between one corner of the station and the other and, owing to the high volume of traffic moving in both directions, the tube workers have decided to section it into two lanes with dividing blue barriers. Thing is, during the rush hours there's the occasional lull from one direction in which one side is rammed and the other is nearly empty. This was the case yesterday, when I found myself being forced to trudge slowly into the busy lane. I accepted my fate and began ambling along with the rest until a man brushed passed me on my right and dashed through a gap in the barrier – swiftly shimmying into the opposing lane. From then I saw him overtake everyone in our lane as he raced down the empty expanse to our right and disappeared, free as a bird.

It was one of those moments when, despite whatever hyperbole I've spouted about shifting my perspective on life, you actually *do* step out of the situation you're in and think 'God, how bloody stupid is this!' So much so, in fact, that you feel like the most enlightened man on the planet.

I flashed back to the queue at the cash point; to that time I'd conceded (despite knowing better) that the rules of the pool table really *were* winner-stays-on; to the time I was told by my Granddad that I couldn't throw rocks in the pond 'just because'. At the ATM the queue was already laid out into four short lines because someone had clearly made that all-important decision already. At Kings Cross though, it would be me who'd make the move. True; I'd been inspired by the man who'd already seen what a farce this cattle march was, but as I darted through the next gap in the barrier and sailed through the empty air in the adjacent half of the corridor, I certainly didn't feel any worse for copying him. I was walking in the footsteps of a pioneer… of a bloody prophet.

Now I was the enlightened man. …One of few.

As I write this I still wonder what was going through the minds of those other people, sticking to the fate decided for them by the traffic-managing powers-that-be at London Underground. My small act of rebellion couldn't have gone unnoticed. I imagine that the rest of the cattle were thinking either:

"Why does he think he gets to do that when we have to keep to this side?"

Or

"I wish I could do that."

Either way, I hope that my very meagre and initially meaningless act of anarchy blooms in their minds the way that the importance of the cash point queue has in mine, and I hope that the next time they make their way to work they each realise that it's *their* life they're working through. It's entirely worth them actually making those small decisions for themselves. I hope that when they do, they always take the bravest of the options available to them – no matter how insignificant the outcome. If I've managed to plant the seed of that tiny notion to those 50 or so people then walking on the wrong side of a barrier at Kings Cross would be more important to me than this entire book.

Well, almost.

***

About an hour and a half later I arrived at Heathrow, with barely a shadow of the enthusiasm for adventure that'd set me off in the first place. It's amazing how that length of time sat in the same tube carriage will do that to you. Actually 'amazing' probably isn't the right word.

'Inevitable' is better.

Heathrow Terminal 5 is a new and futuristic building with an abundance of glass, carbon fibre and neon blue lights that all band together to try and prove their space-age future-proofness to the scurrying masses, who really don't care either way. I'm sure that in thirty year's time it'll look as dated a view of the future as 70's office block interiors do now, but it's markedly impressive at the time of writing and, quite frankly, that's good enough for me. The back wall of the terminal is a huge glass and metal patchwork that looks like the edge of the Martian city in *Total Recall*, except with a lot more air and a lot less explosions.

The theory behind an 'airport' – that it's a port for people to board and use aircraft – is generally more glamorous than the reality, which involves too much queuing and endless waiting around, but this new terminal almost makes things as impressive and romantic as it perhaps should be. I bet that in 500 years' time people are just as bored and nonplussed by spaceports. But then, people are all spoilt bastards.

At any rate, I was going abroad. Somewhere. Problem was that for the life of me I couldn't see how to go about it. I've been to an airport before, been on a plane and know all about the process of checking in and boarding. This is all well and good when you've got somewhere in mind to go to and a flight booked, but when you're turning up on a whim it's frustratingly difficult to know what to do.

In the movies people are always* storming into airports and demanding the cheapest flight to wherever in order to catch their sweetheart and stop the wedding/save their life/say hello. In the real world, when all you can see is a row of check-in desks for specific destinations and people populating the corresponding queues clutching paperwork, it becomes a bit confusing as to how and where this is done. I thought about waiting around for a film crew to come and shoot one of those scenes (and then following them to the appropriate desk), but decided the chances of that happening on that specific day weren't in my favour.

*'Always' might be a bit of an exaggeration, but I've seen at least two films where it's been done.

After walking up and down for a long time – to the point where I'd passed a suspicion-laden security guard so many times that at one point I could've sworn he'd radioed for back-up – I decided that asking someone at the BA customer desk was probably the best course of action. It probably would have been too, had the queue not been about ninety people deep. Apparently a flight had been delayed by a day and the general public weren't too happy about it.

I needed a rethink.

Fortunately the architects of Terminal 5 had catered for such problems in their design, having the forethought to build a pub *before* the rigmarole of check-in or security. I promptly went in and obtained a pint.

I'll tell you now, dear reader, without further time wasting or illusion, that - due to a heartbreaking lack of conviction on my part - I never made it any further from home than the airport. I'm sorry to have raised your hopes about some kind of exotic adventure, Eastern-European misadventure or anything of the sort, but rest assured that I wouldn't have written about all of this if there wasn't a point. Unsurprisingly, I find the whole fiasco of packing, getting to the airport and ultimately failing to travel anywhere quite embarrassing, so if there wasn't a point to it all then I probably wouldn't have mentioned anything about it *at all*. I certainly didn't to Tim, Jenny or May, who all had enough trouble swallowing the wasp sting story as it was. For the purpose of this book I'd have probably worked the cash point and King's Cross revelations into a fictionalised account of a mundane day out, had they not directly led me to the events that followed.

I wouldn't waste your time or mine with a pointless anecdote. Not on purpose anyway.

Earlier on I wrote about how those small, insignificant actions spawn subconscious choices that can often turn out to be quite important. I believe in the importance of these actions more now than I did two days ago simply because if somebody hadn't sped up the queuing at the cash point by taking that bold step, or if I hadn't raced past the rest of the herd at station, I probably wouldn't have met Monty.

iv) The art of...

That's how authors create suspense. You build up to something genuinely interesting, half-mention said thing and then leave the chapter at that. I'll do it again, look, and you'll be powerless not to read on:

If somebody hadn't sped up the queuing at the cash point by taking that bold step, or if I hadn't raced past the rest of the herd at station, I probably wouldn't have met Monty.

v) ...Suspense

Now *that's* good book writing.

vi) The _____ Death of Alan Bell

As I was waiting for my turn to get served, the chap in front of me was shifting the contents of his pockets around in the hope of finding enough for his drink. His search proved fruitless and so, rapping his knuckles on the bar, he asked what the minimum card spend was just as his drink arrived.

"Five pounds," the barman replied.

"Ah," he said, dejected. he turned to me and gently asked: "Would you like a drink, young man?"

This obviously caught me off guard. Normal people don't offer strangers drinks. I wondered if he'd read that list of things to do before you die and was trying to buy a round for everyone, just to cross it off. Or whether he was mental. I glanced at his leathery hands expecting to see fistfuls of Rohypnol.

"Erm… well if you'd like to put it on your card I can pay you back?"

"No don't be silly, I've offered to pay for it now. I

can't go back on that... It'd make me appear a charlatan." He turned back to the barman, who looked quite bemused. "This chap will have a..."

"[Generic lager] please," I finished.

"A [generic lager] please." The barman poured me a pint and handed it over, extending his other arm to take the man's credit card.

"Many thanks," I said as he stared down at the chip and pin reader. He was about fifty, with a suit on his skin and a wry, warm, knowing smile on his face. His hair was a tousled grey and his voice was slightly raspy in a trustworthy manner - like how you'd want a grandparent to sound if he was also your accountant… and a Michael Palin impersonator on the weekends.

"That's quite alright, but I'm afraid you're now going to have to keep me company until I can check in. Or until you can, whichever comes first."

This kind of thing had never happened to me before. Obviously I'd spoken to strangers - otherwise I wouldn't have any friends - but other than those instances I'd never done it for longer than it takes to tell someone the time or give directions. There was something intriguing about this man, though. I had a feeling bouncing around that it was either going to turn out to be a very pleasant experience or he'd bludgeon me to death with his suitcase, but that it'd be intriguing either way. Having had a disappointing experience at the airport thus far I was glad for some company and the chance for some intrigue.

"Oh… I've arrived very early. …But I'll certainly sit with you until you have to go," I said, thinking of ways not to explain that I was at an airport for no good reason. "Alan. Alan Bell." I shook his weathered hand.

"Pleasure to meet you Alan. Please call me Monty."

We sat down in a quiet, dark corner and, just as I was busy running through every topic of conversation I could readily think of in advance (in case things ran dry), he leaned in toward me and said slowly, without blinking: "You've got a very red aura."

"I'm sorry?" I leant back in my seat. I began to speak again, drawing breath, but he interrupted.

"Your aura. It's bright red. Is something the matter with you? It's nothing serious is it?"

"Erm. Well…"

"I'm sorry that's very rude of me, isn't it?" he asked. "Perhaps I should start off with more traditional pleasantries in future." He let out a distinguished chortle, which seemed to relax the situation despite this talk of auras having dashed all my pre-thought-out conversation-starters. I suddenly felt like I'd known this man for years. Suddenly, he could talk about auras all he liked. He didn't, though. "What is it you do, Alan?" he asked, no doubt trying to rescue my perception of his sanity. …As if the posing of one normal question would immediately erase the memory of an aura-related one.

"I'm actually unemployed at the moment," I replied, choosing my words carefully.

"Oh. Is that by choice or...?"

"I'd say so. I think it's by choice when you decide to just stop going to work, isn't it?"

"Ha! Why yes I suppose it would be." He went to speak again but I had to cut him off as he drew breath.

"I'm sorry but... what does a red aura mean? I mean, I'm familiar with the… the concept of auras, but you said mine's red. What does that mean?"

Needless to say, when a stranger tells you you've got a red aura you're unlikely to let that slip by the wayside.

"Well I'm not an expert... I'm an office manager, truth be told." He laughed and tapped my knee. It wasn't sexual, don't worry. "I do, however, think I have a knack for picking up on people's auras and such nonsense." He laughed again, but in a more self-aware, nervous way. The very fact that he called it nonsense told me that he wished he'd never said anything in the first place. It also meant that he wasn't trying to make money from whatever gift he thought he had, which was good because I wasn't keen to give him any. I'd always thought 'auras' were the subject of hippie hallucinations, so the fact that I was talking about them with a clearly erudite (albeit eccentric), perma-suited businessman - the likes of whom must've had the swinging 60's pass him by without making a sound - was odd. Very odd. "What's so special about May? Is that how long you're going away for? Until May?" he asked.

I must have looked terrified. I stared through him in such a hot state of bewilderment that he looked behind himself as if I'd seen a dinosaur eating its way through the queue for BA customer services. "I'm terribly sorry, Alan. Have I said the wrong thing?" He looked worried. "I sometimes... I sometimes say the wrong thing when I read people you see."

"No, no it's just..." How to explain to a stranger what the three letters M, A, Y mean to me? After a moment's worth of hot flush I decided that, since I was quite confident I wouldn't ever see this man again, I should buy us both a second drink and tell him absolutely everything from the very start.

So I did.

I told him about my health, and that I'd done little but potter about drinking for months now. I told him about not telling anyone anything about my health for seemingly misguided reasons, and about moving into the house. I told him about Tim and Jenny, about Tim's acting, and about meeting and falling in love with May. I told him that I knew how much of an absolute shit I'd been and was continuing to be to the girl – even if only in my own head. And I told him about this ungodly body of writing.

He mentioned that I 'didn't look ill' amongst a few other shocked or acknowledging sounds and phrases that I can't remember, but mostly he just sat and listened intently. Then – in a time considerably shorter than if I'd sat and read this entire book aloud – I was done. My head hurt. I necked four fingers of lager.

"Well... I hate to say it Alan," Monty sighed, "but that's all a bit of a mess, isn't it?"

"You could say that, yes." I was ashamed but cleansed. Actually talking to somebody about it felt stunning.

"But it is a bloody wonderful mess." He smiled, flashing every tooth.

I looked up at him. He continued smiling and chuckled to himself as he took a sip of his drink, doing that shaky head thing people do that asserts a 'my oh my...' kind of story acknowledgement. We sat together in the silence that the act of slowly sipping a drink allows, and I let him digest all the information I'd just vomited over him. I went over it again myself. It felt so unbelievably good to talk about it, yet just as immoral as I'd thought when heard aloud. "You're wrong, by the way," he offered up. I pulled my gaze from the table.

"Wrong about what?" I asked. "I'm fairly sure I heard the doctor right. If I didn't then I've been doing an awful lot of worrying for nothing."

"I mean about May."

He looked at me like a parent. Like a parent about to tell you something you both know they're right about. "I'm not sure if not telling anyone about your condition is noble or stupid, but you've made that decision for yourself. May, on the other hand... Alan, she's so important to you that I saw her. I read her. I saw her like you were sweating out photographs of her."

"I-"

"You cannot," he interrupted loudly, raising a finger in protest, before repeating himself in a hushed tone. "You cannot be angry at yourself for being in love. Nor can you stop it – try as you might. Love is by far the most important thing that human beings have, Alan, and if you can't see that as a dying man then there's really bugger all hope for the rest of us, is there?!"

"Yes, but what if I only *think* I'm in love with her though?"

He grinned. Reaching into his jacket pocket, he grabbed his wallet and swiftly pulled out a dog-eared photograph.

"This is my wife." He handed it to me. She was a middle-aged woman with short blonde hair, holding a puppy in front of a studio screen. She wasn't particularly stunning. But then, looking back on it, perhaps she didn't need to be to me. "We've been married for 34 years," he explained, "and I love her now just as much as I did the first day I saw her. I don't love her any less than that day, but I don't love her any more either."

Just as you'd think, I looked confused. "I certainly know her better than I did that day, of course, but when I met her and heard her speak and saw her walk, something very powerful hit me like... like a wave - clichéd as it all sounds. It's never gone, never changed - that feeling of being... of being hit. Do you follow?"

Sadly I did.

"Sadly, I think I do."

"Then that's not *thinking* you're in love. That's *being* in love, Alan. Full, face-aching, heart-chewing love. I'm sorry if you see it as a bad thing, or something to forcefully remove from your person, but - dying or not - you love this girl, May, in a way that most people would be envious of. Please don't be angry at yourself for it. Enjoy it, if only as... if only as a blind man would enjoy seeing for one last time. 'Tis better to have loved and lost, after all." He raised his glass and, as a natural response, I'd clinked it with mine before I'd properly had a chance to understand what he'd meant. All I knew was that it put me more at ease than I'd been for a long while.

A moment passed, and then he asked me something

surprising. "So what is this masterpiece going to be called then? Your book I mean."

"I- I've no idea."

And I hadn't... In all the time I've been writing this book up until that moment, I'd never actually thought about it as a proper book with any real gusto - mostly since I'm aware of the difficulties in getting work published. Admittedly I've been talking to you, dear reader, as my dear reader (and killing off demographics at an admirable pace), but that's been more a release to keep hold of my sanity than anything else. No offence. It's a bit like when people name their diaries. As such I'd not bothered to even put *thought* towards a proper title, which I suppose says a lot about its quality; starting as you mean to go on should probably involve an actual start.

Either way, if this does get published it would be really wonderful. You know... Wonderful in a posthumous kind of way.

"Well, given the way you seem to be taking life on, may I make a suggestion?

"Please..." I really liked this man, and talking so openly about dying, lying, May *et al* felt so liberating that I wanted to rip all my clothes off and throw a fit in a puddle of my own tears. I'd probably have gotten a tattoo of his face on my heart if he'd asked me to.

"*The Bohemian Death of Alan Bell.*"

"I like it, Monty," I said, beaming.

"Some of my best work," he replied cheerily as he finished his drink.

As he returned it carefully to the table, a voice came over the loudspeaker announcing that the check-in desk for his flight to Copenhagen was just opening. As testament to the fact that it's buried deep in our human (or British) nature to do anything possible to get ahead in a queue, Monty jumped to his feet with scant disregard for his present company and shouldered his bag. "I'm sorry Alan, but I'm afraid I should go. The sooner I get through security the sooner I can enter the Business Class lounge and take liberties with the free wine and assorted nuts."

"Fair enough," I said, standing to my feet. "It's been a real pleasure to meet you Monty. Probably more than I can explain without sounding scary, in fact."

"Trust me Alan, the pleasure has been all mine. Listen; I'm further into my fifties than I'd like to admit but I've never had to say goodbye to anyone in a knowingly final way before. I trust that if I just wish you all the luck in the world and give you my most manly of handshakes that will suffice?"

"That sounds like a plan." I didn't ever want him to leave. I wanted him to move into my house. I wanted him to adopt me.

"Your aura's turned a vibrant green now," he said.

"That's a sign of balance and peace."

"Excellent," I replied, not knowing what better answer there was. I wondered why this man was so receptive as to know – on some levels – all my inner workings and feelings and yet not realise how much I wanted him to just come back to Tufnell Park and sort my life out. He probably could have done so with nothing but a cheerily old-fashioned work ethic and a rolled up newspaper.

Alas, he would be gone from my existence seconds later. The last thing to do was to watch him stride off towards the innards of the cavernous airport.

"I'm sorry, Alan," he said as he grasped my hand. "I'm afraid I never asked you where you were going?" I looked him right in the eye and smiled more sincerely than I've managed in some time.

"I'm going home, Monty."

6. SEPTEMBER

<u>Shopping</u>:

Tea
Milk
sugar
A punnet of berries
More fruit. Bananas this time.
As many vitamin supplements as will look normal at
the till
Beer / cider
Port
Cheeses
Frozen meat; two of every animal
Soup
Rice or some sort
You've run out of gin

<u>Things learned</u>:

- Jenny's second toes are longer than her big toes.

- Apparently, 'Squoze' isn't a word.

- Doing what you want is ok, so long as you can't help
but want whatever it is you want.

<u>Favourite Text</u>:

Jenny: "There's a squirrel in the garden. I gave him some monkey nuts AND HE TOOK THEM! Can I keep him? I'd like to name him Frank. Thank you."

i) **Make up, perfume and a speedy exit**

I'm sure it sounds like a pathetic statement but I've started to really appreciate the feel of things. Railings, the bobbled bit underfoot at the edge of a tube platform, how you reach for a specific part of each different door you habitually open or pull shut, brickwork, wind, books... keyboard keys. The list goes on and on. Is this a symptom, I wonder? I feel like I'm not just 'appreciating' them more, but like I'm more highly receptive to them - as if my sense of touch has been heightened somehow. I like it, either way. I spent a good hour last night lying on my bed slowly running an open palm back and forth across a ripple in my duvet, and it was magical.

Perhaps that *is* a pathetic statement.

They say you only fully appreciate things when you lose them. I've always thought that, while that's probably true, it's a really upsetting fact about the human mind. I'm sure it takes a stronger brain than mine to continue being amazed by something once it's become commonplace.

I'm sure that, despite whatever occasional bickering might take place, Tim and Jenny are still amazed by each other. I can see it in their eyes.

I spent yesterday helping Tim paint the lounge. The previous occupants must have been either blind or lacking that part of the brain that keeps you upright, because the walls had an impressive amount of weird stains all over them. We decided on Thursday evening that a nice light blue would make the place seem a bit homelier and by 9am Friday Tim had been out and bought paint, brushes and rollers. I'll be passing this book on as the main proof that I existed, but I couldn't help but smile at the thought that whenever these three look at the paint adorning these walls, they'll think of me.

...Assuming they don't have to move out of course. Or want to, due to painful memories of that lying bastard they used to know. Perhaps I should leave them another year's worth of rent. Sorry guys, if you're reading this. It seemed like such a good idea at the time - not telling you about all this. I'd rather like to carry on now though, since it'll be pretty much the only thing I've ever done that I've managed to see through to the end.

"How's the book going then? Will you remember

me when you're rich and famous? Can you buy me a dog?" Tim asked as we started, somehow already covered in blue paint despite only opening the tin lid some seconds previously.

"Yeah I should think so," I said.

This was a lie. "When I'm a famous author I'll get you to paint my mansion."

This was an even bigger lie.

Painting the lounge was a monotonous job that took nearly all day (with several liquid pitstops) but I can't be bothered going into any further detail about it because, quite frankly, nothing exciting really happened - save for Tim solving the *Countdown* Conundrum in what seemed to be less than a second. I think he must have blacked out into a trance when it happened, because as soon as he'd solved it he suddenly adopted a look like he'd just been born. Born as a fully grown man. With glasses.

May came home at about six and passed through the lounge. She said that we'd made a good job, pulled her tights up by pinching the back of her right thigh and went to her room. She'd been in there a long time, until finally she re-emerged and mentioned that she was going out. Tim and I sat with beers on the sofa, watching as she left. She left incredibly quickly.

Not only did she leave quickly but she smelt nice. She smelt nice, she'd done something to her hair, she was wearing more make up than usual and was dressed nicely. Now, fair enough; she could have been going anywhere, but the speed at which she left and the palpably sharp feeling of guilt and shame clinging to the fresh paint made it all so apparent what was going on. Tim and I looked at each other.

"Do you know where she's going?" I asked.

"Search me."

Moments later, so soon in fact that she'd passed May in the street, Jenny arrived home and slumped down on the sofa between us.

"Did you see May just then?" Tim asked.

"Hello to you too."

"Sorry, hello, love you, yeah. Where's she off too?"

Jenny stuttered, looked at me protectively and looked back at Tim before slowly and guiltily emptying out the slew of vocal inevitabilities that I'd already figured out. I'd known it as soon as I smelt her. She was wearing date perfume, or at least the volume of normal perfume that women wear on dates. My stomach already knew it too - its line of defence was to turn violently upside down and, in doing so, punch my heart up to my throat like the bell in a fairground strength test. I'm sure it must keep most of its things in my throat, such is the frequency it's up there. If you really need to know; he was some bloke she'd met at work, apparently. A PR man or some such bullshit. His name was Dom. Dominic.

"I'm sorry Alan. She asked me not to tell you," said Jenny. "She said she felt really bad about it."

Clearly she didn't feel that fucking bad about it. I'd feel bad about strangling a baby seal to death with a belt made from baby fingers, so I don't do it. Not only do I not do it, but I don't permeate the air around a roomful of vegetarians and new mothers with '*Alan's Strangling Perfume*' beforehand. By far the worst part about all of this, of course, was that this knee-jerk reaction to coddle me meant that Tim and Jenny knew it was May who had ended our relationship. It also meant that they think I'm still hurting about it. Which - credit where credit's due - I am.

I'd tried to keep quiet about how much the whole thing had knocked me, but their reaction suggested I might as well have a poster saying 'May, please take me back' on my bedroom door. Maybe they're both endowed with aura and mind-reading abilities akin to Monty's.

No, actually forget all that. By *far* the worst thing was that May was off on a date with a man that wasn't me - a man whom she obviously had amorous intentions towards. Jesus, it hurt.

"She can't feel that bad about it," I said, sulkily. It

was all I could say, really. I was trying to sound like a man who couldn't care less, and failing miserably. Jenny motioned for Tim to leave the two of us alone for a talk.

The truthfully sad thing about friends is that, no matter how much you think you can trust someone, people will always find a way to justify telling their secrets to other friends. Secrets act as a primal, fundamental currency - as some kind of magical key to popularity. Thus, I knew as soon as Tim left that the bare bones of anything I said to Jenny would - even with empathetic filtering - eventually get back to him and back to May. The *really* truthfully sad thing is, though, that I didn't care. At that point I just wanted to talk to someone. I wanted to talk to Monty. I wanted to cry on his dandruff-dusted, pinstriped shoulder but I couldn't, so Jenny would have to do. At least, I thought as she turned the TV off, at least she'd have some understanding of the lawless inner-workings of the female mind. More specifically May's.

The first thing I asked seems like a really pointless question in hindsight, but I suppose it was just one of those instances where your masochistic side likes to punish you for no apparent reason.

"Have you met him?" I asked. My voice ramped up in pitch as it tailed off.

"No," she replied. "Only seen a photo." The lights in the lounge were dim and the atmosphere suddenly very sombre, like there'd been a death. I pictured May and Jenny in their pyjamas; a teenage slumber party stereotype unfolding all around them. May shows Jenny a photo of Dom and words like "dreamy" and "perfect" are bandied about. I didn't know this man's surname but in this nightmarish fantasy May was scrawling it all over her pencil case, prefixed with 'Mrs' - probably next to the scribbled-out mark that had once read 'Bell'.

I came so close to asking what he looked like (in a critical sense), but realised that that really would give the game away in terms of my still giving two shits. A cool air must be maintained, I told myself. Since Jenny had engineered this talk to make sure I wasn't so manically depressed by the situation that I'd go and kill myself, I needed to try and show her that I was ok and mentally sound. Of course, the skilful lovesick dog knows there's a way of doing that while pumping for information at the same time. I was more inclined to go and kill this Dom character than myself, anyway.

"How long's this been going on then?" I asked, more bitterly than I'd have liked. As the words left my mouth the thought that worries me to this moment formed in my head; what if this wasn't their first date? What if they'd met whilst May and I were still a couple? What if she'd realised *then* – whilst I was in cloud-cuckoo land – that he was better, more appealing, more confident, strapping and 'cool' than I was?

What if he had been the reason I'd lost May?

Reading my thoughts, Jenny answered me with words to the effect that I shouldn't worry - that this had all happened after May and I had broken up. I can't remember the exact wording, since that masochistic side was busy clouding me with dread and self-doubt. Jenny couldn't be sure. It'd only been a month since we'd broken up, after all. If this Dominic was anything like me he would have taken at least a month to conspicuously flirt before vocalising the subject of a date. With a text message.

But then, thinking about it, that might be why she's with him: because he's not like me. I bet he swept her off her plimsolled feet.

It might have been because I was too obviously disregarding what she was saying from then on, but Jenny soon stopped our talk and stood up to go and get changed out of work clothes. She mentioned that the lounge looked fantastic and left.

So there I was: a man with a light-blue living room, wracked with self-pity and self-doubt - a man whose ex-girlfriend had cheated on him with a man named Dominic. Probably. Well, maybe. The point is: as short a life expectancy as I now have, it really doesn't need to be shortened with this level of stress.

I knew I'd better have an early night. Jenny cooked me a sympathy dinner, as you would for a child who'd broken his favourite toy, and as soon as it was over I prepared to go to my room and not leave until the next day. I couldn't write anything. Not anything good at any rate. I played sad music low enough for Tim and Jenny not to hear, and waited for May to come home.

I wanted to actually *see* her come home less than I wanted to see anything in the entire world. She'd be happy having had a nice night out, which would hurt, but the worst part was that she might bring him back with her. Up until that point I'd been sure May wasn't the type of girl to bring a man home after the first date, but last night had changed my perceptions of the girl. Not to mention the fact that I couldn't be sure if this *was* their first date at all. It wouldn't have surprised me last night if she'd rolled through the door as a key part of some spherical group orgy. And yet: I waited and listened. Like a self-harming teen waiting for a delivery of knives.

It was last night that I first realised the dual sides of something usually considered rather nice. Most things in life can be taken as good or bad depending on the circumstances, but I'd never experienced it so much as with the sound of a woman giggling. More specifically; May giggling.

When we'd met, the girl's laugh had been one her most endearing qualities. Infectious laughs are two-a-penny but this one was just... special – in a way that I can't fully explain because you haven't met May and because you're not me. Everyone has aspects of the people they love that they find magical, often things that the others around them wouldn't particularly notice. It's why everyone's not all just madly in love with the same person. In my appreciation of May, one of those addictive, exquisite characteristics is her laugh.

If you understand that on at least some level, dear reader, then you might perhaps understand how hard it was for me last night to hear May's otherwise miraculous giggle, knowing that another man had caused it.

Thankfully she'd not brought him home. She sat downstairs, separated from me by one thin floor and one thin wall, and debriefed Jenny on her date. I didn't want to hear, almost as much as I did, but it didn't matter because all I could really make out were the giggles - consciously hushed, piercing giggles that cut right through the walls and right through me.

It was a dark time and I'm not proud, but for 20 minutes I stood exactly still in the same spot by my door and toyed – seriously – with the notion of going downstairs and telling them both that I was dying. I'm sorry to you, dear reader, that I almost did. I'm sorry to myself for being such a selfish bastard as to think that it would help me somehow. I guess the line of thought was that it would spin all their (read: May's) attention back onto me, and not this Dominic - who'd done nothing wrong himself but fall for the woman whom I do nothing but obsess over. Either way, I'm sorry.

I didn't, of course, and I'm glad I didn't. I'm glad mostly because I've no idea what it would have done for the situation at hand that would have been any better than remaining silent. May being distraught would probably only make her lean on this Dominic for support. Either way, I decided to crawl into bed and try and fight for some sleep.

***

This evening, Jenny, May and I all sat in the lounge together and watched TV. Have you ever noticed that the television often has a cruel way of focusing the subject of its programming on the exact thing that it shouldn't? It's not important to write exactly what we watched, but more than a few times the subject matter caused either May or myself to glance tentatively at the other, and Jenny to shift awkwardly. We talked, all three of us, but not a single thing was mentioned about May's date all evening. Not a single thing.

I'm back in my room as I write this. Next to me on

my bed is a photograph of a blonde, middle-aged woman holding a puppy. I don't know if Monty meant to leave me with the picture of his wife or not, but after he'd left I realised that it was still sat on the table, surrounded by empty glasses. All in all I'm rather pleased I've got it. I'm pleased for two reasons. The first is that at least I now know that my encounter with Monty actually happened. I've never thought that the goings on in my head - whilst morally questionable - place me on the dangerous or deluded ends of the insane spectrum, but since my encounter with him was so surreal it's nice to have a piece of tangible evidence to prove that it did, in fact, happen.

The second and main reason why I'm pleased that I have a picture of a stranger's wife is that it reminds me of what Monty said about May. In truth, Monty could have been the most socially retarded person on the planet, but because he's the only person I've *really* spoken to honestly in months, I took every word he said in return as the gospel truth. I've spent more than my fair share of time mentally festering in the wake of a prematurely-ended relationship, and entirely too much time hating myself for still wanting the person I couldn't have. What's different now is that I know it wasn't lust that had me tangled up around May, it was full-on love. Real love.

Monty told me that there's no way to stop loving someone whom you still love, which - now that I think about it - sounds rather obvious. I still love May even though I shouldn't at all, but that magical man at the airport convinced me - with one photograph - that that wasn't my fault. He'd absolved me. Not only that, but I'm also under no compulsion to *try* to stop loving her, which suits me well.

The woman in the photograph isn't particularly stunning, but she belongs to Monty and that's entirely good enough for him. He loves her to the ends of the Earth and he was vocal about how lucky he was to have her. Finding someone you love and ending up with them relies on such a stupidly large set of improbabilities all clicking into place for you that lots of people never manage either. With that in mind, it's possible – nay, probable - that I'm one of the many people who're just not meant to end up with their true love. I'm set to die in a few month's time so perhaps I should just think myself lucky that I at least met mine at all. I can convince myself more easily to love May silently than I can to forcibly stop loving her.

There's every chance that, due to the severe emotional impact of the last 24 hours, I'm poking around for a moral in a set of moral-less events, but to be quite frank I don't care. I don't care because shaping my own moral at this most painful time is the only thing that makes it all hurt a little bit less. I wrote something at the start of this chapter about people appreciating things more when they've gone but, sweet Jesus, did I appreciate her in the first place.

ii) Get out while you still can

I'm having a hard time grasping how a man as enlightened as Monty could get along with the idea of working full-time in a job that required him to wear a suit and carry a briefcase. Human beings are not physically designed to spend the majority of their lives in offices hunched over computers. The medical problems that arise over time from working a 9-5 can be quite severe, for a start. These are as follows:

>Back trauma and pain

>Bad skin from air-conditioning

>Obesity and heart problems from salty shop-bought sandwiches and lack of movement

>Eventually becoming everything you never wanted be.

Of course, there are tonnes of jobs that don't involve ever going near an office but my point is that, invariably, the pursuit of money (to live) leads most people to spend 8+ hours a day, for 5+ days a week doing something that, given the choice, they'd sooner not.

If I've taken nothing else away from my time on Earth it's the rather tragic notion that in civilised society we're under someone else's control from birth right up until we're old enough retire. With retirement age and the average death age becoming closer and closer friends these days, that's a scary thought. Nobody's born thinking they want to have a career, after all, and when six year-olds say they want to be a dentist, a lawyer or whatever it's due mostly to society's harmful and institutionalising influence. If you take it back to basics, what every single person on the planet *really* wants to do is absolutely sod all.

Once born, we're begrudgingly scragged through all manner of schooling until it's time the world decides you're prepared enough to live by your own means without needing your hand held. However much of an anti-establishmental rebel you consider yourself, living by your own means is incredibly hard to do without some form of currency to keep you under roofs and devouring foods.

In theory it's a system that works beneficially for humanity at large, but there *is* a problem with it, stemming from the very centre of the human condition: those damned emotions we're all so lucky to be able to feel. One such emotion is pleasure; enjoyment.

Enjoyment at being able to do whatever one chooses to do is not an emotion that needs to be enhanced by drastically limiting it in the first place.

As emotions go, enjoyment's plenty good enough as it is.

This is why I cannot and will never understand people who stay in the office after hours or who use their Blackberry whilst at home. I suppose higher salaries come with greater responsibilities but surely the best aim in life is to either:

A) 'Make it' in traditional sense and somehow earn lots of money doing something you don't really deem as work.

Or

B) Find a job that pays well enough to live, has an absolutely minuscule level of stress and can be completely and fully left at the office come five o'clock.

Keeping arms and legs together for 'the man' is so horribly constraining for beings with such free will and intelligence that it almost seems like somebody's idea of an ironic joke. In essence, once full-time work has started you're only allowed to be yourself for two days out of every week - and that's just mental. By all rights I think it's a horrific injustice that we're gifted the ability to appreciate messing around and are then forced to spend our entire lives fighting to do so.

I'm beginning to think this chapter is reading like something of an argumentative essay. If this is the case then I'm truly sorry, but I just have so many (mostly angered) thoughts on the subject of occupational work that its hard for me to concentrate on getting them all out *and* making it seem entertaining at the same time. Let alone objective.

Suffice to say there's more to come, so if up 'til now has bored you its probably best if you skip ahead to the next chapter, by which time something very exciting will no doubt have taken place. My bet would be: alien invasion.

***

If you're still here then I can only assume you're as baffled by the whole prospect of being made to sacrifice most of your life for a job as I am. It's a horrible realisation that earning money has become such an intransigent part of our basic survival. It's comparable now to an animal's need to eat. And all we are, after all, is another species of animal. It's completely nuts.

I know I might seem very hypocritical reeling all this off whilst sat on my opulent pile of bank-given cash (thanks Nancy), but I reckon the amount of days I have left to live is roughly equivalent to all those oh-so precious weekends I'll miss out on, so I think we're about even.

It's not as if I haven't paid my dues, anyway; when I was sixteen I got a summer job in a tin can factory. My job was to stand at the side of a huge conveyer belt as it groaned thunderously about its business. If a can had fallen over, it wouldn't get picked up and moved onto the next stage of the intricate can producing-process; my job was to pick the bastards up. For 12 hours at a time.

This - as you can probably imagine - was not glamorous work, but by far the worst part about it was that everybody else who worked there hated me. They hated me not because I was arrogant, or lazy or useless (although in hindsight I probably was); they hated me because they knew that, in a matter of weeks, I would be leaving to go back to the cushty, padded ease of school. Some of the men in that factory had worked five, 12-hour shifts a week for the last 40 years with no end in sight, and there I was with my entire future still ahead of me.

At the time I wondered why they were there, but since age and the world at large have weathered the ever-depressing facts o' life upon me I've come to understand that those poor sods had no choice. They were there because, just like everyone else that has the dubious honour of being born, they needed money to perpetuate that annoying habit of living. They're probably still there, carving out an existence instead of a living.

In an ideal world I'd march back there and tell everyone of them that what they're doing is no way to spend your time on Earth. I'd try to make them realise that living solely to produce baked bean tins is a waste of their precious human lives. I'd order every one of them to throw their overalls in the air and spend the rest of their days lying on the grass in sunny meadows.

I'm idealistic to a fault, though. Society needs can factory workers so that we can all eat food from cans. I know that. Eating tinned food is, after all, something I've gotten rather used to. It's just that us humans have these magical brains capable of producing wonderful art in all its wonderful forms, so surely we should dedicate our lives to doing just that? Surely it must be every man and woman's main aim to create something whilst we're here? Something that lasts as testament to the fact that out of all the billions of people that touch down on Earth, *you* mattered; testament to the fact that there's something that sets you apart? It's incredibly closed minded, I know, but I don't think I'll ever get my head around the kind of people who don't share that view. I know at least one man who doesn't, but that's something for later on.

I think all I'm trying to say is that life is very, very short.

My life will obviously be a fair bit shorter than I'd have liked it to have been, but that doesn't change the fact that if the average person lives for 75 years, they only get to live through 27,375 days. Roughly 13,000 of those will be spent in an office, which means a little over 14,000 odd days are all we have to be ourselves. And you'll be asleep for half that time. These numbers are based on working from the age of 20 to 70 and mean that nearly half of your entire, piffling life will be effectively wasted mastering inane middle-management phrases like 'Going forward'.

In essence, seeing as the human experience is so very short, I'd urge you to please create something whilst you're here. If you're reading this it means I'm not a hypocrite. It means that I've written a book that has somehow got into the hands of others. If writing's not your thing try filmmaking, photography, music or art. If they're beyond your grasp then make a child and look after it. I urge you to do one of these things, dear reader, because when you die that baked bean tin you helped make will have long been recycled and that company mission statement you spent weeks on will have been recycled into toilet roll. When you die, as now I have, you'll do so wanting your life to have meant something to other people. To prove that you connected with the world around you; to prove that you were even ever here.

I suggest you do what you can to make that happen.

This morning, Jenny asked me what I planned to do once I've written this book and ran out of my 'dead Uncle's' money. She asked what kind of job I'd go back to.

"Will you just try and get a similar thing to what you were doing before?" she asked.

I thought for a moment, before shaking my head solemnly and replying:

"I'd rather be dead."

7. OCTOBER

Shopping:

Tea, Milk, sugar
Fruit
Some kind of bland looking, healthy cereal
As many vitamin supplements as will look normal at
the till
Beer / cider
Cheeses
Sausages
Soup
New bin for bedroom
You've nearly run out of gin

Things learned:

- Identical twins scare me more than a lot of other
things, Especially when they dress the same.
Especially-especially when they're old enough to
choose what they want to wear for themselves.

- Tim and Jenny have very quiet sex most of the time
but, for some unknown reason, Wednesdays are
louder than the rest. I'll let you know when I find out
why.

Favourite Text:

Ross: "Just seen some old country gent in my local playing chess with himself and shouting obscenities at the staff. Bit more hair and some tighter skin and he could have been you."

i) Applying film logic to real life

Yet again I am a mess of a human man. I know I said that I'd do more to live an exciting life with the time I have left but… bloody hell. There's no way I'm doing anything of any worth today apart from sweating out alcohol and practicing self-loathing.

I suppose that drinking is how I'm staking my claim at leading the bohemian life Monty mentioned. Or, moreover, the bohemian death. My hair, which I've never had longer than what could be described as 'scruffy', has now comfortably entered 'shaggy' territory, which on the 'hair styles beginning with S' scale is etching ever closer to 'street urchin'. I've also lost a bit of weight, meaning that (as long as it shoots and raps within the next seven months) I'm a prime candidate for acting the role of the latter in a remake of *Withnail & I*.

I'm not sure what all this alcohol - and the occasional intake of recreational drugs - must be doing to my innards now that I'm winding down to a forced stop. Nothing good, surely. Despite several phone calls, I've not been to see my doctor in a couple of months now. I can hardly imagine he'd be recommending the lifestyle I'm living. The hangovers are worse than they've ever been, at any rate - but then that might just be age.

I've been thinking over my plan of action for when it comes time to actually do the dying I've been hyping up so much. I think that if I'm still around at the start of April I'll stick this book on a USB stick, place said stick on my bed with some kind of letter (which is <u>not</u>, I imagine, going to be fun to write) and bugger off to a hospice. Until then I'm more than happy to bum about here and carry on writing until something interesting enough happens to turn this into an actual book. So far all I've got is the end of a rather sticky relationship and an obsessive, unrequited love. Hardly *War & Peace*.

As I write this I'm sat in the garden enjoying the unseasonable sun; it's one of the warmest days we've had all year. I've not been the good little house journalist I should have been but I'll tell you now that Tim's play – the 'weird' one 'about the passage of time' – fell through. He's out here now with me trying to learn a monologue for an audition he has tomorrow. I'll tell him you wish him luck. Well, I won't, but at least *we* know that our spirits are with him.

Truth be told I'm gutted that I won't get to see his weird play. Its more-than-intriguing premise, coupled with the promise made to me by Tim that audience members sat in the right spot would get to see 'at least three boobs', was surely enough of a crowd puller to warrant some time at the Old Vic? Or the Globe?

C'est la vie.

You probably don't need to know this, but there's a weird thing in the corner of our garden that nobody can quite figure out. It looks like a mashed up pile of wet tissue papers, formed crudely into what would pass convincingly for a spot on the face of a giant snowman, only it's made of plastic. If it's the melted remains of something, none of us boast the right forensic qualifications to accurately guess either what it was originally or how old it is. Since the previous tenants seem to have been hell-bent on chucking things about and making mess wherever they could, one can only presume that it's something to do with them. The most curious thing is that it seems to be set really deep into the ground. When you try and lift it up it doesn't budge, as if it's only the very top of an extremely long object – like the way an iceberg only shows a tenth of its mass. My telling you this is really of no importance whatsoever of course, but since I'm sat looking at it right now over the top of my laptop screen I felt compelled to describe it. I hope that somebody someday finds out what it is, what it's for and ultimately if it's meant to be used for good or for evil.

I suppose that really, what with the last few chapters being about nothing in particular and time passing quickly like it usually does, I've been trying to avoid writing any more about the thing that's been preoccupying my tired little brain for the last few weeks: May.

I honestly can't say exactly what's been happening with her and this 'Dom' character, since I haven't asked and she hasn't told. Nor has she mentioned anything about him when we've all been together in the house, for that matter. What I do know is that every now and again she doesn't come home from work until very late, or comes home and then swiftly goes back out smelling of date. Thankfully, I've still not heard his voice seeping through the emaciated walls.

It's her birthday in a week and so much is the messed-upedness of the situation from my perspective that I feel inclined just to tell her I'll be busy. Well... I'd be inclined to do so if I ever actually had anything to do. As it is, it might seem a bit dubious that the only thing thus far this quarter that I've really had to do lands precisely on May's 27th birthday. In the evening.

More to the point, I've got no idea what to get her. I'm puzzled in most *normal* situations as to what the appropriate amount of money is to spend on someone's birthday - let alone a recent ex. It seems to hinge on the person's role in your life.

As a man, the one demographic that's always hard to buy for is female friends. Men just buy other men beers, spirits or novelty receptacles for said beers and spirits. With women who aren't family there's always a tightrope-thin line between spending too much and too little. For those with poor memories; May and I were together for my birthday. She bought me a Moleskin notebook and a pen that I can only assume cost more than she should have spent. Now that we're apart and the friendship is being stretched thin by awkwardness and a lack of communication, I've got no idea what I'm supposed to buy.

"What are you getting May for her birthday?" I just asked Tim. He looked worriedly up from his script.

"Shit, when's that? It's not soon is it?"

"Next week. Saturday. We're going out bowling."

"Oh yeah. Ace." A pause. "No idea, you?"

"No idea."

"Shall we go in together on something?"

"Surely Jenny will get her something and put your name on the card?" I asked.

"No, she said she's got a really good idea for a present and doesn't want me claiming any of the thanks," he said.

"Fair enough."

"What do you think she'd want?"

I know exactly what May'd want. She'd want one of the myriad things she mentioned in passing to me that she liked whilst we were out and about and together. She'd like that green-jewelled necklace, that cast-iron model VW Bug. She'd love that album that she'd never heard of but liked it because it had a funny name.

That's what people in films do, isn't it? He buys the woman he loves that seemingly random present and she falls in love with him because she'd said she liked it several months back. It proves that the hero of the piece loves her because he listens to her intently. Unfortunately, I don't think film logic can be successfully applied to real-life. If you could, it'd mean that winning a woman's heart could be done by simply completing one of the following tasks:

- Spend some degree of money on her

- Wear a leather jacket

- Take part in (and preferably win) a physical fight

- Listen to one thing she said and repeat it back at the right moment

- Be better (in any visible way) than the overtly evil man she's currently with

'Woman' in the real world is a much more complex being. Such is the problem.

I won't buy her something she previously mentioned she liked. I don't want her thinking it's an attempt to win her back.

In all honestly, in the time I've had to think about it I've only become more and more sure of my acceptant reasoning from the night after her first date with Dominic: I'm not supposed to have May. It doesn't fit and it wouldn't work; finding out you're dying and then beginning a relationship is not appropriate conflict resolution. I can't stop loving the girl but that's not my fault and it's certainly not hers, so I'll just keep quiet about it and act like everything's getting better.

I told Tim that I didn't really know what she'd like and that the two of us should sort something out in the week. Going in on a present with Tim is the best way to avoid that moment when she opens a present that's *just* from me, and therefore personal. It'll lessen the blow of the part when she reluctantly has to kiss me on the cheek to say 'thank you'.

It'll also mean that she'll have spent a lot more money and thought on my birthday present than I will have for hers, which goes some way toward making us even for her breaking my heart.

I'm still quietly observing Tim. He's mouthing the words to his script as he reads, and sporadically covering up the words with his palm like a child learning to spell. Jenny's sat with me now. She came out having made some kind of summery cocktail for the three of us. There's talk of an October evening barbecue.

When you live in a house of four people and there are only three of you present it's always glaringly obvious that that fourth person isn't there. It's not like you're at a stadium and somebody goes to the toilet, it's more like being at a stadium and one whole side of the building disappears into thin air. My point? It's very hard for me to focus on anything other than the fact that May's not here - and she's not at work. That fact circles uncomfortably my mind like a whirlpool of clotted blood.

Jenny keeps leaning over and trying to read what I'm writing. If she or any of them ever looked at this mass body of deception the proverbial jig would be up - and yet here I am, sat next to her whilst I write about everything they don't get to hear. It's really quite nerve-racking. If even she scanned and managed to see her name, that would open a huge can of annoyingly inquisitive worms.

I'm acutely aware of the lack of real characterisation Tim and Jenny have in this book, although I suppose in many ways they're the heroes of the piece. My not writing anything massively exciting or descriptive about the two of them must not be misconstrued for them being boring people; they're perfect. I don't write much about them because they really don't do anything wrong, nor do they ever judge or hinder my life as it is now. They are rocks: proper, true friends of the highest order that I'd find it very hard to fault. I can't write about them too much anyway because I'm not naturally a very objective writer. If I try to scrawl on about them for too long I'll end up attempting to find some kind of angle from which to attack them, and they truly don't deserve that.

Tim continues to study his script and Jenny reads a gossip magazine. All three of us sit in the sun and drink a bright pink cocktail. May's on a date - and I love her - but for now, I suppose, it's ok.

ii) Neither of us smoke

Last night was a big night in terms of my own downward spiral towards mental self-destruction. Nights out have a habit of winding up in this book either because they've played host to something fantastic or something horrible. I think I'd drill last night to wherever on that bipolar scale is closest to 'fucked up'. I also think that the older I get the harder it is to have a big night out with friends without something gossip-worthy happening. I'm sure it's the same for you.

It was May's birthday last night and 11 of us went out to a well-respected underground bowling venue* in central London, to celebrate her turning 27. Judging by past successes this would be a recipe for disaster on its own, even without factoring in May's decision to bring this Dominic chap to the party.

Yes, dear reader, I've met him. I've met him, I've conversed with him and I've seen him (although not necessarily in that order). I probably don't need to carry on with explaining why the night was so god-

239

awful, and why this is suddenly becoming The Incredibly Awkward Death of Alan Bell.

*Note: *I'm leaving the correct names of places and organisations in this book. If you're reading them as something stupid like "My favourite" or "A well-respected" whatever, then it's because an editor has been through and changed what I've written for some bollocksey reason to do with libel. Your pathetic libel laws mean nothing to me, silly mortal being, for I am now dead. Either way, if it's been changed I blame Tim and shall haunt him appropriately. I at least hope they left in the bit about IKEA.*

It suddenly strikes me that I've never properly examined the relationship that you and I might have, dear reader. As the narratee, theory suggests that you should listen to your narrator and be inclined to agree with what he says. In that sense I doubt that you have any qualms regarding the legitimacy of my story. What might be the case, however (though I hope it's not), is that you may not actually like me. True: I'm a lying coward, an obsessive and a poor writer - but I do genuinely hope that on some level you can see that I'm trying to be a good man. If you don't like me but are still reading then I suppose that's your prerogative, so long as you're not reading out of morbid curiosity – like how someone would read *Mein Kampf.*

At the very least I hope you understand my love for May. That's fairly important.

As I continue this chapter and detail last night's events, I can only pray that you aren't thinking how good it is that she's with another man while I'm alone. I need you on my side or there's no point in me writing this at all. If I'm not the protagonist here, I'm nothing.

At any rate, the party had been planned by May and Jenny themselves, since May isn't a fan of being on the receiving end of surprises. This seems rich coming from someone so keen on dishing the bloody things out, but hey-ho...

We were to meet her at the venue at nine in the evening, as she had plans up until that point with her precious Dominic. Needless to say, I was in bits all day. I felt sick and foolish; the last thing I need to be doing in my condition is exposing myself to this kind of angst. It was obvious that any decent solution to the problem would involve large quantities of alcohol, so I coaxed Tim into halving a crate of beer with me and subsequently tricked him into drinking almost as much by playing computer games with him for most of the evening. I defy anyone with a half-crate of beer near them whilst playing computer games with a friend *not* to drink it all. It's impossible.

At about eight o'clock, following a brisk shower, I sauntered into my room feeling a few pints worse/ better off (depending on how you look at it), whereupon I played some 'going out' music quite loudly and decided how to make myself appear more acceptable to the general public. No mean feat.

As it turns out, psyching yourself up for a night out is quite hard when you know that among your number there'll be the man who – through no fault on his part – is the embodiment of everything you hate about the world. Even harder when the girl you love is hanging off his arm. I managed to put this thought to one side long enough to motor my arms and legs into the appropriate motions for dressing and ended up in a smart shirt and trousers. This'll show her, I thought, striking poses in front of the mirror.

At one point I think I put sunglasses on.

I remember thinking how good it was to see everyone together in one room; it doesn't happen as often as it should any more and that's a real shame because we're a close group of good friends. It must be a universal experience that the further you get away from the times when going out with friends is your chief concern (school/Uni etc.), the difference between your real friends and your acquaintances becomes more and more apparent. Friendship's a progressive dance, though - people drop off and join in. Generally speaking, you'll stay in contact with the ones you want to stay in contact with.

Drinking ensued but we weren't allowed to bowl until the birthday girl arrived. At half-past nine people were beginning to get antsy and eager to start but Jenny couldn't get through to May. Ross got so bored of waiting that he opened up our three lanes and began writing 'comedy' names for everyone. The ritualistic crashing of pins wasn't luring me, though. As far as I was concerned, May and this 'Dominic' could both get wrapped up in each other's company elsewhere. If they were so in love that they completely forgot about the party, at least that would be better than having to watch them canoodle like we once did.

Eventually, of course, they turned up. Having to meet Dominic wasn't fun and I don't remember it all elegantly enough to describe it with any real objectivity or accuracy. The best I can do is try to depict it with an exact transcript of what I remember my brain saying to me, which would go something like this:

"Shit; they're here. She looks stunning. They're holding hands. She looked at me. They've stopped holding hands. Everyone's talking to her. They're all meeting Dominic. Too much noise. I say happy birthday. I shake his hand. He's a good-looking man. She looks at me. Tim rescues me. It all really, really hurts."

When I turned round to face the lanes Ross had finished making up stupid names for everyone. I'm not sure what benefit listing all the names would garner (in terms of this books place in respectable literature), so I won't. I *will* tell you that Ross thought he was very clever in putting me down on the system as "Bell-end" and that one of the names wasn't so much a witty handle as a particularly frowned-upon swearword. The staff made him change it.

It's now that we get to the reason why last night rests so near the 'fucked-up' mark on the fantastic-horrible scale of nights out. Maybe Ross thought he was doing us a favour by putting us together – in the same way that you'd make an arachnophobia sufferer share a flat with a tarantula – or maybe he's just the completely tactless, socially unaware buffoon we've often called him; I don't know. Either way, when I turned around I saw three lanes' worth of names. The 11 of us had been divided so that there were four in one lane, four into another, and three into the last.

No prizes for guessing which three of our number were in that last lane.

As you can probably imagine, this was pretty much the worst thing that could have happened save for me suddenly developing Tourettes Syndrome and barking out "I've got about six months left to live." I still don't think I'm fully over the shock of that moment of realisation, just as I doubt May or Dominic are.

The three of us shuffled into our lane with disappointed, squeamish expressions and cheeks full of hot blood, trying desperately to ignore the fact that a few people were quietly having a go at Ross in the next lane for being quite so horrifically stupid.

I'd known I'd have to meet Dominic eventually, but I'd consoled myself with the fact that once the initial meet and greet was done I could stay away and get inadvisably drunk all night with the boys. Likewise, I can only presume that May had consoled herself from the thought of introducing me with the promise of having a nice birthday night, successfully easing her new man into the social group. Now it was all ruined. I couldn't work out who I wanted to murder more; Dominic or Ross. Not only that, but I couldn't help but feel like May was blaming me for what had happened. Her eyes looked fierce.

"So Alan," Dominic started, trying to make conversation. "What is it you do? May says you're a novelist?"

We had two games paid for. Talking wasn't going to speed things along and I, for one, was quite happy to race through in silence so I could go and do what I'd originally intended: make fun of Tim's ridiculous bowling stance while drinking.

"I don't really do anything," I replied. "I was left some money in inheritance so I decided to quit work for a year and write a book."

Apparently I really like lying to people; the more the better.

"How cool." May didn't look happy. I wanted to tell him that what I really do is spend the final days of my life writing about how in love I was with his girlfriend. And that this was the without a doubt the worst moment of my entire life.

"How about yourself?"

"I'm in PR."

"Oh right?" I already knew that. And I didn't care the first time I'd heard.

"I only handle boring companies that make studio lights and things though."

Well aren't you Mr Fan-fucking-tastic? Congratulations, May; you've found the man of your dreams. I took a sip of beer and it all tasted like vomit.

In fairness, he was a fairly attractive bloke. About the same height as me, as I recall, and with black, clean-cut hair. He said he played cricket on Sundays; he seemed nice... but that was the problem. He was nice in such a bland way. I couldn't see any appeal there that couldn't be found in me. In movies, the girl's 'second act' boyfriend is always a seemingly cool but eventually evil and chauvinistic antagonist. Dominic was neither of these things, which made everything so much more confusing. Up until I'd met him I'd thought I had it figured out: he'd be achingly attractive and suave; I'd be the man who's always been nice and dependable. I was the man who women realise they should be with at around 30, once they've stopped being frivolous and tire of being treated badly by achingly attractive, dangerous and suave men. Admittedly, I wasn't going to be around by the time May was 30, but at least that role was simple and made some degree of sense. This Dominic was meant to be inwardly immoral – a fact that wouldn't arise until they'd been together a short while but would ultimately end their relationship. He'd lay a hand on her or kick a kitten - something that would pin him as evil. Except he wasn't. He was just a bloke.

Dominic was that dependable, nice, caring man too; for all intents and purposes he was me but with a sharper haircut and a longer life-expectancy.

I just couldn't fathom it; this didn't fit in with the plan at all. He was just so bloody... normal.

The previous exchange of dialogue between Dominic and myself is honestly all I can be bothered to divulge and I don't really even know why I divulged that ...it was pretty boring. Aside from the occasional forced comment on somebody's bowling (a good tension breaker), we remained fairly silent throughout the remainder of our games. I ended up sitting back-to-back with Tim's lane anyway, so I managed to talk to him and the rest of his group – all of whom seemed to be having a better time than us. In case you're wondering: Dominic won the bowling. It made me wonder whether that was what attracted May to him: his bowling prowess. It was the only noteworthy thing about him, after all.

Everybody soon finished making a mess of the claustrophobic bowling lanes and moved towards the main bar/dance area to continue consuming more alcohol than late-twenty-somethings probably should. A DJ was playing all the songs we wanted to hear. Music thumped out of two huge, towering speakers and everyone began dancing the night away under the influence of flashing lights and irresistible rhythms.

At one point I looked over to May, who'd based herself with Dominic at the far end of the dance floor, opposite from the DJ and on the fringe of our group. I've trained myself of late to be able to glance at her briefly without lingering or looking completely feckless - out of necessity. It's a silent, passive form of stalking I suppose, but I just find it impossible to be in the same room as her and not occasionally look at her wonderful face.

This time however, I performed my – probably less-subtle than normal – glance manoeuvre and was forced by what I thought I'd seen to do a cartoon-esque double take. Looking back confirmed it. May was shouting at Dominic and he was shouting back. Upset arm gestures were all over the place, flailing at the space between them and trying to carry their words further than the music-heavy air must have allowed. My staring caught other people's attentions and soon a few people were looking.

Aware of the audience, May ran outside.

Things, as you can probably deduce, had all gone awry. Dominic walked in a frustrated manner towards the bar, whereupon he sat and ordered a drink. Jenny ran up the stairs after her friend. The best any of the rest of us could think of doing was to carry on dancing, well aware that the reason we were all there was outside crying. I was in bits, of course. I had no idea what their argument had been about but I could only conclude that it must have been Dominic's fault. He'd taken my girlfriend out and upset her. I wanted to punch his face clean off his head.

Sometime later Jenny came back down and, in no uncertain terms, demanded that I went upstairs. I wish I'd insisted on not going as - on reflection - my ability to talk coherently had wandered off somewhere, leaving me with only a limited set of slurs the likes of which normally denote mental illness. I followed Jenny (was dragged by the wrist) through the dance floor and up the stairs to the exit, where I was struck with the rush of cool, fresh air and the whiff of cigarettes. I turned and saw May – panda-eyed and drunk. She was smoking. She doesn't smoke. The picture looked wrong and she looked vulnerable, like a child holding a gun.

"You're smoking?" I said. It was statement more than a question, but one with implied shock stuck all over it. I concede that it wasn't the best thing to start off with, given the situation. She must've known she was smoking; I doubt it was much of a shock to her.

"Oh fuck off." She turned away

"Fair enough." I went to turn around and leave.

That was the moment when I realised that my sympathy for the girl had all but disappeared. Yes: I love her, but having been treated the way I have has obviously instilled some kind of dormant anger or resentment inside me that manifested last night in simply not caring that she was upset. I moved towards the stairs, noticing that Jenny had ran back indoors as soon as she'd gotten me there.

"I'm sorry Alan," May said, softly. I remember her voice cracking painfully, as if she was only resting in a pit-stop between bouts of tears. There was a long silence, and then she offered me a cigarette from a small, clearly just-bought pack. I took one. "Now *you're* smoking."

"So... what's up, May?" I asked, reluctantly. I didn't want to be there, but now I had a cigarette and had to be there for at least another three minutes I thought it best to skip past pleasantries. This was especially as there'd been sod all in terms of pleasantries exchanged between the two of us since ever since we'd split up, anyway.

"Everybody saw that didn't they?" She looked so fragile and cold. I kept flitting between caring and not. It was immensely confusing.

"Not *everybody*," I lied. "Do... Do you wanna talk about it or..."

"Not really."

"Fair enough." I think I was pleased, but I can't remember. If I was sober I'd have been pleased.

A pause for a drag.

"I suppose you know that was all about *you*, do you?"

"I'm sorry?" So that was why Jenny had dragged me out here. Was this about to be it? The big confrontation that had secretly but steadily been building? Were we supposed to come to a drunken, swaggering head now and resolve it all? "...About me?"

"Oh of course it was!" Her eyes glistened with the sheen of new tears ready to fall.

"Well... well what about me? Have I done something wrong?" Assuming she thought this was the case, I adopted a defensive, aggressive tone. "You know it was nothing to do with me – us being in the same lane. That's hardly what I wanted to happen."

"Oh, Thanks." Tears dropped again and she shivered, looking completely lost and helpless. It was almost annoying that she could cry and I couldn't; it was like she had an advantage.

"Jesus May, what do you expect? You- ...*We* break up because you don't want a relationship and very shortly after you're here with this other guy? It doesn't feel great."

"I know. I'm sorry…" She seemed taken aback by my anger.

There was the longest of pauses. The two of us just stared at each other without flinching for what seemed like days. The only way I knew time was actually passing was because our cigarettes were slowly burning closer towards the brown. The occasional blanket of smoke blurred the view, and then eventually May caught some in her eye. She squinted her beautiful eyes shut and rubbed them, causing the rest of the tears she was fighting back to fall about just above her cheeks like a red wave. Being able to say what I'd just said felt like something heavy had stopped pushing against my chest, and I breathed like I'd never done it before. It shook me.

"I want you to know," she started, struggling with it all, "that nothing ever happened between Dominic and me whilst… well, you know. …I'm not that person."

"Ok." I didn't know whether I believed her or not, I just sorely wanted the conversation to be over. I wanted rescuing.

"You Don't hate me do you? You can't hate me Alan, please." Tears again. "You're too important to me. Do you hate me?"

Yes. I kind-of do. I love you of course, but you expect a lot from a man you're not very good to.

"No. No I don't hate you." God; drunken women are a mess, I thought. I know they say women shouldn't drink as much as men, but perhaps not drinking at all might be a better idea. When men get drunk all we do is cause physical damage and ruin people's homes. With women there're always feelings and problems that come up and then need addressing. I don't know why they bother.

"Good. I'm sorry things worked out the way they have. I really am."

You and me both, my dear.

"I wish we could go back to the way everything was before," she added.

"Well I'm not gonna lie, May; things aren't ideal." Now there's a bloody understatement. I trod the cigarette into the floor.

"I know."

"It might take a little while before things are back to that."

"I know... I'm sorry." She did that head-shaking thing that *truly* sorry, crying people do. I believed her. What's more I started to feel sorry for her again – this *was* the poor girl's birthday after all.

"Ok." I let a moment go by, trying to decide how to set a tone that'd let us move on. "Well, maybe next time you go on a date you shouldn't invite me into your lane?" She laughed, wiping away tears.

I made a nondescript noise that drew her in for a hug. She hugged back tight, which I wasn't expecting. "Happy birthday," I said.

"Happy birthday," she said back. I laughed and smelled her hair.

Just then Jenny poked her head round the corner. May nodded that it was ok to approach, at which point I told them both that I was going downstairs.

Having had a thoroughly rubbish time up until that point, I took it upon myself to go straight to the bar and order a cocktail and enough shots for however many people were standing round me at the time. I don't know the exact number but, having looked at my empty wallet today, I can only imagine it was a fairly costly endeavour. Avoiding questions about May and dancing with forceful enthusiasm, I soon managed to get back into the party mood. May came back downstairs shortly after, aided by Jenny.

Everybody seemed to try and ignore her in a strangely executed, spontaneous effort to pretend that nothing had happened. The effect was to leave her with no alternative but to go to the bar and talk to Dominic, who at the time was staring intently at the screen of his mobile phone.

I watched out of the corner of my eye, or by full-on

staring (whichever you think is more likely given my alcohol intake), as she threw her arms around his shoulders and began to talk things through.

There are only three things from that point on that I'm absolutely positive about. The first was the dancing; I remember so much sweaty dancing that I can still feel my heart pounding in my chest from it. It's like when you spend a day at a theme park and then still feel the motion of the roller-coasters when you get into bed.

The second thing I remember vividly - so vividly I think I'll remember it forever – is the last chunk of sickening, painful acceptance that lodged into my throat and slid over my vocal cords when I turned to look at May and saw her passionately kissing Dominic. She'd been as courteous as one could expect up until then, so much so that I hadn't even met the bloody guy until the party. It couldn't keep up, I realise that, but all that well-mannered consideration crumbled to bits there and then with one raw thump when I looked at her and realised that the only thing existing in her entire universe at that moment was him. Not me.

Having that image burnt permanently into the backs of my eyes put the final nail in the coffin of what was a pretty shit night. Aside from that kiss, I've been feverishly wondering about the nature of their argument. I can't remember if May explained it better than how I recall or transcribed it, but that's one of the pitfalls of writing the vast majority of a book whilst hungover, and *about* events that happen whilst drunk. She said that their quarrel was about me, but I've no idea what the context would have been. If you're hoping for some closure on this one, dear reader, I'm sorry but there really is none. As I mentioned at the start of this entry, things are fucked up. Last night May and Dominic were arguing about some aspect of my existence, but I can't for the life of me figure out which and it's driving me completely mental.

The third and final thing I remember was that she didn't come home.

iii) Billy's bored dog

At the start of this book I wrote a lot of optimistic bunkum about living life to the full - something along the lines of 'not being bound by society's constraining effects'. Other than the fact that the bank accidentally gave me enough money to sit comfortably in gainful unemployment during my secret ill-health, *and* that I had the briefest of flings with an actual real life woman, I realise that I haven't really done anything that amazing. Until now, that is.

Last night I'd been seeing my old work colleague Paul for drinks in Clapham. We drank our weight in £4 pints whilst sat by an open fire, staying out long enough for me to miss the last tube and have to crawl upon the two-tall red beast to get home. I've gone on about this at length before, but the night bus really is the worst of the oft-unavoidable things in life. I'd go as far as to say it's even worse than death, although having not yet experienced that I'm not sure I can really comment. Suffice it to say, the bus lurched home in its stop-start fashion with an endlessly frustrating stream of people - whom I've since vowed to kill - getting on, only to ride seven metres down the road.

I got off as near to Tufnell Park tube station as I could, whereupon I started to cut a zig-zaggy path home with legs fuelled by several varieties of Dutch beer. The way home involves traipsing through a small wooden square the length of a street, in which the grass is always peculiarly wet no matter what the weather's like. It's pretty precarious work because it's dimly lit and patchy in much the same way my health is. Its poor lighting also provides the perfect hiding place for some of London's most undesirable bastards. At one point - upon entering - I passed a bush which was clearly providing hospitality to some seedy man/woman closeness, which was bad primarily because of the rather worrying noise the female half of the duo was making. It takes an almost commendable lack of social concern to be part of turning what is essentially a communal front garden for the best part of 50 houses into a wooded land of smut, but you'd be surprised at just how many urchins and undesirables litter the place each night. I normally try to cut round it on the path, but I'd done away with enough alcohol last night to remove my normal streetwise sense of self-preservation. Sadly, alfresco shagging wasn't the worst thing in the square at all. The worst thing happened to be a wiry, angry chav with a dog.

Now, if you think back to when we moved into the house, you'll recall that a little chav and his morally void compadre felt compelled to relieve me of one of my sofa cushions at the overall expense of five. Therefore, my experience thus far with the local swines hasn't being glowingly positive.

As a social movement, chavism is generally followed by the young and the idiotic. In this particular instance the chav was clearly about my age, which made him look a bit like a child that'd grown up too quickly. He still had that angry-for-no-reason look about his angular face and he wore the uniform (hat facing the sky, Reebok Classic trainers, Burberry jacket), so I knew what I was dealing with, but he'd reached an age by which he really should have known better than to carry on with his outwardly angry, antisocial ways. His dog, a giant Bull Mastiff (or something), looked as if he wasn't really that into the lifestyle, which was a shame because dragging an innocent animal into such an existence just strikes me as cruel. It just sat at his side panting and looking like he wanted to go home. Or to somebody else's home.

He (the chav, not the dog) said something to me as I drew near but, having put my headphones in at the other end of the park to drown out the bush sex, I had no idea what it was. I stopped and took them out, naively thinking that he might be asking for the time/directions/some change, but as I did this he promptly adopted a square on stance and dragged his dog round so that they were both blocking my path.

"Alright mate," went out the familiar call to arms. Unlike the unguided, generic squawk of last time, however, this was promptly followed by a direct call to action: "Give us yerr wallet."

Now this was amazing. I'd actually gone and found myself in one of those 'muggings' you hear so much about these days. Last time it was a much more temporal thieving - me being caught by surprise and them capitalising on my stupid situation. The difference between that and a mugging is that the latter requires the would-be thief to set out his aims right from the off, allowing for a bit of back and forth - an engagement of two minds - in which you actually get asked to cooperate. If you think about it (which I did), "give us yerr wallet" could be thought of as either an order *or* a request, which is an intriguing concept because it gives you the opportunity to reply negatively.

The Chav (whom I shall call Billy) wasn't brandishing a weapon, which was a big relief in a world where it's easier for kids to get hold of knives than it is manners and where switchblades are given away in boxes of cereal. In the absence of such a weapon, it was obvious that he was relying on the dog for some aspect of menace other than that being provided by his feckless face. Unfortunately for Billy, the dog's expression was as much one of malice as is a sleeping infant's, meaning the element of threat was significantly diminished to the point where all I really had to worry about was some sort of physical ruck. Seeing as I'm in no fit state to be fighting people I suspect alcohol played some part in my proceeding actions, but I'd also like to think that my dying gifted some zealous sense of freedom. Let me explain…

After he'd asked for my wallet and I'd thought about the entirety of what you've just read for a long enough time to make me appear quite gormless, I looked him in the eye and said:

"No."

I think this was the single most brave thing I have ever done. As I said; Billy wasn't armed, but his face was angry and steadfast enough to wring out the 'I don't want any trouble' kind of response that I imagine is the norm in a mugging. I'm not much of a fighter and I'm sure he was more than physically capable of taking me on, and yet - with one solitary word - I'd taken myself and the situation to the point of no return. Probably, I thought, the wrong point of no return. In saying 'no' I'd suddenly flipped a mugging into something that Billy hadn't ever designed on it being – an educated debate of morals and the nature of ownership. I've a feeling that the reason Billy makes a habit of taking other people's things by force is because his brain isn't quite up to debating standards. Mine isn't either, really, but in this specific battle of wits I quite fancied my chances.

"You what?" he trumpeted. "I said give us ya fuckin' wallet. And yerr fuckin' iPod, too."

I don't know whether he had eyes on my iPod from the start or whether my response had shocked him into remembering that headphones are usually connected to one, but either way it didn't really seem as though Billy knew what he was doing. This angered me a bit, as not knowing what one's doing is a trait that usually goes hand in hand with doing something for the first time. If this was the case it struck me that Billy was at an awfully stupid age to first get into thievery. I'm not saying there's a good age to get into mugging, but I think it's comparable to how smoking from the age of 12 seems more understandable than starting at 20. I was also a bit annoyed that he thought I was as good a target as any to begin his life of crime with. Presumably, I didn't look any different to him than an elderly weakling or little schoolgirl.

I realise that this is all just speculation and that I know literally <u>nothing</u> about Billy's actual circumstances (or his real name, for that matter), but he had a dog, which meant he had to have had money enough to feed it. He had Burberry too, which I highly doubt he robbed if only because he'd have had to have robbed it off a fellow chav. All in all, in a very drunk state, I came to the swift (if ill-conceived) conclusion that he didn't really need to go about mugging people at all and that he therefore didn't deserve my wallet.

"I said 'no'. I worked very hard for the contents of my wallet." This was a lie. "And for the wallet itself, come to think of it." This was also a lie.

I'd heard in the past that the best thing to do when being mugged is to act crazy, as it'll throw the thief off course and cause him to retreat. Ironically, I wasn't thinking clearly enough to consider what a crazy person would do in such a situation, but it didn't matter because – as is usually the case – my drunken head sent me off on a bit of an aural roll. Now, normally when I write down what people have said it's done the day after; the involvement of guesswork and paraphrasing can't be overstated. In this instance, however, I remember exactly what I said simply because I spent some time in bed reciting it in my head out of pride:

"I don't know anything about why you and your dog find yourselves in this park at this ridiculous hour," I began, "but I can only assume that you set out to spend the night relieving people of their belongings. I'm on my way home with a pocket full of items that I paid for the privilege of owning and with money that I worked to earn. I can't pretend to understand how or why someone such as yourself managed to go from innocent youth to thieving adult, but in no way does whatever hardship you might've come across in life entitle you to the things that other people have earned in theirs. You're mad if you think it does. Now, you and your frankly bored-looking dog don't scare me so please fuck off out of my way so I can go to bed."

With that said, I took a step round both him and the dog and carried on home, heart and ribs bouncing off one other inside my chest. I didn't put my music back on, in anticipation of hearing Billy's hurried footsteps behind me, followed by whatever sound a punch makes to the back of a dying man's head. But it never came. Billy, as it turned out, was the kind of thief that neither expects or wants any kind of real conflict. He was the kind of thief that relies on the two simple steps that muggings generally follow: he asks, you give. I expect I'm probably the only person in Billy's short mugging career to ever dispute him and I'd like to think that doing so might have put an abrupt end to it... or at least I'd like to think that things could have gone a whole lot worse than they did.

Either way, I don't think such bravery on my part can be fully accredited to the booze that Paul of Clapham forced me to engulf. I might not have scaled any mountains or headed up a political revolution yet, but dying does genuinely give you at least a *small* step back from reality - the likes of which I'll probably continue to fail describing properly for the rest of this book. It gifts the ability to see how completely barmy most of the world is and lends a frightening, if ironic, sense of invincibility. Last night I realised for the first time that not caring whether you live or die messes with your reaction to certain situations - to a potentially dangerous degree. If I've not acted accordingly up until now, then at least last night's made me appreciate that 'society's constraining effects' are no longer my concern where possibly-violent confrontations are concerned.

That's more than rebellious enough for me.

8. NOVEMBER

<u>Shopping:</u>

Tea
Milk
sugar
Baked beans
Frozen veg
Fruit
Cereal with sugar and bad things in it (never muesli again)
As many vitamin supplements as will look normal at the till
Beer
Cheese
Frozen chicken
You've nearly run out of gin

<u>Things learned:</u>

- A night out with a large group of friends is never without incident. The kind of arguments and developments that caused drama at 18 cause even more drama at 27.

- Once your late-twenties start leaning towards your early-thirties, it becomes more and more apparent that you can't handle hangovers like you used to be able to.

- If there's one thing I'll miss about life it's that it's never, ever boring.

<u>Favourite Text:</u>

Tim: "I woke up with a pint and a cold Pot Noodle next to the bed. I had them both. I really wish I hadn't."

i) An unsent letter

Dear May,

Not sure if I ever told you this, but I had my heart broken... nay; destroyed, by the (then) girl of my dreams when I was at school. I told all to a close friend and he suggested that I write a letter to her, telling her exactly how I felt, then rip it up and throw it away. I never did that then, but at the moment I'm feeling a lot like I did back in those impossibly hard school days. Like an angst-ridden adolescent. So much so that I thought I'd give my long-since estranged friend's advice a go. Because I am drunk.

So where do I start? Well, firstly I'm afraid I'm still - after all these weeks - not entirely sure what actually happened, and feel I'm owed some kind of explanation. I'm angry, confused, upset, all of the above and more. You're an amazing girl, May; you're the kind of girl who's achingly beautiful and somehow doesn't know it. You're that most rare of pretty girls; one whose personality hasn't been affected and warped by years of knowing you're gorgeous. I assume that, since this is the case, you've found yourself at odds with love in the past? Found yourself heartbroken? I do hope so - it's a pretty vital human experience to go through. I doubt very much you'd have ever been on the receiving end of break ups if you knew quite how stunning the rest of the world finds you. The kind of girls that do are invariably horrid, and that's just not you.

Cut to the chase; stop beating bushes: I wonder, more than anything, what's going on in your mind regarding 'us'?

You say I 'mean a lot' to you, but all I can think is how hypocritical that sounds after the cold treatment you so expertly delivered before ending things. … Before ending things without any valid reason as to why. I'm sure I'll never properly figure out what's going on inside your brain, and I'm sure that's exactly the way you'd like it.

Your innards must be a glorious and tangled mess of images and colours. They must splash against memories, fall into a net of sounds and float out the other end only as bewildered movements and words... movements and words that only you understand the origin of. It's an exhausting thing to be a part of.

What I do know for certain, loathe though I am to admit it, is that our relationship ending was for the better in the long run. Or at least it would be if I weren't such a selfish man. In theory, you've unwittingly spared yourself from the upset of having to say a final goodbye to a parting lover, but in practice you've ripped the truest love that I'll ever know away from me, and for that I'm irreparably livid.

This is perhaps all sounding a little preachy and self-loathing. Not telling anyone I'm dying has been so much harder than I thought it would have been, and it's definitely now taking its toll. The only saving grace is that so much time has passed now that telling everyone would be more likely to result in a sound telling off, than it would be to garner sympathy. Maybe that's what's putting me off the most? Just as well. I'd hate to be proved to be one of those men who don't finish what they start in that instance where it matter most.

Do you remember when we were at the cinema and were talking about all the classic films that I'd never seen? You said that you couldn't think of a better way to spend a weekend than to lay in bed with me and watch them all back to back. We never did that.

.

What are you supposed to write in a letter? Should there be jokes?

I gather that in the traditional sense a letter is the beginning of a back and forth communiqué, but since this'll never get sent I can't see the point in asking you any genuine questions. Perhaps I should tell you what I've been up to recently?

- Dying (sometimes annoyingly) slowly

- Writing

- Obsessing over you.

You know what? I think there's a really unhealthy attitude towards 'obsession' in the modern world. The select few among society's number who are born mental enough to begin stalking a celebrity that they've never met have dragged 'obsession' down in public standing to something that it's not. Obsession in its original state means being preoccupied with a single topic or emotion. Yes I'm obsessed, I'm preoccupied with love and preoccupied on focusing that love on you. That's not all that bad, is it?

Or maybe it is.

Your birthday night was a mess. I'm sure this is something we can both agree on, but I'm equally as sure that you managed to get over it in the time it took to step one foot in the cab with Dominic. Christ, May, you told me you didn't want a relationship. You told me that as if it was the main reasoning for ending our otherwise perfect partnership.

Aside from the fact that I am apparently the type of person who'd describe a relationship as a 'partnership' (like it's some kind of business arrangement), what am I lacking that this Dominic character has? Is it haircut money? What am I supposed to take from all this? Above all else that I can possibly think of, it's this: you are a coward. Jenny's told me that you didn't like the idea of jumping straight into the shoes of a cohabiting couple, but that's something that two proper grown-ups with rational brains and more than one pin number could overcome with tact. Tact and a certain degree of trust was all it would have taken to make what was clearly a fantastic friendship a fantastic relationship. As it stands you're just a fucking coward.

I think I'm going to stop now because I can't come up with any more ways to insult you, and I've almost run out of swear words. The most pathetic thing about all this by far is that, despite my best efforts to sound mean and verbally wounding, when I picture what it'd be like to say these things in real life everything gets muddled behind a vision of your beguiling face crying. It's safe to say that I'll never lambaste you in this way in real life, simply because I couldn't stand to be the person responsible for those tears and scrunched eyes. Well... not again, at any rate.

With that in mind I'm ending this here. I hope I've given you something to think about May, and I hope you and Dominic end your relationship in a burning fit of unmet expectations. Honestly.

I love you,

Alan Bell

ii) In which Alan buys crockery

I wouldn't want you to think that the only happenings in my life are shopping lists, worryingly infatuated behaviour and birthday parties, but it appears that we're now fully into birthday season. In the interest of sticking to the facts, I plan not to leave out a key one just because it's clustered near another. It's only fair that I remain fair. Is that fair?

The 'I' key on my laptop can't have a lot of life left in it. I've been reading through the past few chapters and I can't help but notice that the letter 'I' has been, well, prevalent to say the very least. Even now in this paragraph, it's been used six times already. As such, I'm going to give us all a break and write the rest of this passage in the third person - all omnipotent, like. As if this were a real book.

This serves the dual purpose of giving you the reader a refreshing break from the 'I, I, I' nature of the narrative and also letting me write at least *one* chapter in a different style, so that when I do finally die everyone can say "Ooh, yes; he was a very good writer," and not just "Ooh yes, he did like to talk about himself a lot, didn't he?"

Enjoy:

Alan awoke to the sound of the world imploding on itself; great crashing sounds thundered from the insides of his brain and from beyond the extremities of the walls. Arriving on his feet and leaving his room dazed, he was pleased to find that the house and the universe at large were both still in one piece. No visible damage to the structure of the building; no absence of the force of gravity.

Downstairs things were less serene and he soon found the reason for his sudden and brash awakening. Tim was standing in the kitchen dressed in nothing but a pair of briefs and the glasses he was presumably born in - a worried look on his face and a sorry-looking broken cardboard box in his hands. About his feet were the remains of Jenny's best plates.

"What the Billy Jean have you done?!" Alan screeched, chuffed that something bad had happened that - for once - he'd not been part of. Tim was much less amused. He stood staring into the space through and behind his friend for several moments before slowly letting the words:

"Help. She's actually going to kill me," escape his mouth like those of a whimpering child.

"Oh God, was that the good stuff her parents got her?" Alan asked, trying incredibly hard not to laugh. "I tried touching that when we were unpacking after the move and she nearly chopped my arm off."

No sooner had Alan said this that he saw the full and utterly ridiculous situation that befell his flatmate. Not only had Tim destroyed his girlfriend's best crockery, but in doing so the shards and shattered stubs had painted the lanky, barefoot bear into the far corner of the kitchen – near to the cupboard that the now torn box had come from. Tim stood unable to move for pointed spears of china. Alan did what any compassionate friend would do; he stood and laughed.

"What on Earth were you trying to do? Are you... are you stuck in the corner?" Alan asked, fighting off fits of giggles.

"Yes." The response was muttered - almost inaudible.

"I beg your pardon?"

"Yes I'm stuck in the corner." Tim, who had up until that moment maintained his grip on the tattered box, threw it on the floor in frustration and looked up at the ceiling.

"Right. Well now that's cleared up I think I'm going to go and have a shower. Laters." Alan turned to walk away from the kitchen door, sniggering as he did.

"Alan! Al! Help me you stupid, stupid bastard," came Tim's riposte. "The plates were supposed to be for tonight."

That day was a Thursday, and it was Jenny's birthday. Tim had told Alan some days before that, whilst he and Jenny had made plans for the weekend, he was planning a surprise dinner for her return from work that night. Alan had apparently agreed to help, but had since forgotten any such arrangement had been made. Either way, Tim was currently pinned to the corner of the kitchen by sharp objects and Alan was stood laughing.

Soon enough the latter had freed the former by way of half-arsed sweeping, and once the numerous shards had been cleared into a box they both sat down in the lounge and worried about what to do next.

Tim was clearly distraught at the thought of telling Jenny what had happened. Tiny beads of cold sweat began forming in prickly blobs around the spaces between his ears and his eyes.

"Her parents bought those for her," he said from deep inside a sickly daze.

"I know, mate. I was the one who mentioned that in the kitchen. Her parents got them for her and now you've smashed them all over the place."

Alan realised he probably wasn't helping things. Consciously changing tact, he switched to a more positive mindset. "Right then," he began. "Here's what we're going to do..."

...Nothing came. The words that usually set up the part of a sentence containing the plan had all been willingly served up by his mouth, but there was no plan to follow. The air expelled in preparation fell back into his throat and the two boys slid into silence again. After a while, Tim declared - with a tangible level of gravitas - that it was vitally important Jenny never found out what had happened.

"She's going to find out at some point, mate," Alan interjected. "I don't think there's enough superglue in the world to put them back together properly."

"I know. We're going to buy new ones."

Upon saying this, Tim jumped up and ran back into the kitchen, sliding about on bare feet as he did so. A plan had formed in his head and jolted through his limbs with enough force to take him into another room before Alan had properly noticed. Tim returned into the lounge and thrust one of the larger chunks of crockery in front of his friend's face, pointy end first.

"All we need to do is find out where it came from and we can buy it all again. She'll never know." A glimmer of hope danced madly about behind his eyes like a lamb on fire.

"OK. Sounds doable," said Alan, who wasn't really that fussed whether things worked out either way, but was quite keen for some kind of adventure all the same. "So how do we find out where it's from?"

"Erm…" A long pause hung in the air as Tim's brain tried desperately to make one cog turn the next. "Fuck."

"You could ask her parents."

"I can't very well do that, can I? 'Excuse me Joyce, I was just wondering where you got Jenny's lovely plates from?' … 'Why you ask? Well it's just that I've dropped them everywhere and need to rush out and buy new ones.'"

"Jenny's mum's name is Joyce?"

"Yeah."

"Right… well."

"'Well' what?" Tim asked.

"I dunno. It's just that that's a proper mumsy name isn't it?"

"Yeah well she is a Mum."

"Just as well then, really."

Tim stared at his flatmate with such a look of bafflement and confusion that Alan wasn't sure if he was about to get a smack round the face or a tearful hug. Silence stuck again for a few moments. "So what do you want to do?"

Looking down, Tim solemnly began to rub his hand across the surface of the china. It was bone-white with small leaves drawn on at several intervals around the rim.

"We're going to get a cab into town, hit up a few likely suspects and ask them if they sell this set." He held the portion of what appeared to be a bread plate aloft like Moses with the ten commandments.

"OK," said Alan, "I think we should both put some clothes on, though. I don't know how much a shop assistant would necessarily trust a hairy man in briefs brandishing a pointy object. Especially if his sidekick was the Dressing Gown Kid."

After (forcibly) the quickest shower any human being had ever had (Tim turned the hot tap on downstairs to try and speed things along), Alan dressed and met his friend downstairs. Tim bagged his plate chunk and the two of them hit the brisk North London streets. A police siren could be heard in the distance, serving only to make Tim feel guiltier about his accident than he already did. He was adamant that Jenny mustn't ever know about the morning's events, but more to the point he was worried about time. He'd got up early with intentions of laying the table and spending more than enough time planning and preparing an elaborate meal. This unscheduled dash around London (without even a guessable finishing time) had thrown everything off track.

He had just wanted to make a nice dinner for his girlfriend and his friends. He hadn't wanted to smash plates, nor did he want to be where he was headed. The more he thought about it the quieter he became and the hotter he felt. The cab ride towards Oxford Street was uncomfortably warm and deadly silent - save for that damned police siren. Jail was probably a safer option than Jenny's wrath, he thought, though he daren't say it.

He needn't say it anyway; Alan saw it slapped across his panicked face.

They arrived at Oxford street for about 11.30. Tim threw a bundle of cash at the driver and ran off down the pavement with scant regard for change. This, and the fact that he'd looked at his watch 19 times in the last 17 minutes were all the clues Alan needed to know that they both had to act with a heightened degree of urgency. He reluctantly chased after Tim, who seemed peeved at having to have waited for Alan for the entirety of the seven previous seconds. Not a minute could be lost, it was clear.

"Right," Tim began, panting. "I'm sure they must have bought them from a big chain." He wasn't sure at all, but he figured that times liked these called for blind guesswork and the optimism it brought in the face of daunting adversity. "You go to John Lewis, and I'll go to Debenhams."

"Ok, except we've only got one plate."

"So? You know what it looks like."

"I'm not about to go into John Lewis and ask if they have 'a china set with leaves on'. Let's just stay together. We've got plenty of time."

"No we've not," Tim replied with a whimper, bringing his watch parallel with his face. "Jenny'll be home in... onetwothreefourfivesix SEVEN hours."

"Exactly. This isn't going to take seven hours, Tim."

Alan was having a fantastic time. He was just enjoying being out with something to do.

The two adventurers cut a sprightly, if ungraceful, dash through the hordes of people and ended up in their first port of call. Alan's fears that Tim's panicked state might cause a scene were soon realised when he grabbed the first shop assistant he saw by the arm and began waving the plate – or as everyone else saw it, a pointy object – perilously close to her face.

"Do you sell this set?" He demanded, sharply.

Shouting didn't help things any. Alan tugged Tim gently by the arm and told him very sternly to calm down. He'd seen Jenny angry before and, while it was admittedly terrifying, it didn't warrant abusing or scaring hapless shop floor staff.

"I'm sorry. He's a bit... hurried." The young girl looked over at Alan, and then back to the nearest till as if she were about to mouth the words 'help me'. "You don't happen to know if you sell this set do you?" He pulled the shard from Tim's gripped hands and showed it to her from a more comfortable distance.

"Erm..." she began. "I'm not sure. Home furnishings and accessories are on the next floor up. I," she glanced nervously up at Tim, in case he was preparing to bludgeon her to death, "I only work in the jewellery department."

Alan thanked her, and in the time it took for the two words to leave his mouth Tim darted frantically towards the escalators. He'd never seen Tim in such a state, nor had he ever seen him run so fast; he could only presume that the meal Tim was planning on cooking was an extremely complicated affair – like one of those Tudor feasts that went on for days. There was still plenty of time, but the dying man was glad for some exercise, so he shot with similar urgency up to the first floor.

When he arrived up onto the next, equally busy, floor of the sprawling department store, it seemed to Alan as if Tim had disappeared. An abundance of Christmas decorations wrapped the place into an unnecessary frenzy of red; the shopper's faces all seemed stressed as a result. It wasn't helping Tim.

He was now rushing round the store trying to see a plate. Any kind of plate. Things would be a lot better, he thought, if at least he could rule out this store and move on. Alan caught up to his flatmate as he was encircling a 20-foot square plate displays like a shark. He beckoned a shop assistant over.

"Excuse me." He was keen to seem polite in the face of Tim's anarchic behaviour. "You don't happen to sell this set do you? Tim, show her the plate. Slowly."

Tim pulled out the plate and waved it under the nose of the young man. At the very first physical hint of a shaking head, he about faced and made a beeline for the down escalators. Alan, baffled at the speed and agility that Tim was suddenly capable of, thanked the puzzled member of staff, breathed out a large sigh and ran after his friend.

Half way down the escalators he received a text message from Tim saying "Hurry up."

***

It was in the third shop that they finally found the design. The two now-desperate men encircled the forty-odd plate displays a number of times (due to a lack of staff so severe that Tim referred to it as 'criminal') before they'd suddenly seen it piled together at shin level on the bottom shelf. The set – which needed replacing in full - comprised of six dinner plates, six bread plates, six starter plates and six dessert bowls and, for a reason that neither of the boys could fully understand, cost no less than £300.

"Jesus!" Alan exhaled.

"Yeah," Tim replied, looking sombre. It suddenly felt as though finding the plates was very much worse than not finding them. "Yeah they're really expensive."

The two men kneeled in front of the set for a while before Alan, who wasn't sure why the hitherto frantic atmosphere had noticeably and suddenly dropped to a dull throb, stood up.

"Right," he said, clapping his hands together and rubbing them satisfactorily. "Lets do it then shall we?"

"Mate," Tim said sadly, "I can't afford these."

"Yeah it's a bit steep for plates."

"No I mean I can't actually afford these." There was a worried look that passed between the two of them. It was then that Tim opened up about why the plates were so important to Jenny, why he'd been so panicked and why it was so imperative that the set be replaced. "Jenny's parents are poor, Al. They've not got any more money than you or me. Jenny'd said for as long as I can remember that – as girly as it sounds – one of the things she's always wanted is a proper, grown-up dinner set like this. She'd asked her parents for some a few times since we started going out, but they only ever said they'd get them for her when we'd moved in together and got a joint bank account." Alan looked puzzled. "Point is, whilst I'm sure that for her parents that was a way of ensuring they'd never have to splash out £300 on a set of plates, for Jenny they kind of represent our... I dunno, our relationship to an extent. I know that's stupid, but these plates were bought for us by her hard-up parents as some kind of seal of approval, or testament to the fact that we're a good couple. I'd no idea that they cost this bloody much." A pause. "I don't know exactly how she'd react to them being broken, but I'd rather she never had to find out since it'd probably really, really upset her. I'm not in the habit of upsetting that woman. Especially on her birthday."

Tim went on to explain that he didn't have the funds in his personal bank account to pay for the plates, and since Jenny was the responsible one with their joint account she'd soon see that £300 had disappeared. Before he'd completely finished, Alan interrupted with:

"I'll buy them." It came out in the kind of voice that rarely, if ever, gets used between two male friends. It was a stern but soft tone, one which showed the depth and complexity of a relationship that normally either lies hidden beneath a layer of irreverent comment or expressed only through name-calling and high-fives. Such was the seriousness and reserved quality of Alan's voice that Tim didn't question it. He was wary and worried, of course, that his explanation of the situation might have been misconstrued as a sob-story designed to garner money, but he was too thankful to really care. The two had too long a friendship for that to truly be the case anyway; Alan knew Tim wasn't a scrounger.

As the plates were being boxed up, as the money changed hands and as they made their way home (on the bus), Tim made it repeatedly clear that he would pay Alan back over time. Alan spent most of the time trying to convince his friend that it didn't matter. Eventually, as the battle of pride grew tiresome, Alan – who couldn't convince Tim otherwise without revealing the state of his health – agreed to take reimbursements as and when Tim could afford it. He decided not to chase these payments, but to put any he received into a separate savings account and organise the money to go back into Tim's account the following May. This plan made him very happy for the duration of the return journey.

With the level of care someone would usually apply to holding a newborn child, Tim laid the table and saw to the preparation of a stunning five-course dinner. When she got home and saw what he'd done, Jenny was suitably surprised and amazed enough to make the whole endeavour seem worthwhile. Throughout the course of the meal the plates were mentioned no less than seven times; every single time Alan and Tim looked at each other nervously. Alan spoke to May and May spoke to Alan; conversation flowed between the four housemates better than it had in quite some time. Tim classed the night as a success. Alan classed it as progress.

9. DECEMBER

<u>Shopping:</u>

Tea
Milk
Sugar
Hot chocolate
Baked beans
Potatoes
Fresh veg
Token fruit effort
Yoghurt or something
As many vitamin supplements as will look normal at the till
Beer
Frozen meat
You've nearly run out of gin

<u>Things learned:</u>

- A shelf falling down in the middle of the night is the single-most terrifying sound in the world. I can only imagine it's much, much worse than any sound you'd hear at war.

- Plates are ridiculously expensive considering they do the exact same job as the floor.

- Polar bears are <u>not</u> in fact all left-handed. That's an urban myth.

<u>Favourite Text:</u>

May: "I've been waiting for a bus for about nine hours. What are you up to? Tell me something interesting."

i) **In which no one mentions crockery**

I can't help but feel like I should be writing more than I have been. I do nothing with my life. People who do nothing with their lives often find themselves in the agreeable situation of little to accomplish and much in the way of spare time. As it draws nearer and nearer to the point where I'll have to put an end to the book, I think I'll grow more aware that I've not written as much about the most important things in life as I'd wanted to, and that I've not documented as much of what I've enjoyed, hated and felt as was initially my intention. This is no doubt the result of a combination of laziness and the fact that I'm just not as good a writer as I'd always hoped I was. Since there's little that can be done about the latter, it's probably best that I at least try to work on the former.

I saw Dominic again last week. May brought him over as Tim, Jenny and I sat watching a film. The two of them joined us in the lounge, snuggling up on the pile of cushions, and the five of us talked and joked and ended up eating a box of breadsticks and a packet of dips. I didn't have as much fun as I pretended I did.

There's a fallacy floating about our culture that says men would much rather have a 'fuck-buddy' than a proper relationship. The few vile men who are happy never to get close enough to anyone to experience something above animalistic lust are probably the ones perpetuating this, but I assure the female readership that it's generally not true. You can have as much sex as you like (that's not me giving you permission), but at one point or another our natural instincts make us hug the person we're fornicating with, and this is where things go wrong for the misogynistic. A hug shared between a man and a woman (who are mutually attracted) is the road to a relationship. It's game over. This is firstly because a hug is a closeness that serves no sexual purpose, but chiefly because during that hug the man will smell the woman's hair.

I don't know what it is in a scientific sense that lives inside the follicles of the female head, but if you like a girl in a more-than platonic way, you'll find that, for whatever reason, her hair has the most magical smell you've ever known. It smells (and I know how clichéd this sounds) like being home - like being safe. I've a very strong feeling that this is why women are (by and large) shorter than men.

I watched with growing amounts of seething jealously for three hours as Dominic snuggled up close enough to breathe in the rich, hairy smell of

May's barnet – a smell I was once privy to above anyone else.

Then, oddly, a week went by and I didn't hear or see from Dominic again. Not only that, but I saw a lot more of May. It's Sunday today, and on Friday I found out why.

All four housemates shared a takeaway and watched old music videos during an impromptu drinking session that began (I think) because I asked Jenny if she wanted to share a bottle of red wine that I'd had in my cupboard since the move. For some reason this then resulted in all of us going to the shop across the road and buying enough wine, spirits and mixers to forcefully overthrow a rehab clinic. It was a bloody fantastic night. Alcohol filled us up to that wonderful brim of fuzzy smugness – that level of intoxication where shaking your head quickly from side to side has an unusually heavy effect on the eyes, and therefore becomes your new favourite hobby. During this time, the following inconsequential things happened:

➤Tim danced to 'This Charming Man', launching into his flower-swinging Morrissey impression and not stopping until a further three songs had passed and somebody needed to ask him to stop.

➤A girl down the road somewhere screamed like she was being raped so we all ran out to help, only to find out it was just a bunch of kids messing about.

➢Jenny trod on a bag of prawn crackers and smashed them all to bits.

➢I fell over and bruised my thigh on the TV unit.

Having to keep the secret about Jenny's plates is quite amazing. As I've mentioned before, being drunk most of the time is not the best way to keep 'mum' about sensitive subjects and clandestine facts. Up until this moment I've kept my ill-health a secret, but I don't really know *how* since I've an insatiable hunger for sympathy and a knack for saying stupid things. Now though, I've got a new secret to worry about spilling. The whole 'dying' thing has - bizarrely - been pushed to the back of my mind in favour of plates. This generally means that I can enjoy myself a bit more than I would. For the time being at least, my head can stop battling against that selfish side - the one that normally tells me to spill the proverbial beans and focus on something else. Smashed plates is a fairly normal secret that a normal person might have to keep. Dying is not.

I think the reason that the plates thing takes precedent in my head is because Tim knows about it too, so there's someone to look at and squirm with whenever talk or the television moves towards the topic of tableware. You've probably never noticed, but this happens quite a lot. More than the topic of death anyway, which seems odd since every living thing on Earth will die, but not every living thing on Earth will at some point need a complete dinner service set.

Having said that, when things were really bad between May and I the TV seemed to be playing nothing but episodes dealing with the very sensitive subject of unfaithful lovers. The human brain must just be trained to pick up on mentions of whatever's at the forefront of the mind at the time. For example: I went through a stage at university (on reflection, probably fuelled by excessive use of recreational drugs) where I was convinced I was the victim of some kind of bizarre conspiracy. Whenever I looked at the time it would be 22:22, 13:13* etc. This went on until I realised that it was only because I'd become so super-aware of these times that my brain was disregarding all the instances in which I saw a non-symmetrical one. And also that I am an idiot.

*Note: *I realise that 13:13 isn't symmetrical, but I can't think of any better way to describe it.*

Whatever the case, safeguarding the knowledge of the obliterated plates is exciting and weirdly relieving. It's nice to have something so trivial be the most prominent thing in my social life for a change.

***

At any rate, once drunkenness had taken hold of our baby-blue lounge, the thing that I originally started this chapter to write about happened. Midway through a classic David Bowie moment, Jenny (quietly) asked May, who was curled up hugging her on the sofa, where Dominic was that night.

"I don't know," she replied, taking a sip of her Malibu (which you shouldn't do lying down). "I haven't even texted him in a couple of days."

"Really?" asked Tim. He was clearly happy to hear it. I don't think he particularly liked Dominic, for no reason other than blind loyalty to me. It's a loyalty that's made the otherwise inoffensive and harmless Dominic an enemy in his eyes, which is the kind of thinking I can get behind.

"Yeah," May replied. "I don't think it's got much legs left in it. Things have… erm… fizzled."

"Ah that's a shame," Jenny said. She then realised that I was still in the room and got flustered by what she'd just said – not knowing where to look. I didn't mind; 'Ah that's a shame' is a pretty natural thing to say in that situation, whether you mean it or not. I kept quiet and intentionally still, while jumping around for joy inside my own head. If Tim had adopted an anti-Dominic resolve in the way a racist doesn't like other ethnicities, I was Hitler by comparison.

The conversation changed topic soon enough but I don't imagine I was any good at concentrating after that because I spent much of the rest of the night inside the confines of Alan's Lovely Private Place of Good Things. She was going to break up with him and, frankly, it was beautiful.

Jenny tells me that it happened yesterday, and that May was indifferent about the whole thing - far from the "mix of emotions" that she *apparently* experienced with me. I don't know if that's a good thing or not. May came home looking defeated at having done the deed and went to her room for the rest of the evening, glancing briefly at me as she sauntered through.

When this happened I was enormously happy, but since I've been thinking about it I've realised that this isn't all that brilliant. You might think I'm impossible to please, but here's my reasoning:

Firstly, I find it very interesting that May suddenly thinks enough time has passed for her to talk about Dominic as much as she likes – in such an open fashion - in my presence. Maybe it's because she'd had him round the house a couple of times and I haven't hung myself, or maybe it's because she'd had him round a couple of times and I hadn't hung him; I don't know. Either way, according to her I'd now put the whole thing behind me, as if I'm basically her nonplussed, gay best friend.

Secondly - and most importantly - is the fact that, whilst I can sit here and write about how fantastic it all is, I can't stop myself from thinking one thing: from my point of view he was a major factor in May and I breaking up. What I mean is, if she's going to tell me she doesn't want a relationship and then a few weeks later start going out with someone, it had better be the most perfect match-up ever known. They had better be soul mates.

As it stands I'm just a bit confused by the whole thing. On the one hand, he's out of the picture now, so there *should* be less awkwardness and less kid glove use. On the other, she's now a young, free and single woman again; it's set up for the same exact thing to happen again.

***

I've just realised that I've been incredibly stupid. At some point Jenny will read this and the jig - as they say - will be up. If I were a better person I'd probably delete every mention of the plate debacle ever happening. Then again, if I were a better person I probably wouldn't keep those closest to me from knowing about my ill-health.

I'm not going to delete it.

What I will do is apologise to Tim and Jenny now:

I'm sorry.

I think it'll be ok, mostly because reading this will probably be something of an emotional read as it is, and I can't imagine plates (however expensive) seeming that important in comparison. You know… not that I'm egotistical or anything.

As was mentioned at the start of this chapter, I'm a lazy, lazy man. Laziness, much like being a fool for love, is a personal trait that's hard to kick - proved here by the fact that I'd rather risk Jenny being upset about her plates than go back and delete a whole chapter. I've not written as much in this book as a man of more ambition would have done, so I don't think I can really afford to be deleting anything. I'm too lazy to spare people's feelings. If that makes me a bad person, I don't really care; I'm dead.

ii) Saying hello to the bird

Sometimes it's easy to wrongfully assume things. A homeless person, for instance, may well have forgotten more about advanced trigonometry than you will ever learn in your life. Another, more relevant example would be: just because a greasy estate agent gives you some keys, you shouldn't assume that you'll be the only tenant. The four of us each signed a contract for our house saying that we would pay a certain amount of money every month to maintain the rights to use the bathroom and conk out on a bed at night. As it turns out though, this contract didn't give the house the kind of exclusivity we initially thought it would.

As mentioned previously, there are things living in the roof. A vivid imagination had led me to believe that it was either a family of very loud clog dancers, or an unrelated group of very loud clog dancers. Either way, I took it as read that whatever was up there had been here long before we moved in. Unless they arrived on the same day as us and we were all just too busy moving to notice each other. Which is quite unlikely.

In any case, I suppose that they'd have as much right to complain about us as we do them, both because we tend to stay up late drinking and because Tim likes to play 80's punk rock on Saturday mornings.

Three days ago I found out the nature of the beasts that have been dancing/playing Wii/hosting Greek weddings above my head, as they simultaneously became bereft of one of their party.

I was awoken on Tuesday at an ungodly hour (about 7am) by a slow, wheezy chirping that seemed to be entering my head in much the same way a drill thrown at my face with the power button scellotaped down probably would. When faced with a slow, wheezy chirping at 7am (which is an ungodly hour, remember), the sensible thing to do is to find its source and urgently make it stop. I writhed out from under the covers and followed the sound through blurry eyes to my window ledge. The wind was whipping around through the brick tunnel as usual, but it wasn't loud enough to drown the chirping; both noises were fighting each other to get through the small angle at which I'd left the window open.

Lying on the windowsill was a bird. A tiny, scrawny, hairless, half-dead baby bird. It had fallen (or was pushed?) out of the roof and down onto the window ledge. Aside from its occasional pained cheeps, I think it had basically given up hope.

Being the kind of person who is of staggeringly little use in an emergency (as in, will just stand there pointing), I hadn't a clue what to do. I don't know the animal equivalent of 999, but even if I did I wasn't sure how interested they would be in rushing out to save a bird roughly the size of five grapes. I assessed that the fall from the roof must have been about six feet onto the hard wooden sill, which for something so small must be about sixty.

Without even touching the bird, I ran out to the landing and started shouting "is anyone awake?" loud enough for anyone who wasn't awake to be instantly woken up. May came out of the bathroom, ready to go to work. There were white flecks of toothpaste framing her lips.

"What's wrong?" she asked, clearly seeing the panic on my face.

"One of the roof things has fallen onto my windowsill," I replied - that being best collection of words I could assemble out of what had happened at short notice. They all fell out of my mouth rather too quickly.

I dragged her into my room, stood and pointed at the 'roof thing', waiting to be told what to do - be it collect bandages, get a damp cloth, find one of those dogs that carry rum in a barrel on their necks, or mercifully flick it off the ledge towards its maker.

May really wasn't much more use than I was; she disappeared out of the room, leaving me to continue gawping. When she returned I was bent over with my face about an inch from the thing, inspecting it as it flapped a wing dramatically. It looked rightly upset.

"What the hell are you going to do with that?" I asked, realising that she had returned with a spatula.

"Move, move, move," was the reply. I calmly got out of the way and sat on my bed. I was tired; she was in a rush. I became worried that, in a moment of early morning madness, she was planning a sort of improvised fry-up.

In actual fact, her idea was to carefully scoop the thing up off the windowsill onto the spatula (something which is significantly harder to do with live creatures than with bacon) and then carry it over onto a pillow. She slid the little roof thing onto the pillow next to me, gave me a satisfied nod and said:

"Right sorry I'm going to be really late for work. You'll be fine now, won't you?"

With that, she walked out of the room and left for work. I, contrary to whatever animal resuscitation skills May thought I was trained in, was not fine. I had a nearly dead baby animal lying on the pillow next to me and I had absolutely no idea what to do with it. 'Fine' didn't even come into it. As far as I was concerned, things had just gotten a lot worse: now I had a pillow case to wash as well. At that moment, the only things I knew about birds were:

1) That they eat insects and worms

2) That they come from eggs

3) That they don't like cats

4) That one was on my pillow.

Thus, instead of looking for some way to make it feel better I decided it would be best to first get on the internet and research what kind of bird it was. It was a runty looking Chaffinch. A Chaffinch is a fairly common bird in this country, and eats insects. That's all I managed to gleam from all the 80 million pages on the web. That information didn't help much but I reasoned that, since I didn't have anything planned for the day, I could afford to get to know it through primary data. i.e: spending time with it and learning what it likes and what it doesn't like first-hand.

As I didn't know how to help the bird in a medicinal sense, I thought I might as well investigate some alternative new-age cures. It seemed an obvious choice in the first instance to play the bird some calming music as, even if the fall *had* damaged it beyond repair, at least it could enjoy a bit of easy-listening to soothe it into its early demise.

To that end, it seemed to thoroughly enjoy (as much as a bird can 'enjoy' something) the steady sounds of acoustic folk – or more so than other musical styles at least. Its squeaking slowed in frequency to only once every couple of minutes, and I could only hope that it was due more to the relaxing melodies than its overwhelming injuries.

We had made progress.

I scanned for blood and entrails, of which there wasn't much. This wasn't necessarily good news, of course; such a small animal is likely to have very little blood anyway, making that alone a poor tell of the bird's physical well-being. It definitely had a broken wing. Small tufts of fur sprouted from various parts of his body where feathers were supposed to eventually go, but they weren't encompassing enough to hide that his left wing was bent slightly out of shape when compared to the right.

At this point I decided two very important things: firstly that this little bird was going to live (God dammit), and secondly that if it was ever going to fly again then something had to be done quite urgently. Something that involved both my very limited knowledge of medical science and the broken wing attached to the little broken bird.

I left him in Willy Mason's more than capable hands and went to gather all the equipment I thought I would need. The raw materials for bird wing repair were surprisingly abundant in our house, and within ten minutes I had rounded up the following:

•An internet image of an x-ray following corrective leg surgery (for reference)

- Some cocktail sticks

- String

- Aloe Vera

- Cannabis

Before I carry on, understand this: by this point everyone had seen the bird and left for work – in doing so they had abandoned us both in our hour of need. The bird looked to be in a state where it was going to die regardless, but if it did live it wouldn't be able to fly, and therefore wouldn't be very good at living anyway. I had nothing better to do and therefore felt that – however unbelievable it sounds in retelling – if there was something I could do to help I had better bloody do it. I was sure that no matter how poor my understanding of anatomy is, at that exact moment it was probably better than the bird's.

If nothing else I thought it would be an interesting exercise in better understanding the fragile nature of life and death. As well as that, trying to do something good for another living creature might improve my chances of going to heaven – should such a place actually exist.

I began by taking a good long look at the picture that Google had provided me. Obviously my search ('broken leg x-ray') had yielded quite a few results, but I picked the one that looked the most like the injury I was dealing with and that seemed to have been fixed with tools akin to what I had gathered. They invariably involved something stick-like in essence that would act as a splint, and either screws or wire. I had string and, rather than taking apart the TV remote for its tiny screws, told myself that string would probably be adequate.

Obviously, we didn't have any sort of anaesthetic lying around. Cannabis - being the next best thing - would have to suffice, so I rolled up a very small amount. The method was to smoke a tiny bit, and gently ease the smoke onto the bird upon exhaling. This served the dual purpose that it would ease the bird's pain (and racing heartbeat) and steady my nerves for the delicate procedure ahead.

Once this (which I shall call 'Stage 1') was done, I prepared a cocktail stick by snapping it down to roughly the same size as the bird's good wing. The string was then cut in such a way that I had three pieces ready, each about three inches in length. AKA: Stage 2.

Stage 3 was the Aloe Vera. The bird – who was by all counts now looking fairly chilled out from the smoke – was lying near-motionless, which I didn't read as a good sign. Aloe Vera is a plant extract that is known to treat cuts, burns and eczema. It also eases pain and reduces inflammation and is apparently good at dealing with herpes; so I covered him in it from head toe. I'm sure he hadn't contracted herpes by living in our roof but, nonetheless, the slimy gel made him a little bit heavier (almost more of a solid, real thing) and therefore easier to handle.

What happened next wasn't pleasant for either of us, but I suspect it was a lot worse for the roof thing than for me. What (I guessed) I had to do was to physically straighten out his bent wing with my hands. I can imagine that if I had a broken limb - to the point where it was facing in entirely the wrong direction - then someone yanking it straight would probably hurt quite badly.

Sure enough the small, pained thing on my pillow let out a noise that can only be described as the bird equivalent of 'swearing up a storm', before dropping back into a state where he would do nothing but breathe deeply. For bloody ages.

The wing made a noise you'd probably call 'not very nice', but bent back into place all the same.

Following this - in what I must stress were a very tricky and precise few minutes - the bulk of the operation took place, in which I had to attach the cocktail stick to the slimy wing and fasten it tight with my pre-prepared lengths of string.

After the kind of infuriating, impossible fiddliness usually reserved for wrapping awkwardly shaped, tiny birthday presents, everything was done. The bird clearly felt quite sorry for itself – and so did I – but nonetheless I could only conclude that the operation was a success. This was based solely on the facts that:

A) It was still breathing

And

B) That I couldn't see any part of it that I had made obviously worse.

Then, when the room had finally calmed from the franticness of the entire morning's events, he looked at me.

Properly.

The little bird looked at me in the same kind of way that I assume baby people look at their parents when they're first born - that *Hallmark* moment when parent and child bond irrevocably forever. It looked at me very - for lack of a better word - *honestly*. I can't presume that it knew I'd been helping it, as it was nearly dead and almost certainly unable to understand such concepts, but it looked at me in an such an unsettlingly full-on fashion that it seemed prepared for anything that could possibly follow... As if it knew these were dire times. It had nothing left inside it, but what energy it *could* muster was being spent focusing a beady eye on mine. This honest look affected me so much that I stopped what I was doing (rubbing Aloe Vera off my hands) and spent several long moments looking back.

"Hello... little bird," I said.

Predictably, he didn't reply. He broke his gaze from mine, let out one more pained squeak from the bottom of his tiny lungs, and passed out.

iii) The roof thing's fall

The walls that crack and break away
reveal the world at large,
from single slits we force the beaks
to make primary charge.
What waits through shafts, and moistened path and
heat too thick to see?
What waits beyond is newest life, and young identity.

And we spring forth but slowly still,
as bones are sodden; soft.
Still forming like the memories-
and thoughts we'll hold aloft.
The thoughts are fuzzed and fudged away by eyes
that open wide -
that take their place as sacrosanct, bewildered by the
ride.

For this new world that broke away
the old with fettered beak,
has brought us now to colder times

and winds that sing and shriek.
Past the ears that haven't grown, and past the watered
eyes;
past what feet had called a home, now pointing to the
skies.

The only thing to do, we fear,
in worlds that twist and turn,
the only thing whilst falling through
lives we've yet to earn,
the only thing we've learnt to do in moments out in
Earth,
is call for help with tiny tongues; and cheap, and
scream, and chirp.

iv) The only other Bell

The bird continues to live in my room. It chirps and squawks and shifts about in a cardboard box nest that we've made it. The wing was in its splint for a week before May made me take it off; I don't think she could quite see the level of veterinary genius that had been applied. Some people just don't like to admit when they're wrong, I suppose. Either way, a week seemed to be more or less the perfect amount of time, since the little chick's wing looks in much better shape for having not moved than it probably would have if I'd let it flap off the windowsill. The problem now is that I've got no idea how long it takes for a young bird to take flight and live a grown-up life. It doesn't really move that much other than to cry out for food.

We've been dangling worms found in the garden above its tiny beak about twice a day. It eats them and we all gather round with linked arms looking pleased, like proud parents. It's an amazing thing. Admittedly, not one of us was sure whether worms were a breed-specific bird food, but they've been going down too well for us to think of any alternative. Like Weetabix, perhaps?

This isn't exactly The Ornithological Death of Alan Bell, as you can probably gather.

Sadly, the Christmas period arrived and I was forced to go home. Since none of us would be in the house to feed the bird for at least three days, we held a meeting to try and come up with a solution. Jenny said we should take it to an animal sanctuary, but I was adamant that that didn't happen. I didn't think that such places took in common garden birds in the first place, but moreover I didn't want our little friend being institutionalised at such a young age. Plus they'd probably have a go at me once they saw what I'd done to its arm. Tim suggested we build some kind of worm-feeding machine that spouted a new worm out at regular intervals. This sounded like a good idea, until we remembered firstly that none of us are engineers and secondly that we don't live in a cartoon.

Eventually, and reluctantly, we realised that our only real course of action would be to stuff the little bugger up with food on the day before Christmas eve, and then leave the window slightly ajar in the hope that the three days we were all away would bring enough growth and strength for him to make his own way in the world. It was a big hope, of course, but it was really all we could do. With the window open there was also scope for his parents upstairs to hear his noise and launch some kind of rescue party. That would be bloody brilliant to witness; I imagine they'd have a big seagull acting as an ambulance.

As I packed for home the desperate squeaks coming from the box in the window kept making me stop and see what was going on. A lot like with baby people, when a baby bird chirps you're never sure if there's something genuinely, horribly wrong or if it's just making noise for the sake of it. I'm no vet, so I only looked for the obvious ailments; at no point during my packing was it on fire or drowning, so I assumed it was just having a bit of a sing-song.

I pushed the window open out of its stiff wooden frame, told the bird I wished him luck (and a merry Christmas) and left. It was 12:42pm on December 23rd.

***

The three days I spent in my hometown were long. There was no Internet connection, there were no computer games and only five channels on the TV. And, of course, there was my Granddad.

The bus home from the train station took me past places I'd not been to in a long time; the local pub, my old school, the park that – together with large bottles cheap cider – must have helped thousands of kids get through their teenage years unabated. I squirmed in the back of the lumbering thing as it bounced over speed bumps, hoping not to see any of the faces that I'd fallen out of contact with, as if it were somehow solely my fault that neither of us had spoken in years. It's hard to stay as in touch with people as you'd like once you get older, especially when you live some distance away.

Often in films, people who do exciting or unusual things do so without the moral obligation of explaining their actions to their families. People in movies who turn to crime, or become spies or contract killers are never shown as having family members or loved ones who would judge or condemn their actions. In all probability, this is because such scenes would slow down the action or simply prove harmful to the character's choice of actions. Indeed, if you've got a loving family you'd probably think twice about going on a mad killing spree, because your dear old mum wouldn't approve. The result is that these characters are all orphans, loners or social ghosts-out of necessity to the plot.

I hate to fall into a stereotype, since I might as well *be* a character to you, dear reader, but I'm afraid to say that I follow the trend. I imagine I'd think twice about concealing my ill-health if I were part of a loving nuclear family, but as it is it's just me and Granddad – and he's not got much life left in him either.

Granddad's real name is also Alan Bell. It's a family thing that at least one boy from each family generation is called Alan, but there doesn't appear to be a reason for this other than egotism (clearly a family trait) on behalf the Alans concerned. At the time of writing he's 86, so (forgive me for being such a realist but...) I wouldn't be surprised if he's buried next to me by the time this book finds its way into your hands - sprightly chap though he is.

"Alan!" he said, giving me a stiff hug. "Merry Christmas."

"Merry Christmas, Granddad."

We don't get on.

To put it at its most simple, his has always been a world of hard, elbow-grease-excreting work and it's one that I neither fit in or fully understand. He laboured the best years of his life away with nothing to now show for it except his house and a pair of stiff knees. I think it stems from patriotism - that post-war mentality of doing your part for your country - but patriotism isn't a practice I'm generally in favour of in any case other than for sporting events. I think that, to some extent, it breeds the hateful kind of racism. Plus it's fairly ridiculous to have anything bordering on real pride in what is essentially a big chunk of land with invisible lines drawn round it. This is especially as you ultimately don't own or have anything to do with the running of the thing. At any rate, the man had always done his best for Mother England, and worked his fingers boneward for 50 years for a dismal industrial kitchen supply company. Once again: this attitude to the gift of life is not one – as I'm sure you're aware – that I agree with.

We entered his home, the same exact house it was when I was a child with the same mildewed smell, and in the corner of the living room there was still the same box of toys that I used to play with. I sat down with my bags and he went to make me a cup of tea.

Whereas Granddad was never happy unless he was working himself silly for no gain, I've always made it known that I'm one of those idealistic artist-types who'd rather do nothing with my life than waste it. As hard as it would be for him to convince me that I'm wrong, it's twice as hard to try and convince Granddad that there's more to life than being one of society's good little peons. As such we've always been at odds with each other and our viewpoints on life as a whole differ wildly. The problem is, these days the two of us are all each other has, so if we can't at least *try* to get on then it'd be a kick in the face to the memory of all those that at one point surrounded our existence. Even so, we *always* end up having a debate about life views.

I should mention that I'm writing this on Christmas day itself, such is the calibre of excitement and family-fun being had by all.

Today started off with none of the usual Christmas

commotion that I expect my housemates and the rest of the world were enjoying. Instead, the two of us took our sweet time getting showered and dressed, finally meeting in the living room at about 11am. There was a three-foot tall white Christmas tree on a table by the bay window. It wasn't impressive, but at least it was there – he'd put it up for my benefit and I appreciate that. Since I'm the closest thing to a child in his life I suppose he feels it's important to keep up the traditional practices of Christmas, despite the fact that it's usually quite a sombre day for both of us.

He came in with a bottle of pre-mixed Bucks Fizz, a present under one arm and a stack of unopened envelopes under the other. I had my present to him by my feet. He handed me the envelopes first.

"Lots of post for you, young man."

Largely because I'm a child in a grown man's body, I've still not got around to notifying the various organisations I seek custom with that I don't live with my Granddad anymore. As far as banks, phone companies and any governmental or socialised services that need to contact me are concerned, I'm either a 27 year-old loser who never left home or I'm a super-selfless young man who takes care of his eldest relative, instead of seeking a fulfilling life elsewhere. Point is: the kind post that most consenting adults would deem as 'important', for me merely gathers dust on Granddad's kitchen table.

I began leafing through, using the type-fonts and return addresses to recognise which letters didn't need to be opened. It's been my experience that as a general rule you can pretty much ignore any letter that doesn't have green ink on it or isn't in a brown envelope. This is especially true when the last letter you opened from the bank told you they were going to give you lots of free money. After that kind of pecuniary boon it's likely that any further correspondence will only be bad news.

Yes; I said 'boon'.

…And 'pecuniary'.

I had plenty of green-inked envelopes. I opened the first one as Granddad fiddled with his radio trying to get some festive music going. The letter was from my doctor. It kindly suggested that, since I'd not been back at all after being diagnosed, it might be a good idea for me to go in and say 'hello'. Unsurprisingly, each of the four following letters said the same thing, only with decidedly more emphasis on the 'it being a good idea' part. I threw them all in the bin. I was a bit annoyed that Christmas had the audacity to take me away from the house that I so enjoy occupying, so I had no intention of wasting further time in a hospital just so they could look me up and down and say 'yep, it's still terminal.'

I'll go to a hospice at the end, when I'm good and ready... As long as I get my own room.

In case you're wondering, Granddad and I both got

each other jumpers for Christmas. Just like last year.

***

Two hours ago we ate Christmas dinner. It wasn't amazing because I cooked it, but the main thing of note is that during the meal Granddad and I launched into our usual debate about how naive I am and how all art is useless rubbish. Chronologically speaking, this paragraph is the first thing I've written in this chapter, because I want to write about the argument whilst it's still hot in my mind. As such, anything before this exact paragraph (explaining about Granddad etc) was written *after* what follows it... although maybe it's not important for you to know that. I suppose that's for an editor to decide.

"How's your job going then?" he asked through a thick wall of gravy.

Actually Granddad I quit that job when I found out that I have a terminal illness.

"Yeah, ok," I replied.

"It's a good job that. You're lucky. Good to have job security in times like these."

"Times like what?" Seems to me as though people are always keen to claim that things are up the spout no matter what decade it is. Nothing's ever really as bad as the media would have you believe.

"Times when everything's moving a mile a minute." I don't like vagaries, specially not when they're delivered by someone pointing at me with their fork. "Joan next door," he continued, "her grandkid's been made redundant five times in the last two years. You stick at it."

"Why? ...Why 'stick at it'? We both know I don't like working, Granddad. I resent it."

"Yes, well... you've had a fairly easy run of it. I started work when I was 15."

"Yes I know. And you finished when you were 65."

"That's fifty-five years of solid work. Does a man good." More clichés and one-liners.

"Well I'm still writing." Even though I was lying about everything, for some reason I still couldn't let him think that I'd just accepted my fate as another worker ant, or was in any way like him. This argument transcended my physical condition – it was about the world at large.

"Oh yeah? What is it at the moment?"

"A book about a man who's dying." I replied. Inside, the various shades of my personality were all laughing maniacally at the beautiful irony ...and supping ironic tea.

"Sounds cheerful!" He topped up my wine glass. "How much money will that make you? I don't gather authors make tremendous amounts of money." This was definitely treading down familiar territory.

"No, but as I've said before, I don't write to make money. I'd much rather be poor and do something I love than get rich doing something I don't care about. What would be the point in that?"

"Nonsense!"

"No it's true." He didn't believe me.

"What you want to do is work hard enough to be able to do other things on the side. Those things are a luxury, not a living."

I was growing tired of arguing. I told him that if I found a way to sit around and do nothing but write all day everyday I'd probably do it; I came very bloody close to telling him that I'm dying, in an effort to prove my point.

It's strange: with the exception of my Granddad, I assume that most old people must think similarly to me about life. When you're young, the fact that you're going to die is pushed far enough to the back of your mind for you to be able to get on with doing whatever it is you believe you should be doing. When you're knowingly close to death you see how pointless working and being told what to do truly is. I was surprised that this elderly man, at the end of his life, is still sticking to his guns; he still genuinely believes that he didn't waste 55 years of his life.

I was set to carry on, but then something clicked in my mind and I backed off. I suddenly realised the difference between him and myself and the importance of it. We could argue forever on this, but neither one of us would prove to the other that we were right, because we're two completely, instinctively opposite people. Granddad was the person in the tin can factory. He was the man who spent his entire life labouring for his family, and brought a child into the world who then brought me into the world.

I suddenly saw that not everyone can have this insatiable need to create some kind of art, or else nothing would ever get done. Not only would there be no industrial kitchen equipment or tin cans, there'd be no artists as a result of a lack of births (the archetypal 2.4 children family doesn't sit well with the rebellious arty types). These people are just fundamentally built differently: no better, but definitely no worse. I realise I sound so ridiculously arrogant and superior, but I know that I'm a different type of person from my Granddad. I'm a lazy artist, and he's a hard-working doer. You need both, or else who's going to build the artist's galleries?

As soon as I realised this I stopped arguing with him, raised my glass, and toasted a 'Merry Christmas' with a knowing smile. He didn't know the revelatory thinking I'd just accomplished but - for whatever his own reasons were - he joined me in the toast and we smiled at each other for a few moments in… in a kind of mutual respect, born fundamentally out of tolerance. Tolerance of each other is the best we can probably hope for at this stage.

We're now sitting in quite comfortable silence in the living room. I'm writing and he's watching television. I don't suppose that he approves of my 'lazy' attitudes any more than he ever has, but – silently – I appreciate *him* a lot more right this very moment than I think I ever have. His lounge smells of pine.

Please don't get the wrong idea. My granddad is not a horrible person. If I've painted him as such in any way then I've done so accidentally. It's just... it's just that we have very different views on what's important in life. I reckon that's why I love him so dearly.

Either way, Christmas day has been a bit of a moot point, as is usually the case. Since it's just the two of us - and not the busy affair it should be - it's met with some degree of reluctance as a practice from us both. Whilst I've not had the kind of epiphany that would make this a radically different occasion (it's been a dreadfully slow couple of days), I certainly don't have any qualms about this being the last time I see the only other surviving Bell. My Granddad is a loner through and through - legitimately at his best and happiest when on his own, which is just as well really.

He knows he's not long for this world and he's got no qualms about it. He jokes about it all the time - which is nice, because I like to think that's where I get my relaxed attitude towards mortality from. It reminds me that we *are* actually related - that we're family.

It's with the nicest intentions possible that I say I hope he dies on the same day I do.

Merry Christmas.

v) The many other Bells

At the risk of throwing open an admittedly one-sided discussion about nature versus nurture, I wonder how different I'd be if I'd been part of a traditional, 2.4-children family. I'm not suggesting I mightn't be dying, but rather if I'd be similar in terms of personality. I understand that only-children tend to get spoilt, but I've nothing to compare it to so I don't know if that's the case. I was forced to get a paper-round as soon as I was able to, which I can't imagine means I'm spoilt. Maybe that's the reason for my strong objections to work. I used to throw the papers in a ditch at the edge of town, anyway. Or I did until I got fired.

The 'nuclear' family, as seen in the types of television sitcoms devoid of any real issues and jokes, is what I grew up wanting to be a part of because the media told me I should. I don't remember my parents. Would having done so made me a more rounded individual? Maybe with the help of a few stereotypically loving parents and a brother or sister (plus 0.4 of a child), I'd be more inclined to tell everybody I'm dying? I'm tempted to do so most days anyway. I bet that if I had a full complement of family to worry about me I'd probably go through with it.

In the 21st century there's an alarming amount of disparity between this idyllic family image and the actual state of kinship in Britain. The idea of having 2.4 children, for me, only resonates because there was a sitcom on TV in the early 90s that went by that name. These days I think the average amount of children being born in the UK is something in the region of 1.6 per family. Bearing in mind that it takes two parents to make one child, having less than two kids per couple is a recipe for a dwindling population. I learnt at school that this dwindle, mixed with bettering healthcare for the elderly is leading to a more aged population. Probably explains why it's just me and Granddad left, then.

The ideal of having two-to-three kids, loving (i.e together) parents and a variety of small fluffy pets seems to me to be merely that - an ideal. Frankly, I don't understand why that's much better than having 19 kids or none at all; it's what you make work and what you're happy with that counts.

Perhaps fewer kids are being born because people are 'selfishly' waiting around and looking for their proper soul mate, as opposed to 50 years ago where everybody got married swiftly after the third date. Depends where your priorities lie, though, I suppose.

Having children has never been on my list of things to do. I consider myself entirely too selfish to be able to adequately bring up another person - putting their needs before mine every second of every day for some 18 years seems incredibly scary. I'm not sure I could put a child's needs first for an entire afternoon. I can't fathom the appeal. Babies are noisy, useless and expensive things that only really become interesting once they're able to hold a decent and intellectual conversation. I'd say this happens at about the age of 12, but then there's only a small window of time before they turn into teenagers and are suddenly imbued with an almost impressively focused desire to destroy or hate everything around them.

I read somewhere that by the time a child is 18 its parents will have pumped about £180,000 into keeping it alive. That seems like an awful lot of money to just be giving away. I'd rather go on holidays and the like. £180,000 is an especially large amount of money when you consider that people are never exactly *ready* for children in a financial sense. I've heard friends say that they'd like to have children when 'the time's right', but I've never been able to comprehend when that might be.

Do they mean they won't bring a child into the world until they've amassed a small fortune in savings? Or until we're in the right political climate? Until third world debt has been abolished and all the guns of the world have been incinerated?

I can't envisage them ever waking up one morning and thinking in a radically different manner to the previous day. It's not as if they'll leap out of bed and suddenly be 'ready' for a child. In reality, all these couples of child-bearing age are merely at the mercy of both their own biological clocks and relationship politics – if their friends are all having kids they probably will too, just to fit in. It's that simple. Although I should concede that without my parents having at some stage desired a child, I wouldn't be here freely brandishing my ability to slate off other people's decision to have children. That's gratitude for you. I was a child once, after all, much as I'd like to forget it.

It's a hypocritical and quite anti-human sentiment, not wanting to have kids, but I'm ok with it. Not that it matters of course, as I'm basically dead and therefore wouldn't exactly be in the running for dad of the year.

The bird is still here. I came back from Christmas and he was still in his nest of rags. He's the closest thing to a child I'll ever have, and if I can get him to the point where he's the confidence to leave the nest for good then that'll be parenting enough for me. Despite a profound lack of understanding about how the chaffinch body works, I managed to fix his wing and keep him alive long enough to see him actually wander around like a proper little thing. The pride I've earned for doing this is probably comparable to the kind you get from parenthood, although I imagine there's a lot less to worry about with a bird than with a human person.

Either way, he's become an unlikely pet and family member to everyone in this house. Tim, Jenny and May come into my bedroom far more than they'd normally have good reason to just to see if he's about, or to stare at him for a bit. There's usually a look of complete wonderment if he is there - despite the fact that just a cursory look outside will normally gift your eyes about 50 similar common-or-garden birds.

When children grow up and move out, parents experience something known as 'empty nest syndrome', where they become forlorn at the fact that the kids they've invested so much time and emotion (and money) in have now gone, leaving nothing but vacant bedrooms and unoccupied seats round a table. Since this emotional state has been linked through metaphor to when birds grow and leave the nest, I'm presuming that it'll be similarly painful if and when the bird does finally go. There's always the chance, of course, that I'll be gone before him. It'd please my poetic side if we left on the same day, but I don't think I'd be able to communicate this plan in a manner that he'd either understand or agree to. The bigger problem is that I don't think Tim would be able to cope with both of us disappearing at once.

I've often heard the notion bandied about that friends are 'the family of the 21st century'. I happen to agree. Clearly if you're nine years-old then your actual family are probably a better family, but once you've moved out and live - as most people now spend some years doing - with friends, the relationship you have with them becomes just as important as any parent or sibling could be. The defining, fundamental factor of friendship has always been that friends are people you choose to spend time with, rather than being drawn together out of genetic circumstance. My friends don't always see eye-to-eye, but they're by far the most important things in my life and I'd choose to carry on living with them forever if I could.

The main difference between friends and family that goes in favour of the former is that, by-and-large, people are much more honest and themselves around friends than with their family, which is massively liberating. There's a popular philosophical theory that suggests every single person (including you, dear reader) is schizophrenic. It says that we all put on a different personality for every different type of company we keep. I think there's certainly a degree of truth in that. I know people who are one way when with some people and then completely different around others. You could argue, of course, that this is merely a form of adapting to social situations or employing tact, but I think I'm just as guilty of changing the way I act and talk around different social circles - sometimes dramatically - as anyone else. It's the reason why I'll happily lie to my Granddad about my job.

This theory obviously throws up the quandary of 'which one of me is the real me?' If we forget for one moment that I haven't told my closest friends that I'm shortly to die, I consider myself to be a far closer version of my true 'self' (whatever that may be) when around my housemates than I am when with Granddad. Friends tend to judge less than family members, which is freeing enough in itself to strip away a lot of the pretence that we find necessary in some situations.

The group of friends you socialise with slowly changes and unnoticeably evolves through time. People join and others drop out but, no matter what stage it's at, we're programmed somehow to believe that this group of friends is better than any other because they're *ours*. If you go to a busy club or bar you're usually there with a group of friends, but then so is everybody else. Everyone in the world is part of a group of friends and acquaintances that - simply because they are *their* friends - seems to each person involved like the right and proper group of friends to be a part of. We see our group of pals as better than everyone else's simply because we don't know any other.

And are they? I honestly don't know, but I can take solace in the fact that they are at least *my* friends. They love me for the person I claim to be around them - for the impression of me they've soaked up - and I love them for the way they appear to me. That, as rationalised and clinical as it sounds, is plenty good enough for me.

If I were to sum up what family means to me in the

modern world I'd have to just conclude that, no matter what selection of people you surround yourself with, feel comfortable with, feel love for and from and enjoy spending time with - whomever that might be in relation to you - is a better and stronger family than any 'ideal' imposed by the media or anyone else could ever be.

My family are Tim, Jenny, May, my Granddad, a selection of other fantastic friends, a small broken bird and you, my dear reader.

vi) A sonnet for the bird

Sections of him that're meant to be bigger,

Extend to the tips of downy and wings

Grown of patience, wanting and vigour

Stalks now for legs; on gangly strings.

Sprouting with feathers - the bits of him grow -

Now bone turns to claw turns to plume

Take flight little thing, and the air will all slow

Applauding your blossom and bloom.

I know that you'll go because frankly you must

The sky, wrought with clouds, will encase you

Shoot upwards with pride, with life and with lust

And enjoy the sharp sky that you tear through.

A flesh-ridden clump once fell as I stirred -

a downtrodden lump that sprouted my bird.

10. JANUARY

Shopping:

Tea
Milk
Sugar
Hot chocolate
Baked bea-

i) A red wine stain

Life is a very complicated thing. You often find yourself in very complicated situations, or the victim of very complicated feelings. Whilst the ability to explain these feelings might often escape you, the cause for any situation you're in can always be traced back by finding the answers to a string of very small 'yes or no' questions. Everything becomes scarily simple when you look at your actions based on binary results to linear choices – some of which might not even be your own.

For instance, if you're feeling upset because the woman or man you love has dumped you, the route for you being in that situation runs back through hundreds of relatively simple choices. Do you go to the party that you first met them at? Do you think they're good looking when you meet? Do you engage in conversation with them? Do you flirt? Do you pursue things?

On a more basic level, if something *physically* happens to you, you can go back through your day and unravel a very complex web of choices that led you to the exact spot where it happened, and at that precise time.

For May, New Years Eve had entailed a house party with some of her friends from home. She had chosen to go to that instead of celebrating it at Tim's pub with Jenny and I. She chose to buy a cream-coloured dress especially for the occasion. She chose to drink red wine. She chose to stand in a specific part of the house with her red wine that was *just* too near to a clumsy drunken party goer.

On the 2nd of January May had decided that, since there was a dry-cleaner's place near our house, she would get her taxi driver to pull over and wait as she handed over the cream-coloured dress with the red wine stain and took her collection ticket. She chose to send Jenny a text about it on her way back into the cab - a move which slowed her down by microseconds. The cab driver chose to take the main road home instead of the side road that they've been known to take in the past. May chose not to wear a seatbelt.

Today, on the 3rd of January, I've chosen to spend the last 24 hours sat by May's bedside in the Intensive Care Unit of Royal London Hospital. The doctors have said that the coma is caused by massive head trauma. The cab she was in was hit side-on by a London route bus; the taxi driver was killed instantly and May was thrown into the side panelling fast enough to dent it.

They say they can't yet tell if there's any brain damage or any bleeding within the brain itself. Her beautiful face is swollen - red and black in patches - and she just lies there, as still as the bed that props her up.

Tim and Jenny are both at work, and May's parents are talking to the doctors. May's father is a very intimidating man. I think - or hope - her Mother understands why I'm still here.

I have to say that this is not very fucking fair on anybody involved. I don't know why all those choices - choices that were made by both the people directly involved and everyone else who influenced *them* - have all left the most beautiful thing I've ever known lying still in the bed by my side. But they have. Meanwhile, the man who's actually supposed to be dying can jump around and dance if he so chooses. That's not fucking fair.

She's no longer in a critical condition. If she'd died I think I would have stopped writing and deleted everything. Honestly.

Despite any animosity I had for May during the more confusing times, she is far too good a person for this to happen to. She's far too alive to be lying motionless.

***

I doubt I need to tell you how depressing hospitals are, but I've been to this one a couple of times before and it's never seemed quite so grim. I assume that if you're here to celebrate the birth of a child then your brain can overlook the dour, clinical greyness, but when I look around even the brighter colours seem to be covered in a thin layer of hell-sent graininess – as if I'm seeing the ward through an old television set.

I'm sorry, amongst other things, for the fact that this situation overpowers everything in the rest of the book thus far combined, and yet it's the time I least want to write. I don't know what I should say, really, since all my emotion has been numbed to the point where the only thing I can get out is the kind of quantifiable fact that better suits a school textbook. I could try and make up some beautiful imagery but I don't know what good it would do. At this very moment anything poetic I could come up with would just be a facade to cover up a mind that can only keep repeating the things it knows:

I know that she's in a coma; I know that I love her; I know that she has suffered major trauma to the head. I know that I've had to pretend to be her boyfriend to stay here. I know that I've not had a shower in two days. I know that this is the quietest May has been since I've known her. I know that I've missed seeing

338

her eyes more in the last day than I ever have.

Other than that, I'm really not sure what there is to say. I keep pulling out my mobile phone and looking at the photographs of her I have. May is the undeniable centre of every picture: a tiny, gleaming light drawing all the blurriness around it to funnel towards her eyes. I love these pictures. I adore her in every single one.

May's mother's name is Kathryn. She keeps bringing me cups of tea. She wears a broach on her chest that looks like a bird. I was given a puzzled look when I first told her I wasn't May's boyfriend, but I think I have at least been *mentioned* before; she's not made me leave. I'm not going to leave.

May's dad can't look at his daughter lying still without trying to fix it somehow - as if it's his fault. He spends half his time on his phone attending to business, and half his time harassing hospital staff under the assumption that there's some miracle cure that they'll only surrender if you appear to want it more than everybody else, or if you shake them hard enough. I hope he's right.

Jenny cried a lot when she came in. I think they're both coming back later on today or tomorrow. There are three flower bouquets on the shelf opposite my seat. I don't think the nurses, her parents, or anyone watching would like it very much if I crawled into bed with May and gave her a hug until she woke up. I might do it anyway.

***

This isn't supposed to have happened, you know? The ironic thing is that there was a point where I'd actually considered pretending to get hurt to get closer to May again. Now I feel sick. I'm sorry, dear reader, but I can't do any more at the moment.

Aristotle said that Friendship is a single soul dwelling in two bodies. I don't know if that's true because I'm still not sure what my views are on spirituality. I've said a lot here and in the whole book about what I think I know and how to explain it all when, in actual fact, I know very little and can understand even less. What I am <u>completely</u> certain of though, is that I've never felt such a strong connection with another human being as I do with May Cooper, and I know in my heart of hearts that she would say something similar. Or she would if she were here. All there is is the breathing, bloody girl next to me, lying terribly, upsettingly still. And that's not May.

I'm going to remain sat here next to the bed. That's the decision I've made because, until she comes back, it feels like it's the only choice there is.

ii) Fix

Get better, my girl;

sew wounds with ruby looms.

Fix my skin to yours - stitch myself to pours

plant feet into the floors.

Just please get better soon…

Get better, my girl;

breathe not for breathing's sake.

Pin words to outward air - talk nonsense till you're there -

turn gaze to focused stare.

Just please begin to wake…

Get better, my girl;

machines can drone for days.

Your voice should spring and hound - turning, tight and bound

to drown mechanic sound.

Just please make out a phrase…

Get better, my girl,

and smoothen peach-bruised eyes.

Unravel like a rose - she overcomes the blows

drops petals as she goes.

Just please don't say goodbye…

Get better, my girl;

It's what you have to do.

You need to heal and wake - I'm not able to take

the pain you'd leave in wake…

I'm dying before you.

iii) The truth will out

Tim says that the bird is still in my room, but has begun flying in and out of its own accord, treating the makeshift nest on my windowsill as a base of operations. If I were at home I'd probably advise it not to continue with its newfound way of life and love of freedom; the outside world suddenly seems a horribly dangerous place – horrific and unjust. Not that it needs warning of course, given the somewhat tremulous way it began life. This whole thing with May has hit me with such a dire sense of mortality that's bizarrely ten times worse than knowing you're soon to die for medical reasons. Absolutely everything is dangerous: you could die at any bloody moment for the stupidest of reasons. It's as if the world is a trap.

The doctor – Dr Khan – has told me that what they say on television is true; much like being in a deep sleep, people in comas can't hear anything that's going on around them - or at least not in a way that they'll remember when they wake up. I must have looked dejected at hearing this, as he put his arm on my shoulder reassuringly and said:

"...But that doesn't mean that talking to her will do

any harm."

This is a dangerous thing to say to a man who has a lot of very sensitive things to explain to a woman who's bereft of the ability to contest them.

Kathryn and Jenny wanted me to go to lunch with them today. I'm sure they thought I was being melodramatic when I told them that I wasn't going to leave her side, but the thought of May waking up alone in this horrible place has scared any sense of hunger out of me. Her face is still a sort of crimson patchwork, laced together with muddy, darkened gauze and bandages. The hardest part is still not being able to see her eyes. Well, that and hearing her relentless breathing. It's a horrible tease that suggests May might actually be in there somewhere.

The slow rising of her chest and the whisper of delicate respiration - drowned out for the most part by the flecks of her heart-rate monitor and the hectic sounds of an active ward – are the only real evidence that she exists underneath the scarred tissue and bruised bone. Sometimes it overthrows the rest of the god-awful noises coming from all about us, and somehow all I can hear is the all-too-calm sound of her... surviving. Quietly living… in the corner of a dim warehouse. I bet if she were here she'd want to scream just to break the tension.

Scream and throw things.

Now I'm the only one here. The nurse comes in once every twenty minutes or so to check on things and each time she does I'm given a look of disgusted indifference. I've not bathed or shaved properly, nor slept any better than half-hour stints in four and a half days. I can imagine that under the hazy, yellow-grey cacophony of ashen walls and fluorescent lights, I look deathly ill, which, to be fair, I feel like I've got every right to.

There's a sickeningly draconian atmosphere in here. The room, if you can call it that, has been fashioned out of a huge curtain affixed to a rail that encircles the bed. The fuzzy light from the rest of the ward feeds clumsily and garishly over the top and feet march frantically across the space fading in from the bottom. It's an oppressive atmosphere to confess in. But confess I did, nonetheless.

Taking Dr Khan's advice to heart (you should always take a doctor's advice), I talked. I told May's breathing body everything. I told her that I had loved her since the moment I met her, which is true to the extent that I think one could love another based on first impressions. I'm a romantic - which you may have gathered - but, even with this innate sensitivity, before meeting May I never really thought of 'love at first sight' as being possible. Going through what I've been through has confirmed it: such a phenomenon is impossible. What actually happens is that the ravaging effect love has on the sane mind paints a dreamy retrospective in your head that makes you think you did love them - were *in love* with them - right from the very first time your eyes absorbed their heavenly form. This blurry nostalgia, I think, is better than the awkward bodily and vocal awareness associated with the *reality* of meeting people, so I'll accept it as being as close as possible to the notion of love at first sight as you can get. My love-stoned brain *thinks* I loved May at first sight even if I actually didn't, but that's good enough for me.

I told her, despite what everything sensible or rational inside me was screaming, that she was the love of my life. It all sounds like overly emotional bollocks now that I'm writing it up - like a school report about how much of a mental you are - but at the time it all felt like the right stuff to be saying. I told the resting body, coloured in bruises and painted with cloth, that I had never wanted our relationship to end and that (forgetting whatever I'd said to the contrary at the time) she had broken my heart.

Then, and only then, after I'd explained everything I knew about love to an empty set of ears, did I tell May that I was dying. Now that I think about it, that should probably have been the more prominent confession. Having suggested right from the start of this book that I'd be able to see the world for what it is and be brave enough to put emotion to one side, today was yet further proof to the contrary. Further proof that my feelings for May still far outweigh the fear and shame surrounding my imminent death.

Does that make me a bad person? Best not to answer that, actually. Perhaps it's best if you don't label me as good or bad, primarily because I wouldn't like the verdict and secondarily because - unless someone does something horrendously evil - there are usually far too many grey areas between the two sides. I've got my reasons (weak as they are) for lying, as do a lot of bad people. Hopefully they're enough to keep my memory or legacy from being soured too much.

I'm being selfish. This terrible accident is the least about me anything could ever be. This is about May: the girl who talks absolute rubbish, who scrunches her face together and somehow expands it at the same time when she laughs. This is about the most beautiful thing I've ever known, and how the thing that I feel most protective over in the entire world is badly hurt - near fatally, in fact. Her face fades in and out of the red, blood-lined flesh and bandages, but the parts you can actually recognise look peaceful enough... enough to remind me of lying next to her in bed. It would be wrong to force her eyelids open with my fingers, just to see her eyes. I know it would. I feel like I need to do that just to prove to myself that the breathing mass on the bed next to me is actually May – not just something unrecognisable.

I dearly, dearly hope she gets better soon, because without her noisy, brash but ultimately stunning existence, everything's utterly and entirely rubbish.

'

iv) Technology is surplus/ important

The machines in this hospital beep incessantly and carve slightly more of a dent into my temple every single second. I don't hate them, though; the one that turns May's steady heart rate into a steady, audible beep has fast become one of the most important things in my life. It tells me she's sill here. It's as if her heart is actually inside, lying behind the screen. Despite the machine itself having no actual *input* on her health, I'd probably defend that beeping TV set with my life just to keep the reassuring noise and the fluctuating green bar going. Just to have that reassurance. There's little else to do here but sit and think.

The little beeping box is a liar, of course. It's not important. It doesn't help May in any way. It's surplus. And yet all I can bring myself to do is stare at its jumping green line and listen to the beeping noise firing out of it. It's pretending to be May's fragile heart. It's bright and noisy and it makes me feel better, so I guess that's a pretty good impression.

v) **A painfully long month**

Where to start? Firstly: I was there. I alone was there when it happened, and that made it magical beyond any description I could muster.

I was talking to her still body, trying to hear myself over the steady beeping of the machines around her bed. I can't remember what I was talking about but slowly, and without the Hollywood squeezing of held hands, her eyes peeled open and the life raced back into her face. It was May again. ...Or moreover, it was like May had turned up and stepped forcefully into the body lying on the bed, bringing with her a rush of blood and drawn breath.

"Alan?" She asked. I think she asked for me before she'd actually seen I was there. I was silent, save for the sound of my heart thumping against my ribcage. "Alan... where... you're?"

I got up, told her everything was ok and rushed off down the ward, near screaming for some assistance and fighting back tears. Once the doctors got wind that she was awake, I was ushered out of the room and told to sit in the waiting area. I phoned everyone, who collectively said they'd be here as soon as they could, which for the meantime meant I had to sit on my own looking like death, surrounded by the noise and furore of the hospital reception.

Waiting rooms are horrible, horrible places. I appreciate that they serve their purpose, but putting an injured fistful of the general public together in a confined space and telling them to wait for hours on end on plastic seating is, at best, a very bad idea. Even in my should-be peace-loving state of near-death, I maintain that the general public are, by-and-large, a horrid bunch. I often think that having friends must be a lucky phenomenon, based on how little most people would get on when stuffed together at random. Maybe it's just jaded cynicism, but the British public appears to be turning increasingly mental, unhygienic and ignorant to the point where the people I know and love (and you, dear reader… and your friends, probably) must be the only 'normal' ones left. Looking around, there were abnormally loud people, people speaking in the kind of 'gangster' English native to Naarf London (which makes whoever speaking sound like they are profoundly stupid, aggressive and likely to be carrying a knife), and people attempting to speak - unprovoked - to strangers in a very jovial way, despite the fact that people in a waiting room

A) Don't want to be talked to

And

B) Are potentially quite upset about something.

There were people in the waiting area who were talking or playing noisily on mobile phones. There were people who looked like they were scanning the room for anyone who'd willingly engage in an afternoon of fighting, drug taking and/or gang rape. There was even one alarmingly obese woman who was pacing up and down just shouting to herself. I hated all of them deeply, and yet at the same time I was the happiest I'd been in recent memory.

Surrounded by the apparently ignorant, injured and violent public, being beaten down by five waves of oppressive fluorescent lights and withstanding a barrage of noise, all I could think about was that I just saw May's eyes for the first time in nearly two weeks. My heart and breath were strained.

I was also wrestling a selfish thought to the back of my head. A small part of me - the bit that I wish was as small as I usually describe it as being - was thrilled and overjoyed that it was *me* whom May saw first when waking up, and couldn't resist massaging the idea that it might help get us back together.

Even I, Alan the self-centred bastard, eventually managed to appreciate the fact that May being awake was by far the most important thing. I swallowed the stupid thoughts down to somewhere they could be temporarily buried and sat still in a sea of happiness.

…Within an ocean of mentals.

***

Jenny raced through the doors and scanned the vast waiting area for my face. I probably didn't look too happy, since an hour's wait in the cacophony of noise and the company of horrible people had taken its toll. Seeing friends snapped me out of it.

"Alan! Is she OK? Why are you down here?" She looked frantic. Only when she grabbed my arms to shake them wildly did I see that Tim was there too, towering behind her.

"She's OK I think. They said it was fine for me to go in but her parents arrived so I thought I'd let them go in first."

This was true; I had done a selfless thing, but I stress that I'd done so only once I'd convinced myself that May would definitely remember having seen me first before seeing her parents. I truly hoped she would. I didn't want 11 days of losing sleep and looking ill to have been for nothing.

"Ahh. I suppose that's best, though," Tim offered.

'If only you knew the extent of my bizarre and self-serving inner rationalising,' I thought.

The two of them sat with me and we waited. I did my best to answer a slew of questions like 'was she *with it* when she came to?', 'did she recognise you?' and 'did she know what had happened to her?' as best I could without giving away the reality, in which I'd seen her wake up, smiled a lot, panicked, cried and ran off.

After a very long time, May's parents came down and let us go in to see her. It was a strange thing, seeing someone who, for a while, you've only seen unconscious. It's hard to explain, but there's a stitch of embarrassment running through the joyousness - as if seeing them asleep for so long is similar to walking in on them getting changed. Both experiences render people equally fragile and helpless. It renders them very vulnerable. Jenny went in first, leading us in and beaming at her best friend. May smiled back at all of us, there was a pause, and then everyone went to speak at the same time. Both girls began to cry with joy.

"I've had a bit of an accident," May said, finally.

"You're clumsy. You should probably work on being less clumsy," Tim joked in reply.

I stayed relatively quiet. So quiet that in normal circumstances someone would probably have asked what was wrong. There seemed to have been a real shift in the relationship between May and myself; something tangible enough for everyone to silently acknowledge, even if nobody really understood it. May, I suspect, understood it less than any of us, but it was definitely there - you could feel it in the room. It was as if this whole accident had acted as a quick fix. Like someone had pressed the reset button. The shift expressed itself through frequent, strong looks passed between the two of us. It was the deepest I'd let myself look at her for a long time, and the deepest she'd let me, too. I worried for a short while that she'd actually heard me admit all my secrets to her some days before.

"We were so, so worried about you…" Jenny said, wiping away tears as they trickled down to a wide smile.

"I'm sorry," said May, doing the same. We all interjected that she had nothing to be sorry about, with such intensity it was like we were telling her off.

I slumped into the seat that'd long since become my home. It now felt alien to look across and see May looking back at me. It felt just as strange to be sat so close to her. In a very real way the coma felt like it had washed away everything that had happened between May and I since we'd met almost a year ago. And now she was awake, alive and well. It was the most amazing thing.

"Have the doctors said when you can come back?" I asked, hopeful.

"They've said I have to stay here just long enough to be able to get rid of this last bandage." She pointed to the gauze around her head. "Probably less than a week."

When she spoke it was quiet, slow and thoughtful, as if she were trying hard to remember all she'd been told in the last few hours and was terrified of getting any of it wrong. Thankfully, all the noise from the rest of the ward seemed to have suddenly dipped into a distant murmur upon her awakening."There are tests and things to do anyway. Mum and Dad said I should stay with them for a while afterwards, if I want to. Mum says work are ok with me having more time off, which is good."

We all agreed that this most certainly *was* good, in a somewhat overly patronising way - like it was a boring story told by a toddler. I think we were still finding our feet with how to speak to the girl. If Tim and Jenny were anything like me they were probably just amazed that she knew who we all were. And that she'd remembered the English language. Tim held one of Jenny's hands as she was holding May's. I put my arm on May's shoulder and for a moment we were all linked together as the closest group of friends on Earth. It wasn't anywhere near as clichéd in real life as it reads in print. It was Joyous.

vi) **Back to normal**

"Mum says you were here the whole time," she said.

My hands shifted from a folded position to begin picking at fluff on my jumper. For some reason my eyes thought this was more interesting to look at than May.

"Yeah, well… I didn't want you to be on your own if you woke up."

It's a fact that I learned to cope with a long time ago, but I'll never be as cool, calculated, persuasive or erudite as the men in romantic films. Whenever televised love stories get to the point when real talks need to take place, both parties seem to suddenly become very serious and able to produce perfectly worded speeches on the fly. In real life people are made up of much more than just whatever emotion the given scene demands, and exist outside whatever setting the scene lives in. Thus, instead of thinking that what needs to be said needs to be said *now*, you can't help but think about that time that you both laughed about this, or were angry at each other about that. By far the biggest thing stunting serious and heartfelt talks though, is the concept of the future. Beforehand, in your head, you're more than ready to say exactly what needs to be said, but you don't because it occurs to you in the moment that your words will have later repercussions. They'll effect what's said straight afterwards; they'll effect the outcome of the conversation; they'll effect the outcome of whatever the conversation was about and they'll more than likely permanently effect your relationship with those conversing with you. This has the unfortunate ability to override the important part of your head that says 'life's too short to not do exactly what you want to do all of the time' because we're all terrified of making those around us angry. Or worse: losing them. We're terrified of being hated, and terrified of being alone.

Well… that, and the fact that talking is hard. The people in films are good at it because what they're expelling from their gorgeous faces has been written and edited. Talking in the real world doesn't gift the speaker with such thinking time (unless you want to appear to be mentally ill), making saying what you mean when it really matters bloody difficult - especially when you're having trouble breathing over the lump in your throat, and you're being battered by emotions.

This, sadly, is also true even if you know you're but a few months from death, so I didn't mention the word 'love' or any of its equally heavy brothers. What I said was: "Yeah, well… I didn't want you to be on your own if you woke up."

"Well… thanks," said May. "It means a lot to me." She exhaled that last part very quickly from a face painted with blushes.

She was clearly struggling with finding the right words just as much as I was, so she reached out and grabbed my hand. May and I had always talked better when the conversation leant in a more humorous and irreverent direction. We could joke for hours and hours about nothing, but we'd fail to talk about the meaningful things with much aplomb. That said, the women in my life had always seemed to manage it far better than I could.

"So what's it like being unconscious?" I asked, hastily trying to cool the room down with a less pressing discussion.

"Hmmm. Dark. I dunno, that's like asking what it's like when you're asleep."

"Did you dream?"

"…Like asking what it's like when you're asleep and you don't have any dreams."

She grinned. Her legs were stretched out and I could see her feet twirling over themselves restlessly underneath the covers. May's not a fan of sitting around for too long, and she was liking being stuck in bed a lot less now than she had when she was unconscious. "Tell them it's time for me to leave," she demanded, putting her childlike face on.

"It's time for her to leave," I said to the curtain, quiet enough so that nobody who happened to be outside would hear.

"Tell them louder!" Her faced scrunched up, causing lines to form all around her nose and dive into it towards the centre. I laughed.

It was a Thursday afternoon. My experience over the last month was that, for whatever reason, hospitals seemed a bit busier on Thursdays than most other days. Perhaps it's because people are so glad to have gotten halfway through the working week that they're inclined to let their guard down on a Wednesday night, leaving them more prone to incident. Either way, May had thankfully been moved since waking to a ward that was both less noisy and less serious. Even so, the room seemed continually busy. Relieved family and friends visited their recovering loved ones with relentless frequency. It was a much happier room than the last one; even the lights seemed less abrasive.

"So are you going to go and live with your parents for a bit, then?"

"Probably," she replied. "But only out of courtesy. I really just want to go home and back to work, but I think it'd hurt mum's feelings. Does that make me a bad person?"

"No, that's fair enough." I wanted her to come

home too. Everything was back to being nice and good and affable between us. As horrible as the accident was, it'd dragged our friendship back from 'fraught' to 'neutral' - something that, given the complexities of all relationships, was extremely rare. It was like a fresh start. Of course, this had all come at a cost that even I, with a selfishness occasionally bordering on 'evil', couldn't justify.

"I've been invited to the cab driver's funeral this weekend," she said, almost silently.

"Blimey." A pause. "Are you going to go?" Nobody had really mentioned the driver's death in conversation yet, or at least not whenever I'd been around. We'd all privately assumed - as is human nature - that May might blame herself for putting him in that fatal situation simply by being the passenger. She looked at her feet as they twisted and lapped over each other under the bed sheet, drawing my gaze too. They looked like dolphins playing beneath the ocean's surface.

"Would you go with me? I don't think I could go alone." Her doughy eyes were sincere, sad. She looked back at me, expectantly.

"Of course."

It would be the second funeral she'd go to this year, the thought of which was incredibly painful.

vii) Funeral for a stranger

Is a funeral an innately good place to forge a relationship? Men (don't ask me which in particular) claim that weddings are great places to 'pull' because all the women present become hosts to highly charged emotions and underlying jealousy. If that's the case, then funerals must ignite the fear of not living for the now, surely? Or of not dying alone? This is me working under the assumption that a woman 'living for the now' will instinctively go looking for sex, of course.

Yesterday May and I went to the cab driver's funeral. For her, it was a way of absolving herself of responsibility by proving that his family and friends didn't blame her. My objectives were twofold: I was primarily there to be her rock, her confidant and her supportive friend. Unsurprisingly, though, I'm intrigued by funerals at the moment, so I was also going with a view to scope out what they were like these days. That way I'd know what to expect.

The driver's name was David Brook and he'd been a black cab driver for 17 years, having passed '*The Knowledge*' first time after only six months of revising -

something of a rarity. He liked fishing and golf, but only in good weather. He and his brother used to fight over the same women until David met his wife, who 'famously' punched his brother (Stuart) in the nose one night in Hackney. David was killed instantly in the car crash that nearly did the same to May.

As bad as it sounds I couldn't help but think that he was lucky, in a way. I often wish I hadn't been told about my health - it was kind of by chance that I found out anyway. I'm certainly lazy enough to be sure that I'd never have written a book this year; I'd have still worked my job, drank just a little bit less and died without leaving anything in the way of a legacy, but all things considered I'd probably have had a much less stressful year. Without the burden of knowledge, I'd not have spent any time worrying about my unfixable feelings for May in quite the same way I do. I'd also not have spent my time fretting about how much I'll hurt my friends when I go. We've all got to die at some point and, whilst I'd originally thought that knowing *when* was a blessing, the more I think about it the more dying unexpectedly - on a strictly selfish basis - seems infinitely easier. Or less ridden with guilt, in any case.

Mr Brook's family didn't hate May, but - other than a quiet chat from his wife (which I wasn't privy to) - she wasn't overly well received, either. That's not to say there were any scowling glances; it's just that this was very much their day, not hers, and it was one of many conflicting feelings and many rhetorical '*what if*'s. May understood that - going about the day silently and acceptingly. During the service she squeezed my thigh and began to cry a little, so I put her hand in mine and squeezed back. She was gracious enough to make a real effort to compose herself quickly and quietly, knowing that she was only there because she had been asked. Her right to cry was much slighter than that of Mr Brook's family. It was for this reason that we left the wake after one drink. We slipped away to a pub nearby, where we spent the rest of the evening talking.

Incidentally, I wore the tie that I was afraid to burn when I first left my job.

***

It was a cosy, small-town-like pub right on the northwestern tip of London - the sort I'd loved to have discovered under better circumstances. As it was, the solemnity of the day had left us feeling as if we still had to keep quiet out of respect. We spoke with soft, library voices.

For reasons that I didn't very well understand, but that I think pertained to her injuries, May had cut her hair very short. It wasn't shaved, but it was tightly formed around her face with less than an inch of shag. It was a big departure from the girl I'd met, but it focused yet more attention to her eyes, which made her look even more beautiful. I could still see a small bandage poking out of one slither of the rim of her hat.

"These people probably think we're a bit overdressed for a trip to the pub," I said as we fell into two adjacent armchairs. I was trying to think of a subtle way of saying 'you should be glad you're alive' when May drained a huge gulp of a pint of lager and said:

"Can we get really, really drunk? Please?"

I've fully come to terms with the fact that (forgetting that I'm soon running away to die) May is well and truly in the driving seat with regards to anything that happens between her and myself - including anything that we do whilst in each other's company. It may well be that power which women claim to wield over all men, or it might just be me being a weak-willed person, but that control, is and always will be, there. What I mean is: if she says we're getting drunk, we're getting drunk. Not that I'm the type of person who'll ever turn down a drinking session, mind. ...No matter who's asking.

We drank solidly and consistently for hours, while I tried my best to put May at ease over the driver's death. The drinking was just a way to get over it of course, but I reasoned that it couldn't hurt things any; besides 'get drunk', I didn't count counselling tactics among the talents in my skill set. She told me through tears that she'd spent several nights unable to sleep, at the thought of the driver being alive and well had she not hired him for her journey. I told May in return that the driver would still be alive and well had her parents not decided to have a child. I tried to explain those tiny choices that mount up and sometimes lead to catastrophe. I told her that those events can be traced all the way back to the beginning of time if you so choose.

"Unless any of those choices are taken out of malice," I said, "then these horrible events are almost always blameless. Life's too short to worry about things like that, trust me."

By this point my words were trudging through a quickly-drying cement of drunkenness, but I think she took them to heart nonetheless. The conversation soon turned to funerals in themselves. I'd like it noted now that, given the choice, I'd rather be buried than cremated, as I'm not altruistic enough to be content with only taking up a space the size of an urn. Being scattered across somewhere memorable would be an even less satisfying way to be preserved. I've an image of Tim doing the deed into the wind and my remains just spraying all over him.

"If all these people are dying…"

"What people?" I asked with a grin.

"Everyone. You, me… you know… everyone. If people are always dying, surely there'll be a time when we run out of space to bury everyone?"

I laughed. "I suppose so. Doubt it'll happen in our lifetime though." Certainly not in mine, I thought.

"They could always turn the moon into a giant graveyard, anyway couldn't they?" She suggested.

"Yeah I'm sure NASA are working on that right now. Does your concern about a lack of space and the planet and such like mean you'd like to be selfless and get cremated?"

"God no. Tim would probably throw my ashes into the wind and I'd go all over him*."

Note*: I know I'm writing this after the night in question took place, so I'm well aware that to you, dear reader, it could look like I've just typed May's sentiment out claiming it was my own before she said it aloud. I didn't. Well I did, but what I mean is that I distinctively remember thinking it before she said it. Come to think of it, I don't know why that's important … but it is. In fact, I could go back and retype all this in a much more concise way but I just haven't got that kind of time at my disposal anymore, which is also a really nice excuse for the rest of the book from here on in going even further downhill in terms of literate quality. Suffice it to say, we both think the same things. A lot._

She was right, anyway; Tim's an idiot… an idiot with a pinafore. I want to be selfish and take up a reasonable plot of land when I go. Preferably with some kind of plinth or marble statue. A park bench would be good too. Basically, I want to create a sort of centre (or facility, if you will) for Alan-related grieving, where a constant flow of people take a number and then wait for their 10 minutes of intense mourning. People say you can tell the measure of a man by his friends, but the driver's day yesterday convinced me it's easier to tell the measure of a man by how many of his friends cry at his funeral, and how noisily. I don't even think that's me being callous; deep down everyone would like to think that their dying would garner a decent amount of tears. It means you made an impact.

As for my tombstone, I've recently been thinking of having one of the following things carved below my name:

'I'm behind you!'

'I can still see you. What you did last night was disgusting.'

'You're next.'

'If you can read this it means I've died.'

'Read the book for more information'

Any of those would be good. I'll leave the decision up to whoever's in charge.

May and I continued to knock back beer and wine until closing time, at which point we were shouted at by the landlord, whose usual clientele were presumably more demure and refined in their drinking habits. We left and began to travel home. Halfway to the tube May stopped and sat on a nearby brick wall.

"I can't do this any more, Alan."

My heart jumped into my mouth. I worried that the alcohol must have travelled to the spot in her brain that pushes out serious conversations. "My feet are shredding to bits in these heels." She kicked them off, revealing red, swollen toes and a couple of newly formed blisters. I was relieved beyond words. If serious talks were going to happen, I wanted to be the person to kick things off. I wanted it on my terms.

"Do you want to wear mine?" I asked.

"No, no I actually think that'd be worse, if anything. Thanks, though." She smiled.

I like to think of myself as chivalrous when it counts. Unfortunately, my 'helpful' manner whilst drunk usually involves offering the same service over and over and over, and not understanding that what I'm suggesting isn't really that great an idea in the first place. I vaguely remember doing this to poor May for quite some time. After a while of her trying to convince me that - while she did appreciate the offer - her wearing my shoes would slow her down even more, I came to the obvious conclusion (at the time) that if she was going to walk around barefoot it's only fair that I do the same.

It was a freezing cold January night, remember -

almost too cold to be able to breathe properly whilst sober, let alone drunk - but we trudged to the bus and from the bus to home holding our shoes. May would occasionally, when she remembered, suggest that I was an idiot and that I should put mine back on. I really wished I felt that I could have, as I'd given her my socks and I was quite sure that I could feel the sharp onset of frostbite. The thought of having to sit in the bath and pick my blackened toes off of defrosted feet didn't really appeal, but it began to appear more and more inevitable.

I tried to take my drunken mind off of the freezing pain and hard concrete by thinking about other things. We both remained contentedly quiet on the walk home, giving me time to be alone with my thoughts as May was with hers. The problem was that the only thing my brain would jump to (other than the cold and my imminently absent leg ends) was May - and just how much fun I'd had talking and drinking with her. Even the silence we now shared was comfortable. I began to walk through everything in my head; things seemed so good again between us that I genuinely felt born again. Our slate hadn't been wiped clean, it'd been obliterated. Where we went from here wouldn't be defined by anything that had happened prior. I was sure of that.

It must have been a combination of this time to think and the generous volumes of beer parked heavily across my brow that led me to completely forget that I'm going to die very soon, and in turn to do something really very stupid. From what I remember, this dream world I created for myself was really no less stressful than the real one, since I spent the entirety of the way home planning to tell May that I wanted to be with her and, in place of my worrying about death, I indulged in much fretting about the consequences of doing so.

For you to read the next passage and understand that the talk buried within carries social weight, you need to do as I clearly did last night and forget all about the fact that I am now dead. Before you begin: I know; I'm a complete and utter bastard.

viii) Cold feet

There were long, sharp, drunken pauses after every few words that I managed to get out, which must have appeared to be for dramatic effect. In actuality, the staggered sentences were just the product of a complete inability to speak with any kind of sophistication – especially prevalent when expressing serious feelings. Or anything proper. I used these pauses to try and wipe my charcoal soles clean, as giving my hands something of a task early on was one less thing for my brain to worry about. I had asked her 'can we talk?' very bluntly as soon as we'd entered the house, which in my experience is never a turn of phrase that proceeds a good outcome. We sat in the living room with low light and hushed voices.

"The thing is…" I began.

This is always a good start to a serious conversation because it means absolutely nothing (so it can be applied to anything) and it gives you an extra couple of seconds to think about your real opening gambit. "I know you've only just got better," I continued slowly. "…And the timing because of that… is pretty awful…"

Her eyes looked like they knew where I was going; she remained silent nonetheless. "But I've had… feelings for you for quite a while now."

Quite why I needed to word it like that, I'll never know. Why did I need to say 'for quite a while'? Why was I even doing this in the first place? I'll be dead within the next quarter. Dead! I gather dead people find it quite hard to participate in fulfilling relationships. Or ones that aren't massively one-sided, at any rate. I doubt I'd be saying this if our talk had had a decent outcome (however 'decent' it would have been is another matter), but if ever there's an argument against drinking - and against generally being a bloody fool - last night was it.

Suddenly the ceiling seemed to lower by about half a meter, turning the room into a hideously oppressive place to be. I felt sick. I instantly regretted what I'd said, but didn't at the same time. It's terribly clichéd to say that one feels one thing and the exact opposite at the same time, I know, but using that cliché is as well as I know how to describe the way I'd suddenly made myself feel. May looked at her feet and rubbed them gently as she spoke.

"Alan, I'm sorry but we just… I don't think I can."

"Right," I pushed out, glumly; painfully. Just as when she'd ended things with us the first time, I'd heard all I needed to. From that second on I just wanted to leave. I didn't want the rest of the conversation: I didn't need it.

"I'm sorry. It's just… it's just that we've only just managed to get over the last time. I love you," she continued, "and you're probably my best friend, but I can't do this again. We live together."

"OK."

"I'd be too scared of us falling out and not talking again."

I didn't understand her argument. It was either that we lived together, or that she'd be too scared of it not working and us falling out. These were two completely different problems that she'd somehow made one, by way of cowardice. It was enough to illicit a proper interjection.

"But wouldn't you rather try something and find out if it works than just to not do it under the assumption that it won't?"

"I'm sorry, Alan." There were tears jostling to stay within the safety of her eyes, pushed back behind frantic blinks.

It became apparent that May had little concept of the one mantra that dying had forced upon me over and over again: *Life's too short.* Clearly she can't put her fears aside, which forces her to take the choice that - for her - appears to be the best one due solely to its ease. Suddenly, drunkenness forced a time-lapse, and suddenly we were lying down, her teasingly draped across me. We lay on the sofa and hugged for three hours, during which time I interspersed enormous chunks of silence with the occasional rethought argument. It was essentially all the same talk and, as such, it fell on the same deaf ears. I told her that we'd both grown and changed a lot in the last year, and that, now we know each other better, it would be different second time round. It wouldn't just be a lustful, physical attraction. She was mine, I said; she was *my* May, made just for me. It was a stupidly brave sentiment to say out loud, but one that she echoed. Despite all the heady emotion, it made me feel wonderful. It made me feel shit in equal measure. She still couldn't bring herself to do anything about it, because all her better judgement fell at the feet of powerful, overriding fears.

Eventually the gaps in the conversation grew longer and the talking itself became dramatically less important and far less emotionally charged. Going to bed was mentioned, and then she slipped away from me and off to her room.

I can't tell you how long I stayed on the sofa, staring at my dusty feet, before going to bed, but I know that it was quite a while. The soles were very black and very, very cold.

ix) From inside a different room

A cell of boiled blood pushes through,

And spins us into separate rooms.

Please be near me, she demands.

No. I'd rather hide and wait.

I'd rather bide for fate to filter time through my sticky hands -

etch a route with scratchy plans.

And time does so, but it filters more like dust than sand

More like viscous slobbers of awkward space, and

…every bloody one of us can feel it.

And every bloody one of us is loath to tolerate it -

a fireplace burning one side of a beautiful face.

And her beautiful face? It sits where I want to sit, and walks to rooms that I used to walk through.

It seeps through walls and groaning floorboards and laminates a dead man's face with cold, grey loneliness.
A sheen of bonelessness I can't undo.

All I want is to be in there too.

Conversation - when a word *is* flicked with a nodded head - juts:

A greasy knife passed back and forth

through longest nights with jilted talks

Passed a glance she must've caught….

…And then back I retreat,

to my separate fort.

You've never looked quite so beautiful as you do from here.

11. FEBRUARY

Shopping:

Tea
Milk
Hot chocolate
Fresh veg
Fruit
Yoghurty rice
Biscuits
As many vitamin supplements as will look normal at
the till
Wine
Cheese
Frozen meat
You've nearly run out of gin

Things learned:

- After only four days of not bathing, not shaving and
not eating particularly well, the average mid-
twenties male turns into something that the general
public finds quite repulsive.

- In real life, things that go wrong sometimes do get
better.

- I've spent more time in the last year being upset
about May Cooper than I have about the fact that
I'm dying.

Favourite Text:

May: "Hi. My mum and Jenny have been going on and on at me about how long you stayed with me. I just wanted to say thank you and that I love you. It means a spectacular amount to me. x"

i) Being wrong about most things in life

If by some slim chance the person reading this is a willing publisher, I think I'd quite like you to ignore whatever Monty said and publish this book under the title of 'The Disrespectful Death of Alan Bell'.

I'm now avoiding May for something that isn't really her fault and something that neither of us have reason to be upset about anyway, given that in about three months I will disappear never to return. Matters of the heart should not seem so big a problem. The worst part, of course, is that *I've* done this to us both. It wasn't mutual. Things were brilliant - back to how they should be - and I've ruined it by spraying out a large amount of verbal refuse that had no business ever leaving my stupid, stupid head in the first place. I've effectively made the last few months of my being so unnecessarily tense, for reasons that are just beyond brainless.

The piffling ups and downs of two people's

relationship affects the people around them and knowing that I've once again had a detrimental effect on the dynamic of the house hasn't made me feel any better about the whole thing. When there are only four people living in the same, thinly-walled abode, gossip spreads with so much gusto that it'd make the common cold feel slightly jealous. If they didn't hear May and I talk as the talk happened (which is a possibility), May would have told Jenny and Jenny would have told Tim anyway. To ensure that what's being conveyed isn't just from May's point of view, I told Tim myself, who would undoubtedly have then told Jenny who'd then tell May and the whole thing would circle around, feeding off looping patterns of gossip for as long as it can possibly stay alive. The end result is that everyone ends up knowing absolutely everything, which can be as much a negative as it is a positive.

"I agree with you mate," said Tim as he served me another pint. "She's being a coward. I know you two should be together, so does Jenny. So does everybody, really."

"The whole thing's a mess."

"Women are mental," he offered on cue. Push the right buttons and Tim will usually throw out a catchphrase.

"And May's a coward."

"That she is, mate. Oop, back in a sec." And with that he darted across the bar.

Tim was not a natural bartender. He was quite good at the bit where you stand with a dishcloth over the shoulder talking to friends on the other side of the bar, but when it came to talking to strangers, coping with multiple orders and - crucially - pouring pints, he fell on his arse. The job made his forehead sweat. I scooped about two inches more foam than is customary from my glass and wiped it on the underlying bar towel, while he served a small group of women. I wouldn't have complained even if it wasn't Tim doing the pouring; I'll take a free half-full pint over a full one at nearly four pounds any day. My gangly friend struggled almost comically to produce three G&Ts, under his own self-imbued sense of haste and urgency, before finally coming back to me with a stressed pant carrying his breath.

"Is it awkward for you now, then. In the house?"

I was about to say that it was bloody god-awful, when I realised that I've been through all of this before. This wasn't any different from several months earlier, which was probably the most embarrassing and shameful thing about it all; I've failed in any way, shape or form to grow as a person in my final year on Earth. Brilliant.

"It's pretty much the same as last time," I said with a smile, leaving off that it was just as fucking painful, if not more so. Tim probably knew that anyway.

"You know, Jenny said May cried her eyes out when they spoke about it. She feels like she's let you down."

"Well she has," I said. "I'm more angry now than upset."

As much as I hate the thought of making May cry over my selfish requests, I'd be lying if I said that this knowledge didn't make things somehow better. And just between me and you, dear reader, I *was* still upset about things. Very. Anger had merely slipped into the equation somewhere along the line, settling in nicely next to self-loathing and crippling sadness. I can't see how May can want to simply not do the thing that makes the most sense in the world just because, in her mind, there's a chance that it won't work out. All the best things in life require a certain degree of risk. If everyone thought like May does we probably wouldn't have ventured out of caves. Or the womb, for that matter.

Unfortunately for me it appears that May is stuck in her ways, so I've taken the mature tact of avoiding her wherever possible, no matter how obviously I do it. And drinking. For example: the other day I'd been out with Ross and came home tired, wanting to sit and relax in the lounge for the evening. I went as far as actually entering the room before I saw her. Having no acting skills to speak of, I don't think the pretence that I just wanted to grab a DVD and go back to my room was particularly believable. I didn't even really look at the DVDs. I just hastily grabbed one at random. Thankfully I've only been forced - out of circumstance - to sit in the same room as May for longer than a few moments *once* since we had the talk, because she's been spending a bit of time at her parent's house. It wasn't a fun few moments. We sat in dire silence until I decided to go to the toilet and not come back.

Earlier on tonight Jenny showed me a text she'd had from May. It said: "This is horrible. How long do you think it'll go on for?"

I don't know if she showed it to me to make me feel sad, or sympathetic or whatever but just made me more angry. I realised that her turning me down has caused the exact same emotions and atmosphere to kick into being as would us going out and breaking up again - the thing she's so scared of in the first place. I might have brought all this upon us, but by being a coward she's made it infinitely worse. I'm starting to think that we're just as bad as each other.

A pause for thought

Do you know what?

I think some very serious bits have gone very wrong in my head. I don't want to hurt May, and don't want to be angry with her for turning me down when I shouldn't be suggesting getting back together anyway. I have no idea how to either stop how I feel or change the stupid things that I keep doing, and it's driving me mental. I'm living in the real world while falling gently into a fabricated fantasy - one involving even more pain than dying. At least in the fantasy world there might be some slim chance of rekindling things with the girl I love.

I wish I wasn't dying, I really do.

I've discovered through laborious examination of my own psyche that I'd much rather argue with, feel awkward around and avoid May than live the reality of a short life where there's already a definite answer regarding our future together - and therein lies the entire problem.

I daydream. I have done so habitually for as long as I can remember. Daydreams are a great way to get away from the sometimes sad, painful or just boring parts of real life, but a while ago I seem to have flicked permanently over to daydream mode and can't for the life of me figure out where the switch is to get back. I'm so sorry to anyone reading this. I'm just the most bafflingly selfish and stupid man.

I know I mustn't dare blame May for any of this; she's unwittingly right and I'm the most wrong I've ever been but – Jesus help me - I can't stop. It's become glaringly apparent that I've no control over my thoughts, feelings or actions, and that's proving to be a far scarier realisation than my life ending.

ii) Saying goodbye to the bird

As if sensing that I won't be around much longer, or sensing the tension in the house, the bird has gone for good. I last saw it just under a week ago. Since then I've been leaving the window open ajar, braving the fearsome February cold for several days, but there's been no return visit - bringing the rest of the house and I slowly round to the realisation that he probably won't be coming back. I gather that it's nothing personal; he's reached an age and level of health where he should really prioritise finding a real family, or living a life that isn't based so close to human comforts. The small, half-dead thing that had landed on my windowsill had gone a long time ago, anyway. It had been replaced with a real life bird. It grew and learnt to fly. It stopped moving with awkwardly slow gestures and began to tick like a wind-up toy. Its every twinge had a jerkiness to it, as if it were an animated character from a cheap, 1960s cartoon. Or as if it simply lived in a world that ran quicker than ours. I imagine it thought we lived our lives in slow motion.

He'll probably end up back in the loft, such is the circle of life.

I'll miss him, though. Such moments were few and far between since he first crash-landed, but whenever the bird and I were in the room together he had become a sort of unwitting psychiatrist. Times have been troubling and confusing recently at levels that I'm sure go against parameters set out by the Treaty of Versailles, so it was unendingly therapeutic to have something to talk to. Especially something that wouldn't then pass judgement. Obviously this book has been a godsend in keeping me going, but there's no underestimating the value of vocal release. I would spend many evenings on my bed gently chatting to the small grey-brown creature as it tweaked and fiddled with the clothing and rags that made up its nest. Having the bird gave me something else to pass on morals and life stories to, but much more importantly it gave me something to be responsible for, and for a short while something that needed me to be there for it to continue living.

I can only hope that, wherever he is, he gets over his rocky start to life and has a better time of things from now on than I have of late. I don't profess to knowing what constitutes a good-looking bird, but he grew rapidly into a fine specimen with nought noticeably wrong with him, so I've every confidence that he'll find himself a nice wife without much problem and manage to father a handsome set of kids thereafter - each probably genetically inclined to fall onto the windowsill where their dad started off. It's quite sad to think that I won't be here to see it happen, or to foster the next generation of clumsy chicks.

Jenny was rather upset when I told her the news - surprisingly so. For someone who'd originally abhorred the idea of me keeping the thing locked up in my room, she'd come to see it over time as some sort of house mascot. Tim liked it too, and tried on many occasions to convince me that we should call it Brian. I've remained staunchly adamant that it simply be called 'The Bird', and felt that I had the casting vote since I was basically its dad. Giving it a proper name would only have made it harder to say goodbye, anyway.

May, having been my assistant of sorts during those crucial first few hours, had since lived a very separate life from the bird due to the distance between her and myself. Even so, I'd occasionally notice new items in his makeshift nest that had no doubt come from her. We'd all contributed over time to making the young thing comfortable, resulting in a nest compiled from scraps of cloths and clothes, bits of magazines and anything else we thought he might find snug. May's contributions usually came from the gossip magazines she reads (but claims she doesn't). As if aiming to keep the bird abreast of goings on in the celebrity world, she would cut out amusing headlines as strips of paper and litter them around the nest. The bird either greatly enjoyed all of these contributions or found them a terrible annoyance - it's hard to say. His frantic fiddling and organising was therapeutic to watch, but without a detailed knowledge of ornithological behaviour it was always difficult to tell whether he was having the time of his life or merely doing the bird equivalent of weeding the garden. It's nicer to think that we didn't spend our time making his life harder, obviously. Either way, all in the house now suddenly feel at a loss.

The most intensive thing I've had to do today was to decide what to do with the now vacant nest - a task that involved a lot of standing around, leering over the item in question and looking pensive. I felt as I imagine parents do when their child either leaves home or unexpectedly dies, which forced me to look round my own room and envisage the chore my poor friends are soon going to be faced with. As previously mentioned, I'll gift them all enough money to continue living here without having to fill the room, but that means it'll be an empty space with all my stuff cluttered up inside it.

The only two options facing parents in matters such as these are:

• Keep the room exactly as it was the second the child left, forever

• Box up everything and turn the room into a gym

This situation doesn't leave any room for middle-ground options. It's all-or-nothing. Or rather: nothing-or-all. Arguments for the former include sentimentality and the worry that whomever has left will either come back or look down from above judgingly for their having moved on so swiftly. Arguments for the latter include a logical and forthright understanding of 'moving on', knowing that doing so entails purging one's surroundings of items reminiscent of the departed.

In all likelihood, the bird would think I was daft for holding onto a nest that he's no intention of coming back to, and I think the same should probably be said of my room. I doubt very much that the bird's nest contained an even smaller abode for an injured tick he was nursing back to health, but such a scenario would be the only one I can think of where it'd be worth keeping everything as is - out of appreciation for poetic irony and the many layers of life. You could turn the whole thing into an art instillation or something.

It's an ego-boosting notion to think that people might miss you with such fierce intensity that the best way to save their fragile brain from further trauma would be to keep your room frozen in time, but there's a much bigger argument for letting people get on with their own lives and for moving forward. Throwing a homemade nest in the bin with a melancholic expression plastered over your face is, of course, an entirely different and less distressing process than slowly clearing out everything a dead loved-one ever owned, from a room that smells like them, but I can only imagine that that procedure in itself would provide such a needed blast of closure and grievance that it's entirely necessary.

Shortly before removing the nest, I asked Tim

whether or not he thinks I should keep it. His reply was short, straightforward and (for once), helpful. He said:

"I went back home for a weekend just after I'd finished Uni. My Mum and Dad had rented out my room to a middle-aged Caribbean man with a wooden leg, without telling me. I didn't mind because she used the money to put me up in a Holiday Inn, which was a lot comfier than my bed was anyway. And it had porn on the TV."

At any rate, I shall miss the bird. He was a friend, pet and child all in one tiny body; he was a patient and loved one. I hope, for what it's worth, that he outlives me and cultivates a family. I shall miss you, bird. You grew into a wonderful thing: a creature with full control over his own life.

iii) Twill

Just twill and rotten rags it was,

Just jaunted cloths and twine.

Outstripping plume on fragile bone

this home with quick design

Bound together out of need

And fed with softened leaf

A warm and dry recovery

Away from lofty grief.

Juxtaposed the barbing red

And wing that snapped in two

Made from lukewarm weavings, it's

the best that we could do.

Discreetly growing, fixing though,

The bits that nearly broke.

Catching up with squatted home

My feathered, blooded, yoke

My bird soon jutted upwards and

With deftly braving strides

Took towards the brick-red flume

With weighty adult pride

The plumage had now far besmirched

This grotty, knotted twill

And painted him in flying stripes

As well as growing skill.

The plumage had now far outclassed

This weaving, clumping twill

And gifted him his airborne right

To leave my windowsill

12. MARCH

<u>Shopping:</u>

Tea
Milk
Sugar
Fruit
Biscuits
Vitamins
Beer
Cheese
Frozen meat
No more gin

<u>Things learned:</u>

- If you're lucky enough to have had a nice sum of money injected into your account by your bank, keep exceedingly quiet about it. In all likelihood they won't pick you up on it.

- Despite a profound lack of medical training or anatomical understanding, I am fully capable of fixing broken bones to the point where the patient can then go on and live a normal life.

- I was a lot more attached to the bird living in my bedroom than I thought I was.

<u>Favourite Text:</u>

Jenny: "Why is my boyfriend so incapable of tending this bar like a normal human being? There are only three people here and he looks like he's about to break down and cry."

i) Two-for-one

March brings with it the promise of Spring. At the end of this month the clocks will change, bringing an extra hour of light to the currently temperate British evenings. Eventually, the nights will etch further and further back towards midnight, and daylight will persist in larger dribs and drabs. It ekes out summer at a rate of around four minutes per night, but I don't think I'll be around for that. At best, I'll be alive just long enough to see the days lengthen slightly. And perhaps a couple of weeks of the heatwave that, over the last few years, April has brought with it. Time is speeding up. Everything is running at a frantic pace and the only things that serve to slow it down are writing and drinking. When big events happen, they happen quickly. The following is a sentence that I didn't think I'd ever get to write:

It was with one final talk and a barrage of sexual tension that the walls between May and I finally fell over, letting in wave after wave of passionate kisses.

I've spoken before about sticking firmly to the truth in this book, which has meant that being able to describe May and I kissing wasn't something I thought I'd be able to enjoy doing ever again. It happened though. It happened and it's all I can think about, so I feel its more than worthy of being the opening of what's likely to be a very short passage of text, due mostly to it being the first thing I felt inclined to type when I sat down to type. That and some preamble about Spring. I'll try and explain how that sentence came to be as best I can, but I'm still hot-off-the-heels of a late night, much booze and a strong punch to the romantic part of my brain, so you'll have to forgive me if I sound any more stupid than usual.

Last night was a birthday do for Katherine, a mutual friend of our house. Cocktails and dancing. Following the usual drill, the four of us consumed endless bottles of wine and listened to loud music as we suited and booted. We arrived just late enough for it to stop being fashionable, said our hellos and gave over birthday wishes. The place we were in had a 'buy one get one free' offer going on cocktails, but an evangelistic approach to the 'drink responsibly' slogan meant they wouldn't sell two cocktails to just one person, so I ended up having to give one of mine to May to avoid having them both taken off me.

My point was going to be that handing May my spare drink was the most we've spoken for several days, but reading back it looks like I'm setting up to tell you that I slipped her some Rohypnol. I'd like to make it explicitly clear that <u>I did not slip May some Rohypnol</u>. I'm a stupid person but I'm not rapist-stupid.

At any rate, we all drank and danced and talked and had a good time, and Tim (having adequate experience of doing so in the past) helped me stay with a sub-circle of friends that was separate from May from then on. I avoided her quite successfully for most of the evening. I wasn't doing this to hurt her or prove any kind of point, you must understand; the reason for my avoiding her was simply and truthfully because it was easier for me not to have to see her. I struggle to think what I'd have been able to say to her in any case, and doing so would only have made me feel worse about having put her in this situation as it is.

From the safety of our subtle, separate factions the evening passed without incident, which (as with any group of adult friends) renders it a bloody successful night. We reluctantly night-bussed it home and each went to bed, exhausted. Or at least that's what I thought we'd done. What had actually happened was that Tim had collapsed on the floor of his and Jenny's bedroom, while his girlfriend and May sat and had a very heartfelt chat. When May knocked on my door half an hour later, it was the result of a talk that had seen Jenny finally tell her to do what she and everyone else knew to be right, and come up to see me. May had been just as frightened as I'd thought, but a little stronger against that fear than I'd originally given her credit for.

I let her in and she asked if we could talk. My theory on 'can we talk' - that it usually signposts a bad conversation - throbbed inside my head and suddenly the ceiling did that lowering thing again that made the room an unsettling place to be. May sank gently into my desk chair and span back and forth in neat quarter-circles opposite me. I perched on the edge of the bed. It felt like it would be a perch-worthy talk, and one must never underestimate the importance of a straight back in conducting a strong argument. I won't lie: I was taken aback by what she had to say.

"Alan," she started. "I've been thinking a lot about what's happened between us, and how awkward things have been, and I think you're right."

"Right about what?" My back stiffened more, as if I'd suddenly been struck across the shoulder blades.

"About us. I know that I've been too scared, you know? I know now… that you're mine."

Forgive me for not remembering much more of the back and forth that went on for the following ten or so minutes. What's written above is what I remember, but I'm not about to start making things up for the sake of injecting dialogue. Suffice to say, there were many prolonged silences snagged between serious words, and moments where we both went to speak at the same time, caught sight of each other's drawn breath and stopped. She said she wanted to be with me but didn't want it to end badly; that she couldn't face losing me again.

My heart jumped into that specially-carved space in my throat and, for a reason that I don't think I'll ever be able to understand, I told her that it wouldn't.

"Do you want me?" I asked, frankly.

May said that she did, and started to roll off a list of more ifs and buts. It was too late; as soon as I'd had it confirmed that (in theory at least) she wanted to be with me, I launched out of my seat and caught her mid-sentence with a kiss. She kissed back like it was the first and last time we'd ever do it. I don't think I've ever felt as good in my entire life. More than this book, the friends I'd made and the family I'd loved, that moment made everything leading up to it, and the short time that'll follow after, all completely worthwhile and indescribably important.

We kissed for hours. It was daylight by the time everything had stopped swirling madly round in blurred circles, and we laid there in each other's arms for the better part of the entire day - the most satisfied with life I've ever felt, and will therefore ever feel.

ii) You can't make an omelettey mess without cracking a tonne of eggs

Quite obviously, you should disregard the previous few chapters and stop reading if you want to leave off with anything approaching a positive opinion of me as a human man. I do appreciate, however, that it might already be too late to change your view, in which case you'd better read on as I try hopelessly to somehow justify my actions. Thinking about it, maybe I should cut this paragraph out and put it as a warning at an earlier stage? Like at the end of the first chapter? All things considered, it seems likely that it probably *is* too late to do anything about my poor choices and your view of them, so you'd best read on regardless. You can be judge, jury and executioner if you please - although the latter third has already been done for you, so you can put the axe away...

***

I have concocted more plans and ideas whilst lying in bed at night than any human man could put into motion even with the luxury of a full and particularly active life. For some unknown reason, when the comfort of the duvet surrounds me and the world is shut out by pitch blackness, it's incredibly easy to envision myself doing something that - come daylight - I realise I'd never actually do. I imagine it's the same for everyone, though. You might, for instance, decide in bed that you should join a gym. This seed of an idea will flourish into a full-blown plan of action for how to turn yourself into a muscular Adonis, complete with a vivid mental montage of you working out and pumping iron to inspirational music. Come morning you'll realise the major flaw in your plan: you're lazy. Likewise, whilst in bed it can seem likely - no; *certain* - that you'll march right up to the person you're secretly enamoured with and tell them you love them the very next morning. Morning breaks and you remember you're a coward.

I don't know what it is about the night that instils such inappropriate confidence in our abilities, but I hate it. The night is a lying, falsely encouraging bastard.

Last night I was lying awake in bed as May slept next to me. I laid my hand on the groove where her waist pulls in between her hips and her chest and gently stroked her pale, soft skin. I shifted upwards began slowly stroking her short, black hair, which - with the benefit of being sans bandages - now looked even more gorgeous and right than I ever thought it had. Since meeting May her thick, long hair has shortened to a boyish cut, and my boyish bonce had lengthened to a bohemian shag; if that's not sufficient personal journeying to count as 'character development', I don't know what is. I fingered through her locks and hated myself.

How different would things be if my illness showed any tangible physical symptoms? I'd not be able to hide anything then; everyone would know that I was very clearly on the way out and I'd be the subject of some seriously ill-deserved sympathy. Aside from the obvious pain and discomfort that such symptoms would bring, it strikes me that the illness making my mind up for me would have been fucking bliss. I wondered how different things would be if I weren't ill at all. If that were the case then I'd have everything I ever wanted with absolutely nothing to feel ashamed or disgusted or scared about. A month suddenly seemed like a dreadfully short amount of time and, for the first time, I really wished that the doctor was wrong. I closed my eyes to a tight squint, concentrated painfully hard and wished. For the first time, I really wished I could live.

Is lying to every single person you know - holding out on revealing that you're dying until you actually do die - worth it for the continuity and sanctity of a book? At the start of all this I thought it was. I justified it with totally selfish reasons regarding what I believed to be art. If we're being honest, I could have probably written a book about anything. I could have written a book about magical elves that had to battle a huge monster, or save their town, or take a road trip to Vegas. I could have written a book about Mr X and Mrs Y falling in love, without it necessarily being my doomed relationship with May, completely verbatim. Moreover, if I were a good writer it definitely *would* have been one of those things. As it stands it's the diary and last testament of a man who painted himself into a moral corner, refusing to get his feet wet to walk himself out of it, despite having more than enough time to do so.

What's sad is that despite all these realisations, *and* the bold claims of living for the now and without constraints, I still can't tell them - out of nothing but a fear that they'll hate me. How pathetic is that?

It's more than that fear though, isn't it?

Is it?

I genuinely don't know. I'd really like to think it's more a case of me not telling them for a sense of closure on the challenge I set myself that windy afternoon in Hyde Park. I've now happily resigned myself to the fact that my initial decision was wrong, but - out of a bizarre mix of the aforementioned fear and sense of accomplishment - I feel like I must keep the lies going. I'm now living by waiting for the right moment to run off to die like an injured cat. This is not a good way to live.

When I started this book, the egotistical part of me

had ideas on being canonised in eternity, as some kind of hero of the modern man - a mythical tour de force in contemporary literature. Through no one's fault but my own, this hasn't exactly come to pass. In discovering as much about myself as I have, I've realised that all the stupid human bits of my brain I thought dying would silence are by far stronger than anything else in my personality. I do incredibly selfish and stupid things, and I do them often. I am not a hero; not a modern legend. I am not even a particularly nice man.

The problem is probably that I am a man in the first place. Humans are nothing if not flawed; when it comes down to it, self-serving personal desires are what drives me, and I hope to god that they're what drives everyone else too. If I can believe that everyone else would pick themselves over others only half as much as I do, then I wouldn't die loathing myself in quite the dramatic fashion I currently do.

It's a bit scary, really. The point of this book should have been to discover, experience and describe in my last year of life all the wonderful, magical things that humans do and are capable of, but I've fallen at the first hurdle by exposing myself as a truly nasty piece of work. The book's only real purpose of late seems to be as a vehicle for apologising and explaining my actions, all a pretty futile attempt at absolving myself of responsibility for treating everyone like idiots.

Some people are never happy, I suppose. I've wanted for so long to be able to lie with May again as lovers, but now I've got there I'm struggling to deal with it. It'd be perfect if it weren't for the trifling matter of my health. Hurting and lying to May is obviously terrible, but the damage won't just be confined to one person in the long run. One person would be OK - manageable. The extent of my secrets spreads across a big group of friends too, remember. And Granddad - who, unless he dies within the next 30 days, is more than likely to outlive every single member of our family. That's probably not a thought anyone should have to live with. Or die with.

Tim and Jenny, too will probably need a fair chunk of time to turn anger into sorrow. The whole situation is ridiculous and the more I think about it the less able I am to fathom why I've done and continue to do it to myself and those around me.

I used to struggle with cross country running at school at all stages of the race, but my aching legs and pounding heart would always turn into boulders the second I could see the finish line. Every race gets harder when the end's in sight because you know you'll soon be able to, or have to, stop. With the final weeks seemingly flying by, I've found myself questioning my motives and my sanity with equal weight and intensity. Everything's broken in my brain and its all playing through in a manner almost as dramatic as I make it sound. The only things I know I've done well in the recent past are:

• Feed myself

- Drink alcohol, take recreational drugs

- Walk and talk when needed without falling over

- Paint the living room

- Buy some plates

Not an overwhelming list; I'm sure you'll agree. The only thing I've managed to do consistently well over the last *year* is lie. I've mastered the art of deception - something I could have put up on the list (and 'deception' is a nine letter word so I'd score well for it), but it's a word I've been doing my best to avoid using. Deception it is though, clearly. The Deceptive Death Of Alan Bell.

You know that sinking, dangerous feeling you get crawling around your innards when you lie? It's the fear brought on by living in the time between telling the lie and the lie being found out. That time could last a lifetime or an hour, but it is always finite; the lie will *always* get found out, and the horrible feeling is you knowing that when it does you'll be in a (varying) degree of trouble. I'm not saying 'don't ever lie', because lies are an integral part of living with other humans. I merely want you, dear reader, to understand that I've been living in that terrifying space now for almost a year, and it's a horrible place to be.

Some sound advice: if you do *need* to lie, please don't do so with such a wild untruth that you'll go down in history as a deceptive bastard - especially if you're going to be so impressively stupid as to write a book as evidence chronicling your malevolence.

Back in the bedroom, I turned to face May as she slept - watching her for as long as I could stay awake. As still as she was, there was something hugely different about how she rested compared to when she was just a breathing body in a hospital bed. I wished that Monty could meet her. Maybe, somehow, after I'm dead they'll track him down and he'll fight my corner as everyone else shouts horrible words and throws faecal matter at my grave. I wished the bird could see us. I wished he could see the resolution of everything I'd spent endless hours talking to him about.

In the hospital, the empty girl in the bed next to my seat would sit and listen to me talk about all the surreal facets of my life. It made me truly appreciate how much talking helps council people; it's by far and away the most natural and satisfying way to vent. The bedroom felt ominously silent by comparison - the one constant being the steady sound of May breathing.

I wished she was truly unconscious again, just for half an hour or so. There were plenty of new things I'd love to talk to her about, all on a topic of conversation I'd only like to open if I was sure there wouldn't be any ramifications or arguments. Telling the truth is so much easier when you're cushioned by the safety of the other party not actually being able to hear what you're saying.

I pulled my fingers from her tousled hair and let out the quietest of whispers.

"Sorry," I said, desperately. She didn't stir.

iii) Keep calm and carry on

'Unseasonable warmth' is probably how you'd best describe it; a window of a few days wherein late March is basically August and jumpers turn into halternecks and t-shirts. Given the choice, I'm more inclined to wear the latter.

We made a conscious decision to make the most of it as only the British know how; by staying out until it's far too cold to still be wearing a t-shirt (or halterneck) and waking up the next day having been scarred with horrible sunburn.

"Alan Bell."

"Sounds familiar," I replied.

"Do..." She stopped talking.

"What?" I asked, digging my chin down into my neck to see all I could of her. She was draped across me in some anonymous field in Hampstead Heath, and from that position all I could manage to see was the top of her head as it lay facing sideways, from a distance of about half a centimetre. I kissed her hair.

"No it doesn't matter."

"Oh you can't do that," I declared.

"Do what?"

"You can't start asking me a question and then stop. It's only going to make me want to know what you wanted to know more than ever." Convoluted sentence, but true nonetheless; I had to know what she was going to ask. I'd have killed to know. She slid round to face me, propped herself up on her elbows and gave me a kiss. Her elbows concentrated all her weight into two small points on my chest and it bloody well hurt, but I tried not to let that show.

"No it's really wanky."

"Then I definitely need to know. What was it? Do I...?" She was always going to tell me, but it was clearly one of those things where pretending that you won't at first - that you'd thought better of it - would adequately excuse you from any possible embarrassment.

"OK FINE. Do you... think we're... like..." she did little inverted commas with her fingers. "'...Meant to be?'"

I smiled a stupid, stupid grin and May Cooper dug her beautiful face into my neck, as if trying to escape from her own words. "I can't believe I actually just said that."

A moment passed where I didn't say anything, she didn't say anything and we both lay there motionless in the evening sun. It was about four o'clock and, while there were less people around than there had been earlier in the day, we seemed to be surrounded by couples. Perhaps they were all having the same conversation as us, caught up in the romance of a sunny Spring eve in the park and each loose-lipped enough from wine to start getting all lovey-dovey. Perhaps.

"Honestly?" I said, "I've thought about it."

"And?" She lifted her head to look at me expectantly.

"I don't know." She dropped down again sharply. "I try not to think about stuff like that too much because when I do I get too rational, but..."

"But?"

"But... I dunno. Maybe there are, say, 15 people in the world during your lifetime that you're perfect for, and it's amazing luck if you find one of them."

Then, in a moment of Hollywood romanticism the likes of which I never thought I'd actually be part of, I looked her dead in the eye and, trying to sound soft yet masculine, loving yet cool, said: "I think I've found one in you."

I think this was enough. We both stopped talking and kissed. We kissed for a long time, with a perfect balance of love and physical attraction driving each new kiss from the end of the last. It made my lips sore in the best possible way, and for a lengthy window of time in a warm and still March evening, everything was right, everything was as it should be and everything was finally brilliant.

"I suppose I agree," she said after a while, sitting up to scan around. "It's just... don't you ever feel like we're... a bit... better than everyone else?" She bit her lip and looked at me worriedly as soon as the words left her - guilty for having said them. I knew exactly what she meant, but felt hungry for compliments and longed for her to elaborate.

"How so?"

"It's just. This. Us. It's just amazing. Like we're a better couple than them." She pointed across at another couple, who were lying together just like we'd been. "Or them," she continued, "or... especially them."

"I know what you mean. This..." I rubbed my face up against hers so our cheeks were touching, my mouth pressing against her ear, "just feels very right." We hugged.

In the cold light of the morning after it's easy to imagine that every other couple in the field was having the same conversation, all wrapped up in that arrogance that love and warm weather so expertly brings to a couple's view of themselves. But if they *were* having that same conversation then I can quite expertly say that they were wrong and we were right. Or more specifically: May was right. We are special and better. We're better than the world. We're better than any description of love that anyone has ever managed to dump together using useless, useless words. We have one of those 'through the ages' kind of loves that you feel the entire world deserves to know about. It should be plastered across the front page of every newspaper. 'THIS IS IT,' the headlines would read; this is the very definition of love, made so real and powerful by Alan Bell and May Cooper that those outside can only read about and hope to one day experience even a tenth of it. A hundredth of it. May Cooper and Alan Bell love each other in a way that was completely right. It was as much a real and powerful force as gravity. It took forever to get here, and then it took mere moments. And it just felt so right.

It would all be so perfect if only I weren't lying to her, and if only I weren't so soon going to have to leave. And if only – if fucking only – I wasn't going to die.

Tim and Jenny toddled back towards us. They'd been sat for a while on Kite Hill, where the view of London rumbles on for miles, dotted with tall buildings and netted in smoggy mist. May saw them coming from a way off, turned to me, kissed me once again and said quietly and hurriedly:

"I'm sorry this took so long. I was a bit of an idiot but we got here in the end. I'm yours, Mr Bell, and I'm not going anywhere."

As we sat, a chaffinch landed nearby. It jerked and danced about and rubbed its head on the grass, before quickly fluttering up onto a nearby branch. From there, the little thing looked about with its brash movements and clockwork ticks - first at the horizon and then, for a while, at us. I won't insult your intelligence or mine by pretending it was our bird, but it didn't really need to be. Just looking at this creature, for barely a minute, reminded me of something important: despite myself, I have done at least one good thing in the past year.

iv) For the reader

Things are genuinely getting quite scary now. Knowing that death could strike through the window and knock me down at pretty much any time has made me become noticeably ill with stress and fatigue. Having never taken a massive interest in them before, I can't tell if my hands *are* now any different than they used to be, but they look thinly skinned, or the veins more obvious somehow. May says I should stop worrying about whatever it is I'm worrying about - even if I don't want to tell her what it is - because it's made me lose anything resembling an appetite. I promised I would. She's also asked that I cut back on the drinking, which I thought I had anyway. Suffice to say; it's embarrassing when your girlfriend tells you that you drink too much, so I promised to give it a bit of a rest.

"Thanks," she said. "I just love you, and worry about you. You know?"

I did know.

***

I'm leaving soon. I don't know exactly when because it usually takes around two days after I initially say I'll do something for me to actually do it. Thus, I've not put a date on it because there's not much point. Every time I walk into my room my eyes are drawn to the suitcase that's vaguely visible under my bed. It stares back in sympathetic acknowledgement of our upcoming journey together. I'd pictured leaving home with one of those polka-dotted sacks tied to the end of a big stick - the kind prevalent in hill-billy American stories - but there's enough that I'd like to take with me to whatever hospice I decide to check into to necessitate a suitcase.

It's a nice suitcase, anyway; it's leather. I suspect that if someone took a picture of me hitch-hiking whilst carrying it, it would make quite a good album cover. At some point soon I'll have to drag it out, fill it and quickly disappear, which - despite having been the plan for quite some time now - is a terrifying prospect. The last year has been a bit like when you embark on a long school holiday or exciting chapter of your life; people say it'll fly by but at the start it seems like it'll last forever. It comes round soon enough, though. This has come round more than soon enough.

Needless to say, talking and being with May is proving hard. The relationship, as far as she's concerned, is going perfectly; we laugh, we talk, we dance (a bit) and generally have a lot of fun, but underneath it's all cracking into shards. It's to the point where I almost can't wait to leave just to stop having to lie to her. I've got her back and she loves me - she told me so - but I'm so upset by the situation and that I can barely say it back. My heart is in bloody ruins. Tim mentioned the other day that in the summer we should organise a trip to a theme park. I silently agreed, nearly imploding with guilt. Shit, as they say, has suddenly gotten very real.

You'd be surprised at how often we as people talk about the future. You probably haven't noticed because you're not actively aware that you won't be around when the time in question came, but it's all the bloody time, trust me. I keep having to swallow down spongy lumps of regret. Jenny too, who's become nothing short of a surrogate mother to me whilst I've 'felt under the weather' is an amazing person to have to leave forever. She's got into the habit in the evenings of making me sandwiches for the following day's lunch when she makes hers. One day my sandwich just won't get eaten and they'll all be at a loss not only as to why, but to where exactly I am. The whole thing's a mess and I'm sorry, I truly am.

For quite some time now there's been a wholly negative vibe running through the narrative of this book. I've written at length about what a terrible man I am and revelled in the relieving self-pity that jotting everything down allows. That said, I'm very aware and concerned that for you, dear reader, what started out as a jovial read about a dying man who would try and do some interesting things has swiftly turned into a wallowing, depressing uphill struggle - meandering turgidly between apology and yet more wrongdoing. While there's an argument in suggesting that if you've made it this far you'd probably sit through another hundred pages of self-hatred without breaking sweat, we're coming towards the end now so I should probably try and lift your spirits a bit. If only as thanks for putting up with everything. *I* didn't know what I was getting myself in for at the start, after all, so I'd be pretty amazed if you did.

We'd best talk about the positives: what I've learnt, my achieved objectives, and what's been good about my last year on earth.

Firstly, I should probably question how successful this whole thing is as a book. A while back I declared that I wanted it to be seen more as a story than a diary, which is still true. My initial aim of leaving something behind that wouldn't die quite as easily or quickly as I have has always been very important. There'd be nothing more tragic than a wannabe author dying before having written a book, no matter how poor and morally dubious his efforts.

Luckily for me and my complete lack of

imagination, the necessary tropes of an interesting story (conflicts, character growth etc.) have all been put nicely in place for me over the course of the year, with minimal effort on my behalf. Primarily there was May, whom I met and moved in with because things were all decided and arranged by people with a more active interest in living comfortably than I could ever pretend to have or act on. I swiftly and irrevocably fell in love with the girl, but - like all the best love stories - things haven't always run smoothly. Saying that our relationship has at times been a bit rocky is like saying that London is a bit livelier than the Sahara desert, which ticks a promising amount of boxes on the 'love story' checklist. I'd decided it would be as such some time ago, though - that's why I dedicated more page space to May's terrible accident and our ups and downs than I did to, say, going to the shops (which I've done lots).

The problem is that I've crafted this doomed romance with the help of real life events, and now that it's so close to the end that I can almost hear funeral music, I just know that it's not going to end in a satisfying way for you, the reader. I truly don't mean to trivialise the horrible thing I'm doing to May and my friends. I know it's terrible. But striving to make this book a good book is one of the only ways I can get my mind off it - not to mention that doing so is the only way I can think of to justify my actions up until this point. The point is this: other than downing tools and running away in a blurry slither of tweed and hair, I've simply no idea how to put a finish to it.

I suppose at this stage in the game I should just be

happy that I've managed to write such a grand amount of words without it just being my own name over and over again, even if I have used the letter 'I' approximately nine billion times.

And at least I'm aware of my own shortcomings.

Forgive me for sounding like a teacher or snobby superior, but (assuming you count yourself as having actually benefited in any conceivable way from reading this) one of the biggest things from this year that I'd like you to take away with you is a better grasp of how people react in unusual situations, and when their personal wants and needs jostle for the deciding vote. I've learnt a hell of a lot more about the human mind than I ever thought I would, or perhaps wanted to. I know I've always been naïve and idealistic about things, but when we started I was genuinely under the impression that knowing my sell-by date would free me up to do whatever the bloody hell I liked without caring about the social - or even legal - effects. This wasn't the case at all and shows a profound lack of understanding of one thing: fear.

The way humans live together now - under such civilised social rule - really does make it hard to do anything out of the ordinary without a lot of scary ramifications. I know that cause and effect dictates everything in the universe, but when it's applied to a social scenario the effects that your causes *affect* make it very hard to do anything brave, even with such a heightened sense of mortality. True: it *could* just be me being a coward; it *could* be the case that knowledge of an imminent end in different hands would have led to headline-making activities and daredevil japes, but I'm willing to bet almost everything I own that it's not and that it wouldn't. I gather it's all just a condition of the way we're brought up and programmed. What I've learnt is that being scared of telling certain people certain (read: difficult) things, or acting out of your normal realm of comfort, is not necessarily something that's made easier by knowing you're about to die. Thus, I can only conclude that it's up to *everyone* to live each day like it's your last. If we all did that then doing the things we're scared of wouldn't be anywhere near as scary, even if it would mean we'd probably all be a lot less polite.

Trying to make sense of society as a whole has been one of my favourite games. All I can really conclude is that human beings are a fascinatingly bizarre species - one that really shouldn't:

A) Have gotten as far as we have

B) Be allowed to carry on as we are

And

C) Go unsupervised, ever.

We're a scared, selfish, brutish, hateful, confused and clumsy species who live all clumped together by virtue of an archaic concept of 'safety in numbers', and also the fact that some people are better at some things than others - despite most of us not really liking or understanding anyone else. It's a system that works, but only barely. We've introduced and enforced laws that try and keep us on the straight and narrow, under the idealistic understanding that things'll be better if only we all sit down, behave and try to learn about trivial stuff and better ourselves. This, even though our media spends most of its time glorifying the stupid, the pretty and the talentless. It's all strangely beautiful to look at when you take a step back, as I sometimes - only sometimes - have done. The best bit about all of it though, is that as much as the human race can seem like an innately ghastly and wasteful disease on the planet's surface, our ability to love makes us appear entirely special and magical.

Love, as it turns out, is a frighteningly powerful thing, and it's taken a stranglehold on this book. Don't worry: I don't intend to go on at length about it here as I've already done so, but in both loving and being loved properly for the first time, it's become the most important thing in not only this book but in my final year of life as a whole. It's an embarrassingly obvious and clumsy conclusion to reach, but if I had to summarise what I've learned about love, it would be this:

When you have, or are the benefactor of, true love, you can feel it as much as you can feel anything in the physical realm - and you'd kill to keep it. No matter how strong or free of boundaries you think you are, love can and will make you do deeply, overwhelmingly stupid things. No matter how unusual the circumstance, human beings are incapable of ignoring what the heart wants. We're slaves to that - slaves to the most powerful, profound and ill-understood force there is.

More than my uninformed philosophising and hypocritical evangelism, though - more than anything else at all, really - what I'd really like in the end is for you to treat this book as a window into the life of a young man who you'll never meet, and who never really did much to change the world whilst he could. For better or worse, I've always been honest in these pages, resulting (again, for better or worse) in a body of work that is totally, completely and irrefutably the written from of the mind and soul of the now deceased Alan Bell. It's a body of work I can only hope you've enjoyed. There will be no twist ending; no magical cure. The words will simply peter out and I will leave. But I do hope you've enjoyed it.

We're not quite done yet; I'm giving myself another week or so. But this seems like as good a time as any to say a heartfelt 'thanks' to you, my dear reader. It's been an absolute, unmatched pleasure.

13. APRIL (Again)

Shopping:

Tea
Milk
Fruit
Vitamins
Beer
Gin for the road

Things learned:

- I do, as it turns out, have the ability to finish something I've started.

Favourite Text:

May: "I love you too."

i) The thing inside

We're very fragile things, human beings. We're the summation of slippery bags sewn to ivory twigs and wrapped in a leathery film. A knock or fall of even the slightest nature can break any part of that delicate structure, or kill it outright. Likewise, a tiny virus smaller than we're able to see can nest within and crash the entire galumphing system. When you think about how stunningly dangerous the modern world is, it becomes a surprise that people aren't dying left, right and centre in far larger numbers.

If you really wanted to, it'd be frighteningly easy to make yourself dead. What with cars essentially being speedy death wagons, trains being the same only larger and faster; and knives, rope and medicinal pills being easily attainable, it's madness that we don't take going out into the world on a daily basis much more seriously. Venturing to the shops should be a task met with careful planning and the correct level of protection. We're so complacent about meandering through the streets and standing on platforms next to speeding trains that by rights, death should be happening all around us at all times.

It's this thinking that makes me question the intellectual prowess of anyone who fails a suicide attempt. I'm no fan of suicide (it's just lazy living), but - should it be your aim - it seems impossible to be unable to put a world wrought with peril to effective use. It's like being in a kitchen and failing to cook a meal. People who *do* kill themselves are selfish anyway; it's not as if some of us have the choice.

I have - as you know - spent some time questioning what happens after death. I've still not made my mind up as to whether it'll be God waiting for me when I go or a grave-full of hungry maggots. Should the latter turn out to be the case, I don't think I'll ever be able to comprehend the notion of not existing any more. Or certainly not in less than a month, at any rate. When you're born you come into life following nine months of energetic growing. What I technically *was* before that, though, is anyone's guess. I don't imagine 'not existing' is a concept that any human mind is able to fully grasp, due to the fact that we're all so egotistic, but it's frightening to think of a time before you, erm... 'were'. The same is true for birth, death, the beginning of the universe and what happens in every part of the world that you can't see from where you are. It's all very frustrating to not know.

I suppose that's as good a segue as any on to the subject of drugs (it's not, clearly, but I've all but given up caring). I've mentioned my occasional recreational use before and promised myself that at some point down the line I'd explain the full extent of it.

I find it quite hard to talk about drug use without sounding massively hypocritical. In the extremes, hard drugs can be tremendously harmful to you and (in some cases) those around you. I suppose that where you draw the line all boils down to figuring out what you think we're all on this planet for in the first place. What I mean is: should you be the ant, working hard and getting the most out of life in a traditional sense; or the grasshopper, who gets stoned off his tits long and hard enough to avoid any of the pain and hardship that life can often throw at you?

I reckon that if you have a desire to cultivate human relationships *and* have a good time of life, it's probably best to maintain a happy medium between the two, but I suspect that the latter attitude is becoming more and more favourable as people become less god-fearing and more aware that ,in many areas, society is flawed beyond repair. As it is, I partake in occasional and balanced usage of cannabis and impressive amounts of alcohol, topped off with obscene amounts of caffeine to fill in the valley carved by the first two. It's a cocktail that leaves off hard drugs for reasons to do with money, fear and what my social circle finds appropriate. I agree that a dying man should probably adopt a more willing attitude to new things, but I've stuck to marijuana because it, at least, comes out of the ground without the need for a chemical lab.

Drugs have been rife in civilisation since civilisation began, which leads me to think that it's only the will of 'sophisticated' governments that's deemed them 'wrong' and has painted that opinion onto the face of the masses. I don't mean to start a revolution myself (I haven't the funds, the military contacts or the time), but I'd suggest that, so long as you inform people of the risks and benefits with equal aplomb, it's only right to let grown adults get on with whatever it is they want to do. It'd be interesting to see how different the world would be if cannabis were as common as grass. There'd probably be less in the way of buildings, technological progress and general get-up-and-go, but there'd most likely be a lot less war as well.

Unless mass paranoia set in, of course.

Health - and the battle for it - has had a constant place in all human history. In the extreme, disease has culled both civilisations and young writers - acting as a natural defence against over-population. Of course, since we've all become genius chemists things have changed. There are still enough diseases and illnesses kicking about to kill people of all walks of life (of which I am evidence), but we've got to a point where we actually understand why that is, instead of hastily blaming God or something vaguely faux-science like 'imbalanced toxins'. Crucially, we understand the human body a lot better than we did even 20 years ago. This means that we're able to fix simple ailments that in days of yore would've killed off even the hardiest of men, and also that we're able to ensure people live on and on for years longer than we're perhaps supposed to. This is why women go through the menopause at 50 and men begin breaking down from the inside not long after; like most similarly sized mammals we're not, *strictly speaking*, meant to live much longer than that. Our constant strive for longevity being what it is, though, people are now living towards the 100 mark with alarming frequency and it's putting a strain on the population as a whole. Having said that, I can appreciate how easy it is to be on the outside. Looking at a granny with 37 bionic limbs and a hip made of bicycle parts and saying 'you should just give up' is a lot different from actually being that granny. In that case the option to carry on living for that little bit longer before greeting the great unknown must be the only obvious one. It's that survival instinct that's got us where we are today.

I don't want to die, after all; I've just accepted that I must because there's no alternative.

I feel it would be naïve of me to write a chapter on health and not acknowledge that - while the body can break around you in a more noticeable way - a large part of what we consider 'health' is to do with your mental well-being. If anything, the brain is almost as fragile as the body. Endlessly trying to understand and react accordingly to things that happen to and around you puts it under enormous strain - the results of which can be just as harmful as being physically paralysed.

This year's played havoc with my poor brain for

more reasons than one. By far the most noticeable damage has been done by affairs of the heart, which has left me at times devastatingly upset and unable to function properly. I'm not familiar with the point at which the tissue and muscles that grip together and form the brain connect to the part of you most people would call the 'personality' or 'soul', but I do know that when the brain interprets bad news it somehow makes you feel physically unwell. Sometimes this is worse than physically hurting yourself can be.

Please don't get me wrong, dear reader. I'm not trivialising the real mental illnesses – the ones that properly cripple the human experience. Clinical depression, Alzheimer's, autism *et al* have always frightened me deeply. I've huge respect for the power of the brain. It's so bloody important that when it does go wrong in such an extreme manner it's justly the stuff of nightmares. I'm running away to die very shortly, but at least throughout this year I've had complete mental wherewithal - something I'm endlessly grateful for because it's allowed me to write this book. Truth be told, I would rather be dead than to be unable to understand the things that happen around me. Wrong though they might be, I'm thankful that I've been able to make my own choices about how to live the remainder of my life and keep control of my own movements. I'm thankful that I've been able to experience death with a full deck of cards.

So where does all this leave me? I'm a man dying of a disease that I don't fully understand because I've not seen the point in doing so. I know the name of it, but since I'm loathe to explain it I feel that telling you would be a waste of both of our times. I suppose the only way to bow out is simply to advise that you appreciate your health… in whatever capacity you can. Obvious, I know, but by now you really should know better than to expect to genuinely learn anything you didn't already know within these pages.

None of us knows for certain what happens once the bag of meat that carries your eyes around ceases to function, so the only fitting thing to say is: as long as your heart's willing to beat, bloody well let it.

Now, if you'll excuse me, I have to die.

ii) Some pointless home truths

•*My name's Alan Bell, and I...* Tried the guitar, tried photography, tried painting, gave up, and began to write.

•*My name's Alan Bell, and I...* Can no longer remember my parents' faces when I close my eyes.

•*My name's Alan Bell, and I...* Once threw a toad at a wall and killed it. I don't know why.

•*My name's Alan Bell, and I...* Like spaghetti, but not spaghetti westerns.

•*My name's Alan Bell, and I...* Am right-handed but left-footed.

•*My name's Alan Bell, and I...* Once scared off a mugger.

•*My name's Alan Bell, and I...* Am in love with a woman named May, whom I met just before the month of May.

•*My name's Alan Bell, and I...* Saved the life of a bird,

and then watched it grow and disappear to create a life of its own.

•*My name's Alan Bell, and I...* Never did swim with dolphins.

•*My name's Alan Bell, and I...* Have written word after bloody word for the length of an entire book to try and justify my actions to those who'll hate me when I die.

•*My name's Alan Bell, and I...* Love all those who'll hate me when I die.

•*My name's Alan Bell, and I...* Have, despite what I'd like to think, spent my entire life desperately wanting to be liked.

•*My name's Alan Bell, and I...* Am quite heavily self-involved.

•*My name's Alan Bell, and I...* Am running off to die.

iii) London is living, and I'm leaving London (Part 1)

You have to be in the right frame of mind to properly enjoy this city. Walking around at pace with somewhere pressing to be is only likely to make you angry and frustrated, and will drive your focus squarely towards the floor in front of your marching feet. If you've the luxury of having nowhere in particular to be, or at least no specific time to get there, your gait slows enough to bring your eyes up, granting you the pleasure of soaking up what's become of a city 500 years in the making. The buildings from edge to core are all entirely different; old and new are tied together with laces of brickwork and littered with grandiose. Swirling flourishes scrunch up under windows and morph into roofs. There's just enough space dedicated to parks as there should be – just enough to stop the city from feeling dead, while at the same time making each one feel like a rare treat. The whole town darts madly from carefully planned architectural excellence to aesthetically happy accidents. London really is a beautiful city.

Today I'm suffering from the most severe headache I think I've ever had, but as I slowly and purposelessly tread around the town's innards I almost can't feel it. This place has been a truly wonderful home.

I had a really long dream the other night that was basically just me having a normal day at home writing. It seemed to last the entire night. I gather that dreams are normally meant to be comprised of fantastical or aspirational elements in the face of a usually dull life. Thus, I can only presume that having a dull dream means I'm subconsciously aware of the altogether unusual events happening in my waking life, even if trying to get to grips with them on a cognisant level is proving entirely futile. What I mean is: this a bit too real for me to fully grasp - like trying to *actually* understand how far away the Earth is from the Sun, or what a billion pounds is.

I'm in a grassy square in Mayfair, sat on the floor trying not to think about it, even though 'it' is why I'm here in the first place; I wanted to wander round town properly one last time in and enjoy it. I'll have to travel through briefly to get out when I make my escape in a couple of days' time, but in that instance I'll be trying to get somewhere and will be irritably rushing with my nose to the floor. Today, then, is my last official visit to the very centre of London and I intend to remember it for however little I've got left in the best light possible. I'm doing this by slowly traipsing through its meandering lanes, alongside busy roads and by soaking up the old along with the very new. It all mixes perfectly.

I was stood under the London Eye earlier – the colossal Ferris Wheel parked on the water's edge – looking about the town; St Paul's one end, Big Ben and the Dome on the other. London is framed with magnificence, littered with random clumps of historic and modern importance that are all impressive enough to make you feel part of something just by standing underneath it all. That feeling appeals to me. The feeling that some of your blood is owed to your surroundings, that you'll be almost welded into such a remarkable place forever just by having lived here is something I've only tried to enhance by writing this book.

I'm not suggesting that this literary mess entitles me to a blue plaque, or that London owes me anything, of course. Moreover I owe London, since this book is very much a product of it. From the most residential, suburban reaches to the famous landmarks and even the night buses that I hate with so much vigour, every part I've been to or in has shaped me, shaped events and has therefore shaped my writing. For that, I sincerely thank it.

The walk from the Eye to this grassy haven was longer than it should have been, purely because I stopped and sat for around 10 minutes at each of four benches along the way, simply to watch it all buzz by. I'll never get my head round how many people there are. Sitting anywhere in central London and watching them ebb and flow through the streets is near maddening. The sheer number of people coming from each direction – especially in places like Oxford Street – is endless; they just don't stop coming from either side. It's easy to imagine that everyone on the planet is just passing through on their way to whichever country it is they're meant to live. Or that it's a kind of purgatory that loops round: walk down the street far enough and you'll end up back where you started.

With such an extreme density of human traffic, people-watching in the usual sense becomes impossible. Attaching a back-story or invented end-destination to this many people isn't doable due to the limits of the human brain. Trying to do so worsened my headache, so I simply concluded that everybody was going 'somewhere' and moved on to where I am now.

As luck would have it, today is stunning. I'd have been happy to wave London off in this relaxed manner in any weather, but it's definitely all the sweeter with the benefit of balmy April sun warming the town from the top down. It means I'm not inclined to move on just to stay comfortable – it means I can maintain a slow approach to my ambling. Shadows beneath the buildings keep one side of London cool, while the other soaks up a dry, dusty humidity that's thickened with the fog of black cab exhausts. That dust and fog doesn't reach the middle of this grassy square though, which is as warm and quiet as a greenhouse. I don't want to leave, so I'll stay here just as long as these exact conditions do.

In two days I'll drag the old leather suitcase out from under my bed, pack it with whatever I deem necessary for as much as a month spent dying in a hospice and disappear off to find one. Since I want to leave London on this high, I think I should like to find a hospice in the country, so as to spend my final days surrounded by a bit of nature and other such clichés in peace and quiet.

All this was supposed to happen today, you know. I'd arranged in my head for this to be the day that I went off and did my disappearing act, but there are still things to organise that I've failed to tick off. I've been lazy. Even in running off to die I've been lazy, which is dangerous if only because I could very well go to sleep tonight and not wake up. That would pretty much ruin everything.

Since I've got some life admin to take care of (re: this book and the love of my life) before I go, I've pushed my leaving date back another two days. This is me being generous to myself. In truth, what needs to be done could be done today and I could go tomorrow, but I'm putting things off out of idleness and fear. It has, however, given me the chance to do what I'm doing right now. To enjoy London properly for the last time. I'm thankful to myself for that privilege.

Later I'll be meeting Tim for drinks and lies, but that's not for several hours and means that I've got the interim time to sit and think about everything that's ever happened to me. Ever. The saddest thing about that is that it feels as though four hours is ample. I've written very little about my life before this book, but that's only because there wasn't an overwhelming amount of it. Suffice to say, what I've written over the past 12 months has probably been as good an Alan Bell highlights package as I could have engineered, even if the word 'highlight' might be a bit of a stretch.

As is fitting with my luck and overconfidence, as I write this I can now see dark clouds oozing in from behind me. Regardless, I'll lie here for as long as I can and think about things in the unseasonable warmth, surrounded by the throbbing heartbeat of the extraordinary city. London's heart has a tireless beat that's helped keep mine pumping for as long as I care to remember.

iv) A sent letter

Dearest May,

I've been meaning, as much as 'meaning' will allow, to avoid starting this letter by saying "this is the hardest letter I've ever had to write."

And now, predictably, I've failed.

In truth, I don't think I've ever written more than three letters in my entire life. When the competition's that small, finding one competitor to wildly differ from the others in any respect (let alone difficulty) is pretty likely, but I suppose that's wildly beside the point. Suffice to say, this letter is incredibly hard to write because I don't have the slightest idea how to start it properly.

I doubt it matters. A letter like this is destined to be an absolute fucking mess either way. An uncontrollable discharge of inane words, served up within oceans of guilt.

If you're reading this May, it means I'm gone. If you're reading this it means I'm a coward. If you're reading this it means I'm more sorry than I think I can describe with any combination of the now ineffectual words that I know exist. For the things I've done - and more importantly the things I've not done - I am eternally sorry.

Saying that I'm sorry - a written form of apology - is by far the most important thing I could ever do with the English language. That I'm sorry is the most important thing I could ever write.

The last time you and I saw each other - when we sat and ate dinner together, held hands in front of the television and then held each other in bed - was the last time you'll ever see me. The last thing I remember you saying to me was a sleepy but heartfelt 'I love you', and that's more than I could have asked for.

I'm dead, May. I've been dying and am now gone - a state of gone-ness I've been building up to for just short of a year.

I suppose, taking all sense of poetry out of the situation, there's no better way of saying it than to do so bluntly. I have had a silent, invisible passenger living inside my cells for over 12 months, slowly killing me, and now I've left our house to die. I have been quietly dying and I've not told anyone.

I can't imagine what such horrific news must be doing to your beautiful mind. Unlike nearly everyone else on this planet, I was gifted reasonable warning about my own death; with the help of medical science my expiry was pinpointed as more or less one year. That was April last year, and in that time I've managed to paint myself into quite a magnificently stupid corner. I chose, in my own inexcusably selfish way, to keep this information from Tim, Jenny, yourself and everyone else that I know. I chose to do so for reasons that I can no longer properly remember or understand, let alone agree with, and yet here we are, at the end of my last year on Earth with a legacy of lies and mixed emotions. I am dead, May. Death has me and I am truly, truly sorry.

Before I go on, I need to dispense with some reluctant practicalities. It has to be now as I don't know where else it'd go and there are important things not to leave off. I have set up a bank account with enough money in it to pay the rent for my room for another year. The details are on the USB stick attached. I've no idea what the three of you will decide to do. Maybe it'll be the case that you can't face living here another moment? If so, please put the money towards your new lodgings. Or a holiday, or something that won't make you all feel horrible. Please tell Tim and Jenny that I love them more than most people love their family. Tell them I'm sorry. Please tell my Granddad nothing. Tell him I'm busy; tell him I hate him, just please don't tell him he outlived everyone. Also on the USB stick is a very important document. It's the book that I've been working on. It's a book to which I suppose this letter is the end.

Reluctant as I was to tell you all the subject of the book, I can't imagine that anyone guessed what it was truly about. The book was and is about you. And about me. It is the story of my death and it's the story of us. And it's only struck me very recently that it is probably the most horrendous gift anyone has ever given.

If you ever find the courage to read it, the last thing I want to happen is for you to think that I left off thinking of you as I did earlier on. The book was never, ever some juvenile way of getting back at you. Quite the contrary: the whole thing is, as I've come to realise, an enormous love letter to you, May. It's a shrine in written form to the thing that I loved most in the entire world and an explanation and justification as to why - by all rights - I shouldn't be allowed it.

I thought I'd begun this book for myself. I thought, in my naïve innocence, that it was all for my own personal growth, sense of expression and dreams of becoming something in the world of writing. I was wrong, of course; the months that waned between then and now showed me in blindingly obvious form that it's for *you*. And it always was.

This is the song I could never write you, the picture I could never paint for you, the film I never made for you and the lifelong partner I simply can't be. Here's the absolute limit of everything that's within my power to give you, and it's still so much less than you deserve. In many ways it's a punishment you've not earned. Within the pages of this book are my side of our story. It doesn't have an end because I've been too selfish to give us one, and for that I am so unendingly sorry. Nonetheless, it's our story and I want to give it to you now... at the last possible moment. While there are a number of things I wish I'd done differently, there was nothing I could have done to change the fact that I was dying in the first instance, so I've given this to you instead of the lifetime of love I'd rather you had. I've given you me in written form.

Please keep it.

Jesus... It's you.

It's taken me this entire bloody time to realise it but I think I've just figured it out. By writing with such bias and inelegance, with wit that you've given me and about such private experiences that you and I have shared, I've alienated anyone who would ever want to read this book and made you cripplingly unlikely to ever push for it to be published in the first place.

It's you. You're my 'dear reader'. If ever you do read the shambolic musings I've committed to paper, then I hope you'll come to understand what that means, because to me it suddenly means the world.

The most important thing now, taking rage and sorrow and regret and all the other horrible things my memory should rightfully bring forth for granted, is that I felt nothing but overwhelming and almost indescribable love for you from the very moment I knew that I could. I don't mean to try and make matters any worse than they already are, but my god, May, I loved you uncontrollably and completely in a fashion I didn't know this universe could tolerate. I loved you as if it was something I needed to carry around with me - much more than just an abstract feeling. It's been misused and led down dark directions, but I loved fully, May, and it was all for you. For that reason alone you made my short life worth more than any number of additional years could do justice. I can only apologise that it's come at the cost of making you as confused and shockingly upset as I think I have.

I've spent the entirety of this last year in a state of acceptance about dying. At no point did I really feel hard done by. It was just something that had happened, or was happening. That was just the way it had to be. The thing is, only now - when I realise that I'm saying a final goodbye to the person I always want to see - do I feel so fucking cheated by the world. I'd like to think that by not telling you about all of this I didn't affect the way things panned out between us. We have recently - up until this very moment - been a couple once again, and I know for a fact that it's not out of pity or remorse. It's out of genuine, requited love. I also know, though admitting it carves my throat, that doing this to you is unendingly cruel and selfish. If I could excuse it in any way, it'd be with the fact that I was able to experience true, joyous love for a time. You've unwittingly given me the best parting gift any human being could ask for, and I'm thankful for it almost as much as I am indescribably remorseful.

I'm struggling more now than at the start of this damned letter to find a balanced and worthy way of saying 'I love you' and 'I'm sorry', so I gather I'm coming to the very end of what was never going to be straightforward, clean or easy. They're the only two things I mean to say anyway - for whatever weight those words actually carry.

I love you, and I'm sorry.

If the book I've knocked together with uneasy, fidgety words does nothing to rationalise a year's worth of misguided actions, then at least let it teach you how not to live your life. Charles Bukowski once said in praise of a book that "It was good to read. It made you realise that thoughts and words could be fascinating, if finally useless." If that's the case with this, then I suppose at least that's something. I've foolishly tried to explain many things that I know nothing about, but the one thing I think I managed to talk near sufficiently about is love. By accident I learnt and divulged more information about the true nature of love than I could ever have hoped to do with any other subject. I know it's not an excuse for my ill-conceived actions but I now know that - no matter how extreme the circumstances - none of us have any control over love. If you learn nothing else from ever having known me, May, please make it that. Please apply it in the future.

I think the biggest problem with life is that it makes you tired of it. It never bloody stops, and you get exhausted, but then very suddenly it does. There are 270 tube stops on the London Underground, and in my life I only went to 19. Even if you *were* in a position to willingly take my advice, it'd be a hugely hypocritical and clichéd sentiment to suggest that you should go to all of them, or swim with dolphins, or gamble until you regret it, or climb a mountain, or see the world or do anything like that, so I think all I can say with conviction is: spend the rest of your life doing what you want – doing whatever feels right. You can't help your feelings, May, so ignore whatever the world says and just do everything and anything you bloody well want.

The last thing I remember you saying to me was a sleepy but heartfelt 'I love you'. That's all I could have ever asked or hoped for. I love you too, May Cooper - so much more powerfully than an entire book could ever explain or apologise for.

Yours forever and always,

Alan Bell

v) London is living, and I'm leaving London (Part 2)

Moistened sills reflect a town built upward from the earth,
Where tiny lanes lie with roads and talk of London's birth,
And tempered with a suited sky, which - mournful now with crying eyes -
Soaks into a cobbled guise;
Spreads the city's girth.

It looks to times when angled glass was absent in consent,
No modern substance scratching sky to mark a new ascent
Unruly structures hold the land, stalked by birds that never planned,
To nest inside a hero's hand -
But view the town's extent.

The view creeps down to alleyways that wind a dreary aisle,
Pulse-less veins that trickle now with cells in single file,
Where boroughs thrive with vivid heat, and people carve new London's beat,

It forces change in older streets -
Adopting newer styles.

They cater now for varied tastes that tarnish older
paint,
Cracked like clay that etches across colours pale and
faint,
We walk the slopes that shadow lows, and corners
stopping traffic flows,
To circus lights in garish rows,
Void of all restraint.

Sweep downwards to where dragons make a home in
sunken lairs,
Dug out with plans of missing all the parks and
concrete squares,
So history and art go by, without imprinting on the
eye,
Blinder than the crow can fly,
Then freed by winding stairs.

A ribbon draped transversely through also leaves a
cut.
London town's main artery that breathes its seeping
gut.
Slashed where bridges sew the wound, nocturnal
waters whistle tunes,
Breaking grey with black lagoon,

The laceration shuts.

Our gaze is taken now beyond, and up across the
banks,
Where structures shine in different hues, and kindle
darkened flanks,
One eye keeps a careful watch, and time is kept by
mighty clocks,
And weary now the city flocks,
To sleep in towered ranks.

'Death is the only pure, beautiful conclusion of a great passion.'

- D. H. Lawrence

The End

.